Combustion

The Fall of a Kingdom

Books by Jordan S. Keller

Ashes Over Avalon Trilogy
Wildfire
Burnout
Combustion

Coming Soon!
Failing Gravity

**For more information
visit:** www.SpeakingVolumes.us

Combustion

The Fall of a Kingdom

Jordan S. Keller

SPEAKING VOLUMES, LLC
NAPLES, FLORIDA
2024

Combustion

Copyright © 2024 by Jordan S. Keller

All rights reserved. No part of this book may be reproduced or transmitted in any form or by any means without written permission.

ISBN 979-8-89022-173-5

For Charlie
You know this book wouldn't be real without you

Chapter One

The morning was a lie.

It was neither good nor bright. At least not for Abigail Turner who felt like a hostage strapped inside the passenger seat next to her too good and too bright companion. San Arbor passed by the windows in streaks of wood, brick and pavement. The other commuters didn't give the car a second look, or the occupants inside. It was a nice change for Abigail who otherwise lived under a constant media lens. Without her mask, she was invisible. She ground her teeth together wishing the invisibility transferred to Lancelot.

For as easy as a distraction he was for her, Abigail found ignoring him painfully difficult this morning.

"You know," Lancelot said as he parked the car outside her apartment building, "We wouldn't have to stop by your place every day if you kept some stuff at mine. I've got a couple of drawers in the bathroom cleaned out for you and the extra closet—"

"Lance," Abigail warned, shooting a look as sharp as daggers across the console. "Don't start that again."

"Come on Abbs." He smiled at her and probably believed the simple grin would ease away her mood. "It's been almost a year since, well since things happened, and I don't even know what we are. At least keep a toothbrush over."

Smoke oozed between Abigail's fingers as she gripped the door handle, her powers flaring with her emotions. "You're my coworker."

Abigail left the car before she could say anything more. Whatever rebuttal Lancelot had was lost to the door slamming shut. She probably heard his defense by now, anyway. He seemed to bring up the subject weekly. Abigail was no closer to leaving anything at his place today than she was six months ago when her overnight visits became routine.

The doorman wished her a "good morning," and Abigail replied with a nod and rode the elevator to her floor. She could smell woodsmoke as soon as she entered the hallway despite the monthly carpet shampooing. Every trace of soot and the scent was removed from the path between the elevator and her door, but it never left her memories. Or the inside of her unit where both still clung to the drywall. When Abigail unlocked the door, it crashed into her.

Her apartment hadn't changed in a year. She didn't think she had changed in a year, either. The same painful grip seized her chest as she saw the bed, the scorched patio, the discarded boots just inside the closet, the twin toothbrushes on the sink counter. The apartment looked like he could come back at any time.

Abigail wasn't sure if she kept it that way as a memorial to Thomas Sanders, firefighter, or as a warning against Cinder, Flame Villain.

Barely a year passed since he died in a fire of his own creation. Barely a year since Abigail couldn't save the man she loved. Barely a year since she'd heard the rumble of his voice, felt the softness of his hands, witnessed a crooked smile claim his face. Barely a year since Cinder scarred her a second time. Except now his scar only stained her mind. No one saw this one twist and damage the hero.

Pictures of the two of them threatened to cut Abigail and make her bleed memories and lies of what she once had. The woodsmoke smell was suffocating. The ghosts were emerging. Abigail tore through her closet for a change of clothes, washed her face, and exited the apartment before she lost control. Before she dissolved into the dark, into the loneliness, into the sadness.

She squeezed the melted pendant hanging on a chain beneath her shirt and felt the rough texture of what had been her engagement ring bite into her hand. The subtle pain grounded her. Thomas was dead. Cinder was dead. She was alive and had a job to do. Abigail returned to the lobby with a smile that could pass as genuine and rejoined Lancelot in his car.

"Hey," she greeted, hoping to restart their morning. If she was using him as a distraction, she could at least be nice about it. "Thanks for waiting for me."

"Did you think I'd make you walk?" Lancelot asked with a chuckle.

"I would have. I didn't mean to yell at you."

Lancelot merged into traffic. "Yes, you did, but that's okay. I shouldn't pressure you to move in if you're not ready."

Abigail didn't address whether keeping an extra set of clothes somewhere meant she was moving in. Instead, she said, "Thanks."

"The offer is always on the table." Lancelot winked at her. "I'm here for whatever you need. But can I ask you something?"

"Sure." She was prepared for any number of questions except for the one that came from his mouth as casually as if he asked about the weather.

"Why that guy? Of all the people in the world, how'd you get wrapped up with a crook like the Flame Villain. Weren't there warning signs of who he really was?"

Abigail stared at him not knowing what to say but knowing the exact emotion that simmered under her skin. Irritation. It was hot, angry, and it burned up her spine before flaring behind her eyes.

In her silence, Lancelot chuckled to himself and added, "If that's the reason you don't want to move in, you don't have to worry about me, Abbs. I'm as real as they come. A good guy inside and outside of a mask. There's no evil plots when it comes to me."

Abigail formed an evil plot of her own that involved throwing Lancelot out of the moving vehicle. She pinched the bridge of her nose until the mental image faded.

"Stop the car," she demanded.

Lancelot paused in the middle of the sentence she wasn't listening to. "Why?"

Abigail bit down the truth of her wanting to get away from him before she roughed up his pretty face and pointed at the coffee shop coming up on their right. "I forgot I told 'Xcal I'd bring him breakfast this morning."

"Okay, sure." Lancelot changed lanes and followed his superior's orders. "But hurry up, or we'll be late."

Once outside the car, Abigail took a deep breath and exhaled a stream of blue smoke. The action momentarily lowered her internal temperature and anger toward Lancelot. She entered the coffee shop to find more momentary solace. She felt like a coward, choosing to run from the situation before she either combusted or realized she was powerless to do so. She hoped while on patrol something big happened. Something with an easy outcome. A simple task for Avalon, Dragon Slayer to accomplish. Thwarting bad guys seemed way more enjoyable than the remaining commute to work.

Among the coffee shop's bright green interior, Abigail caught glimpses of herself and her team. Merlin printed coffee mugs lined a shelf, each bright red and covered in tiny magic wands and pointed hats. King Arthur had his own line of tall, reusable mugs styled like his golden crown. Posters of Lancelot hung from the ceiling advertising the drink of the month. At the counter, Abigail found ground coffee in two new flavors dedicated to her and Excalibur. "Dragon Breath Heat" made with chili peppers, and "Armored Giant" flavored with black currant and orange.

Neither sounded appealing.

"What can I get started for you?" the woman behind the cash register prompted.

"Just two large black coffees, please." Abigail fished for the bills she had in her front pocket. "And the Lancelot drink of the month."

"It's a popular item." The woman inputted the order and accepted Abigail's payment. "Name?"

"Abigail." It was the truth, but as she said it, it tasted just like all the other lies she told that morning. She found comfort knowing she'd be in her mask soon. That she'd be Avalon soon. A hero that didn't get hurt in the ways a human did.

The woman handed Abigail her change, which she dumped into the tip jar, and said, "They'll be up at the end."

Abigail moved with the other patrons to the end of the counter and waited for her drinks. A teenager beside her clutched a newly purchased Merlin mug to her chest like it might vanish. The man behind her ordered a cup of "Dragon Breath Heat" with extra cream. Peeking over her shoulder, Abigail saw the man wore a windbreaker that matched her costume's color scheme. She turned her attention to the TV behind the counter as the man moved down the line.

The morning talk show hosts were signing off, but their farewells were cut short by the flashy intro of the national news taking over. A grave looking anchor sat behind an orange desk. He tapped the papers he held before beginning his report.

"Another member of Hero Enterprises has been slain."

There were no accompanying graphics or shift to a field reporter to soften the severity of the announcement. Abigail couldn't look away.

"The Guppy was discovered murdered in Tennyson City's shipping yard this morning. Local authorities are still investigating but have declared foul play based on the state of the body. This attack comes two weeks after The Swordfish's death. Currently, it is unclear if the two murders are connected, but local authorities believe the same villain is at fault for the hero and her sidekick's deaths. Hero Enterprises has not released any statements."

"Abigail! Order up for Abigail!"

Someone touched her arm, and Abigail spun around with a hand forming into a punch. The man wearing the Avalon windbreaker jumped back.

"Sorry ma'am, but I think those are yours?" he pointed at the three drinks on the counter, his hand shaking.

Abigail snapped out of her fighting stance and grabbed her drinks, muttering an apology and exiting the store before the anchor finished his story. She already knew the important part; another hero was killed.

Lancelot examined something stuck between his teeth through the car's visor mirror when Abigail returned. She set the drink carrier containing the two black coffees on the floorboard and handed him the foamy concoction topped with blue sprinkles. He accepted the drink and closed the mirror.

"It's your drink of the month," she absently explained as Lancelot turned his examination from his teeth to the drink.

"Shouldn't it be a little more manly?" Lancelot asked. "It looks just like the unicorn one they had a couple months ago. Just the sprinkles are different."

Abigail didn't reply. She fastened her seat belt and secured the other drinks on her lap. The car rumbled back to life, and the coffees bonked together as Lancelot bump the curb at the exit. At a red light he collected his drink from the cup holder and was about to take a sip before eyeing Abigail's two untouched coffees.

"Hey," he asked, and Abigail looked at him, his problem-solving grin had returned. "This thing isn't poisoned, is it? I see you're not partaking in any of those, either."

"I wouldn't poison my whole team, would I?"

"Probably just me." Lancelot kept his grin as he slurped down the drink.

Abigail sighed, his grin having a small effect. "The other one's for Merlin. She had patrol with Excalibur last night."

"Still trying to get on her good side?"

"If she even has one."

Lancelot pulled into the parking garage of the Hero Relief Center. "Maybe I'll share the secret of finding it later."

"I don't think I want to know. I'll see you at The Round." Abigail exited the car before Lancelot put it in park.

Chapter Two

At twelve stories, The Hero Relief Center wasn't close to being the tallest building in downtown San Arbor. That title belonged to the Grand Hotel which launched more than thirty stories of art deco design into the skyline. The HRC was the busiest building in the city, however. Serving as the headquarters for the Round Table Knights, the business side of hero work took care of the marketing, costuming, payment, public relations, endorsements, and merchandising. The building housed a museum and gift shop for visitors, and the newly constructed health center servicing all heroes and employees on the ninth floor.

Abigail used the coded employee elevator to bypass the lobby and public floors to reach the level containing hers and the other Round Table Knights' offices. She stopped at the open door of Excalibur's office and cleared her throat before entering. The twin coffees in her hands prevented her from knocking on the door frame as she usually did.

Excalibur took protecting his secret identity more seriously than any of the other Knights. Every part of him was covered in a medieval inspired suit of armor. His helmet contained a voice changer, and his padded gloves rotated through different fingerprint molds each month. Abigail had seen his face in passing but didn't know anything personal outside the alias he used.

It didn't stop her from trusting him with her life.

"Morning, boss."

"Is that for me?" Despite the cold, automated voice that trickled from the helmet, he sounded hopeful.

"It sure is." Abigail set one of the coffees on his desk and eyed the report he had been working on. "Is that from last night?"

"You missed a good night." Excalibur produced a metal straw from a desk drawer and pierced the coffee lid like an oversized caffeinated juice box. "Merlin and I had an attempted robbery at the auto dealer. Four people, each trying to drive off in a Lexus. They didn't see us coming."

Abigail whistled. "That does sound like fun. How far did they get?"

"Only about four exits down the interstate. Merlin trapped them with some goop, and I chased down the runners."

"I still don't know why people even try to commit big things like that knowing we're here."

"Desperation, I reckon." Excalibur shrugged. "Or stupidity."

"I'd agree with the stupidity. Is Merlin still here?"

"She's at The Round with King." Excalibur glanced at the clock hanging between two rapiers on the wall. "We should be headed that way too, almost time."

Abigail set the other coffee on his desk. "Would you mind giving that to her? I still need to change, but I'll be right up."

"I kind of like the new Avalon look you have now," Excalibur laughed. "Very retro."

Abigail looked down at her T-shirt. In her haste to leave her apartment, she hadn't noticed what she grabbed out of the closet. An animated version of herself and Excalibur grinned up at her with matching swords. It was the first shirt made of her when she was Excalibur's sidekick. That seemed like a lifetime ago.

"It is a nice shirt," she agreed.

"I still have mine, but I don't think it fits me anymore."

"Too many fast food endorsements?" Abigail joked and left Excalibur's office before he could fire back.

Like the other Round Table Knights, Avalon's costume mirrored the Britannia theme of the heroes. Her golden greaves and gauntlets matched the golden cape attached at her shoulders. The dragon emblem on her chest was polished, her hair pinned back by her red mask, and her signature sword strapped against her hip. This was the truth Abigail needed to remind herself of. She was a hero. She was Avalon, the Dragon Slayer. She saved people.

She would save people.

Abigail was the last one to arrive at the Round Table, the meeting room for the Knights, and she closed the door behind her before taking her seat between Excalibur and Lancelot. Across the granite tabletop, Merlin raised her coffee cup in a small toast toward Abigail. The subtle motion was as much of a *thank you* as Abigail would get. She accepted the tiny victory with a nod and turned her attention to Quinn Samuels.

Among his masked employees, President Samuels wore his own costume: a three-piece suit. It took Abigail several months to realize he always matched his cuff links with his tie and handkerchief. Today all three were steel grey and glinted against the otherwise dark outfit. He set a folder in the middle of the table. Several papers spilled out between the manila cover.

"Good morning, everyone," Samuels began. "Let's get started by congratulating Merlin and Excalibur for their quick work last night. Minimal damage and minimal injury."

"It would have been *no* damage if bucket head watched where he was going." Merlin tossed an accusing finger at Excalibur.

Excalibur didn't let her insult penetrate his armor. "I didn't know your magic spell would be slippery. The way it caught the cars I thought it was sticky."

Merlin sighed. "When the chemical bonds with aluminum it becomes viscid, otherwise it retains its slick state."

"You expected me to know that?"

"You would if you picked up a book once in a while instead of a sword."

Abigail was sure only Merlin would consider paging through a molecular chemistry textbook as light reading. Last Christmas, Merlin had gifted everyone a pocket-sized chemistry book. Abigail hadn't read hers, but it was at least kept on a proper shelf where Excalibur currently kept his desk leveled with his.

"Regardless," President Samuels regained control, "It ought to keep Benton happy."

At the head of the table, King Arthur groaned at the mention of San Arbor's mayor.

"Why is it our job to keep him happy?" Lancelot asked with a similar groan. "He targets us any chance he gets."

"We have to be the bigger person," Abigail reminded him, earning a smile from President Samuels. "San Arbor loves us and needs us."

"And that's why his proposed ordinance won't make it past city council." President Samuels promised the heroes. "Restricting you all to predetermined situations would be bad for everyone."

"Not to mention impossible," Lancelot said. "Who would be in charge of assigning those conditions? Would we have to test into new options?"

"We're not going to worry about that because it won't happen." Samuels returned his attention to Merlin and Excalibur. "I know you both were on patrol last night, but I need you to stay an hour after and answer some media questions downstairs."

"Just an hour," Merlin confirmed the agreement. "Not a minute more."

"It shouldn't even take the hour." Samuels attempted to please the Witch Knight. From a remote he pulled from his pocket, Samuels powered on one of the television monitors on the wall. A picture of two masked individuals came into focus. They were dressed in matching blue and green wet suits. The woman's had a long-nose fish stitched onto the front, and the boy had a smaller fish on his. Both wore armbands that sported the logo of Hero Enterprises.

"You may have already heard about the two homicides in Tennyson City."

"The Swordfish and her sidekick The Guppy," Abigail said. "Have they been linked together?"

"Not officially," answered Samuels. "But Hero Enterprises is leaning in that direction based on the attack. They were killed in the same way. It's safe to assume it's by the same individual."

"Who could kill The Swordfish?" Lancelot asked. "Doesn't she have full water control? Isn't Tennyson City next to the ocean? Gup has it too, right?"

"It was an ambush." Merlin determined, analyzing the documents from the folder.

An image slid toward Abigail as Merlin discarded it back onto the table. Abigail turned it upright and regretted it. The image was gruesome; A mangled body strung up by wires between two shipping containers. The face was too bloody to make out, but the costume matched that of The Swordfish. Abigail slid the image back to the center of the table with the others.

"Multiple attackers caught her off guard, it had to be the only way," Merlin completed her analysis. "Lancelot is right, someone like The Swordfish and Guppy would be in their element near the water. No ordinary person did this."

The room turned cold and quiet. Samuels cleared his throat and the Knights shot their attention back to him.

"This is a tragedy. The HRC has already sent our condolences to Hero Enterprises. I know Tennyson City isn't close, and this death won't affect our city, but we need to learn from it." Samuels turned off the television screen, removing any evidence that proved The Swordfish and The Guppy had lived. "Later this week there will be training for the five of you. It must be completed, understood?"

"Yes, sir," Lancelot audibly agreed with everyone else's silent nod.

The photo of The Swordfish's body snuck out of the stack of papers Merlin reinserted into the folder. Abigail reached across the table to flip it over. Tennyson City had one of the largest hero companies in the country, giving it the nickname of the safest city in the world. Abigail couldn't believe something so awful could occur there.

"Where are we going today, Quinn?" King Arthur asked, sounding far happier than the room should have allowed.

"You, Avalon and Lancelot will be teaming up at a press conference. Play nice with the media—" Samuels raised his hand, quieting King Arthur and Lancelot as they began to protest "—Yes, Benton will be there. No, you do not need to interact with him. Yes, this is mandatory, and yes you will all be reassigned to patrolling districts when it's over."

"Does this thing only last an hour, too?" Lancelot asked, unsatisfied with at least part of Samuels' answers.

"Probably a little longer," Samuels answered. "San Arbor Energy is releasing information on their new electric grid plan. Dox-Con is putting on this event for them. I suspect it's to help them win favor and the bid for the project later this year."

"Do we support Dox-Con?" Abigail asked. She wasn't too familiar with the technology company now residing in a new high rise building downtown.

"This isn't about the HRC backing any horse. I want you three there in case something happens. It's supposed to be a large crowd."

"And because of the cameras." King Arthur crossed his arms.

"Yes, that is a bonus. Kiss a baby if you see any."

Only Excalibur laughed at Samuels' joke. Probably because he didn't have to go.

"We'll make us look good," Abigail promised the president, eager to get the mission over and done with. The sooner the event was over, the sooner she would be protecting San Arbor. Tennyson City was states away, but she wouldn't let whatever evil residing there populate her city.

Chapter Three

Abigail did tire of the metaphorical leash keeping her and the other Round Table Knights at the beck and call of the media. When she wasn't doing good for her city, she was their show dog, jumping through interview-shaped hoops and smiling on command. It was the least important part of her job, the first part to lose the shimmering glow of hero work, but she couldn't deny how good she was at it.

As she, King Arthur, and Lancelot floated to the ground outside the press conference's barriers, the attention on Dox-Con's extravagant event shifted away from energy and onto the heroes. A small boy ran to them, his green Dox-Con checkered balloon escaping to the sky in his excitement to be the first one to greet the heroes. He tripped on the curb, but before the boy could fall into the road, King Arthur scooped him into his arms. Lancelot appeared on his left with the lost balloon retrieved by his telekinesis, and Abigail stood on his right assuring the boy's safety.

It made a wonderful photo.

King Arthur kissed the top of the boy's head before setting him back on the ground. "Is your ankle okay?"

The boy stared up at King Arthur with big eyes. "It's okay. I'm Gerald."

"Well hello, Gerald." King Arthur shook the boy's tiny, outstretched hand. "I'm King Arthur, do you want to meet my friends?"

The boy nodded eagerly, almost losing his balloon a second time. Abigail crouched down and tied the balloon around his wrist before it could fly away again.

"This is a pretty cool balloon," she commented when she was finished.

"Thanks! Do you want to play rock-paper-scissors with me?" Gerald asked.

Abigail readied a fist. "I would love to. Ready. Set. Go!"

Gerald comically bashed his rock overtop Abigail's pretend scissors upon their release.

"Looks like you got me. Good job!" Abigail said. "Best two out of three?"

"Gerald!" shouted a woman pushing through the crowd that had encased the heroes. "Gerald!"

"Is that your mom?" Abigail asked.

A blush claimed his face, and Gerald nodded.

"Did you run over here without telling her?"

Gerald nodded again, but this time his bottom lip trembled.

"Don't cry, we'll get you back to her." Abigail stood and pulled Lancelot to them. "Lancelot can fly you right to her."

"It would be my pleasure." Lancelot telekinetically plucked Gerald off the ground and the boy giggled until he landed in his mother's arms. "Think we can leave now?" he whispered to Abigail.

"Fat chance." Abigail didn't deny the same wanting Lancelot felt. She waved at one of the cameras that flashed in their direction. "We have to at least see the speaker."

Lancelot groaned. "Since King already met his baby kissing quota, want to tackle this interview with me?"

Abigail eyed the reporter Lancelot nodded at in the crowd. He pushed his way to the front, armed with a single microphone, and adjusted his tie. "Is Channel 9 not here to get your exclusive?"

Lancelot scratched his cheek, but Abigail saw it flush pink before he could hide it. "Monica doesn't seem too interested in me anymore. 9's working King over, anyway."

Behind them, King Arthur answered a question asked by Channel 9's main field reporter, Monica Langford. The woman who was once obsessed with Lancelot hadn't given him much attention for months. Abigail felt she was somewhat to blame for that.

"Take the lead." Abigail nudged Lancelot toward the reporter on their side of the crowd.

He paused for a few selfies and autographs before making it to the reporter. "Are you missing your camera crew?" Lancelot asked him.

"No sir, only need myself and this baby." The reporter flicked up the side switch on his microphone. "Dominic Desoda, with San Arbor Air-One. How are you doing today, Lancelot?"

"No complaints, Dominic, how about you?"

"Excited to see what San Arbor Energy decides to do with their new electric grid project. Many suspect the company to begin phasing in free wireless internet across the city. What do you think about that?"

"I think that's a good way to promote better communication and education."

"Is it a better priority than strengthening the current and failing electrical lines that customers are currently experiencing black outs with?"

"Well, no, I don't think it should replace that work."

"Is the HRC here to promote that agenda?"

Abigail shook her head watching the interviewer try to entrap Lancelot in a buzz worthy quote. The *gotcha journalist* never seemed to run out of questions for the heroes. Abigail finished signing the back of a cellphone, returned it to its owner, and joined Lancelot before he could answer Desoda's question. Lancelot's back relaxed as soon as their elbows bumped together, and a sigh blew out between his teeth.

Here she was to save the day.

"The Hero Relief Center doesn't want to speculate what *could* be happening before anything is announced." Abigail addressed the reporter without any hint of negotiation. "We're here to hear the news the same as everyone else. Whatever San Arbor Energy is unveiling, I'm sure it will better everyone's life in our city."

Dominic Desoda fumbled, flipping through his notebook for his next talking point.

Abigail took the opportunity and attacked. "Thank you for your time, Mr. Desoda. It was nice to meet you, but Lancelot and I need to get back over to King Arthur."

"See you next time!" Lancelot quickly added with a smile before backing away with Abigail. "Thanks."

"Can't let my partner fail," Abigail whispered back.

"Or the company?"

"One may have a bigger priority," she admitted.

Ahead of them, King Arthur wrapped up his interview with Channel 9 and faced Abigail. He was smiling, probably the same smile he used for the entire interview, but it didn't reach his eyes. They were cold, bored, and tired. King Arthur offered a head nod as a form of instruction, and Abigail and Lancelot fell in line behind him, wading through the crowd armed only with their plastered smiles and passing high fives.

The Dox-Con building twisted into the sky and shimmered as morning sunlight caught against the angled curves of the tower. Three structures on the top resembled a trident and shook violently in the upper air currents. Abigail wasn't sure if they were practical or a decor choice. The tower was a new aged skyscraper that quickly outpaced the others in terms of design, but not in terms of class. It was a shiny thumbtack among a field of clovers. Black and green checkered balloons marked the building's entrance and decorated the small platform where people in suits were getting settled in uncomfortable looking folding chairs.

The heroes arrived at the aisle in front of the platform, walking between the rows of chairs filling with citizens, reporters, and employees on either side. All of them turned to face the Round Table Knights. Abigail readied herself for the next gauntlet. She waved to a pair of kids closest to her, her flaming hand making the kids *ooh* in delight.

"King Arthur!" A woman jogged down the aisle before anyone could advance on the heroes. She was dressed in black, held a clipboard, and a curling wire connected an earpiece to a radio on her belt. "We have your seats reserved at the front. If you'll follow me."

"Front row seats?" Lancelot asked with a smile. "Too bad we couldn't score these at a Majestic's Football game."

"Second row, actually," corrected the woman. "The first row is for Mayor Benton and a few members of his staff."

"Miss?" King Arthur gently touched the woman's arm as she led them to their seats. He waited for her to face him before he continued. "We have the front row seats. Mayor Owen Benton and his staff are to sit behind us."

A blank expression cloaked the woman's face. Her bottom lip slipped momentarily while her mind was elsewhere. Her blue eyes became dull. She looked like a doll; lifeless and controllable.

"Here are your seats." She pointed to her right where the front row was clearly marked off for Benton and his staff. The woman plucked the name cards off the seats and switched them for the ones labeled *HRC*.

"Thank you." King Arthur passed Abigail and Lancelot to reach his new seat. A purple shine faded from his brown eyes.

Abigail took her seat and waited for the presentation to begin.

The unnatural hue of King Arthur's eyes should have bothered her, but she was used to the color change when his power of sway activated. In her first year working with the Round Table Knights she rarely saw him use his ability to mentally control his targets, but now it was becoming too common to see the purple gleam around his irises. From stopping a get-away-driver to changing seats with the mayor, King Arthur resorted to his abilities more often than not.

And more often than not, it wasn't for hero work.

Abigail learned to ignore the clinch in her abdomen when she saw him use it outside of hero work. She knew nothing she could say would stop the abuse of his power. And worse, she feared he may use it on her. Once would be enough in her lifetime.

At least *she* could be a good hero. A noble knight like the legends they stole their names from.

A Dox-Con representative, marked by his green and black checkered tie, cleared his throat at the podium and silenced the audience before giving his welcoming remarks and introducing the actual press conference speaker.

Despite sitting six feet from the man, Abigail hardly heard him as a gust of wind ripped through the grounds and screamed its way to the top of the Dox-Con tower. Abigail did hear the three prongs on the roof bash together, however. A second gale ripped away one of the balloon bouquets and littered the blue sky with black and green orbs.

"We most certainly did not need all of this fanfare," spoke the speaker from San Arbor Energy, "but it is appreciated. Thank you, Dox-Con. SAE is very excited to announce our plan to update the current electrical grid which will improve power and communication lines across the city and into the various districts."

Combustion

A thundering snap sounded above the crowd. In an instant, everyone's eyes were off the speaker and on the falling piece of metal. A thirty-foot prong from the roof plummeted to the ground.

Chapter Four

The scene around Abigail slowed, but she still wasn't fast enough to save everyone. She leapt behind the row of seats, yanking Mayor Benton from his and shoving him down the aisle away from the incoming missile. His staff quickly followed without the aid of the heroes. Her skin prickled as Lancelot activated his powers near her and mentally pushed all the speakers off the stage moments before impact. Frantically, Abigail grabbed the hands, arms, shoulders, anything she could reach of strangers and jerked them out of the landing zone.

She didn't remember there being this many people at the start of the press conference, but everywhere she looked she found more people to save.

And she was running out of time.

The prong crashed through the center of the platform and tore into the ground. Its base teetered upward before collapsing against the Dox-Con building, shattering glass and steel. The entire tower shivered as the front half caved in. Window shards flittered to the ground like rain, ceiling tiles dropped and shattered against the floor, people inside moved through the dust like ghosts.

One of the ghosts stumbled out of the building between a hanging doorframe and a mess of sparking wires. He fell to his knees while gripping his chest and coughing painfully and uncontrollably.

Abigail evaded prong fragments protruding from the ground and other hazardous debris as she ran to him, arriving at his side with a baseball slide. She flipped her fire-proof cape over the man's head and shot a fireball at the wires above them, soldering the ends and silencing their sparks.

"You're going to be okay," she promised him. "Can you walk?"

The man tried to speak, but another coughing fit stole his words. He answered Abigail with a nod.

She helped him to his feet and guided him, his shaking hands holding onto her arms for support, from the tower to a safe section of the lawn. She ordered a bystander to stay with him before returning to the tower. Her body slowed as she approached the fallen prong. From this side, she saw the limbs of those caught underneath and blood squeezing out between the spongy earth and compact metal. Abigail's throat swelled and instead of continuing forward, she wanted to puke. On her left, King Arthur examined the carnage with his arms crossed over his chest.

"What's the plan?" Abigail asked, desperately keeping her eyes glued to his face rather than the scene behind him. She found stability in his stoicism.

"Keep doing triage. Paramedics will be here soon." King Arthur squeezed her shoulder, gently shoving her toward a person sitting on the upturned lawn with their head in their hands. "Let's be heroes today."

Abigail nodded and got back to work, keeping the blood-soaked ground out of her line of sight. She crouched next to the woman in question and tried to assess her through her hands. Her knees were caked in earth, and the backs of her hands were carved in thick lacerations. Blood trailed down her arms and dripped off the points of her elbows.

"Ma'am, my name is Avalon, and I'm here to help you. Can you tell me what hurts?"

When the woman didn't answer, Abigail coaxed a hand away from her face. She was missing an eye. At least it was hidden under the bleeding head wound above it. Abigail ripped her cape until she had a long enough piece to wrap around the woman's head. Blood darkened the golden fabric.

"I'm going to help you stand." Abigail didn't wait for the woman's approval.

She heaved her to her feet and guided the woman to the growing assortment of the injured. Some made it to the self-assigned triage station on their own, others gripped onto each other and staggered to the area, and a batch of people were gently lowered to the ground by Lancelot. The pile was a good sign, Abigail thought. It meant they were alive. The wail of sirens penetrated the chaos as ambulances and firetrucks neared.

"Gerald!"

Abigail snapped her head in the direction of the mother's voice from earlier.

"Gerald!" the mother shouted again, moving frantically around groups of people. "Gerald where are you? Have you seen my son?"

Abigail ran to her, and the mother snatched Abigail's hands, commanding all the hero's attention.

"Please, you have to find him," urged the mother. "He ran away from me when the announcement started. He was heading toward the front of the stage."

Abigail doubted the little boy wanted to see the San Arbor Energy speaker up close. Gerald was trying to find the heroes. Now she would find him.

"We'll get him." Abigail told the mother, then switching to her ear communicator said, "Guys, we have a missing kid. The boy from earlier."

"I'm in the air," replied Lancelot. "I don't see him yet."

"There!" the mother's shriek sounded through Abigail's earpiece.

Combustion

Abigail followed the direction of her pointing hand. Gerald stood inside the Dox-Con tower just below where the prong teetered inside the building. Wisps of dust concealed him as he wandered between hanging lights and broken ceiling tiles. He seemed unaware of the dangers. Abigail sprinted toward him. She would pluck him from the rubble before anything could happen.

The prong groaned as it settled and slid further inside the building, kicking up a storm of dust and dirt. Abigail lost sight of Gerald behind the avalanche of building materials. The mother's screech sounded behind her. The boy's cry sounded ahead of her. Both pushed her to run faster. She was losing sight of Gerald behind the rubble.

"Avalon." King Arthur clutched her arm with an iron vice grip that stopped her as she ran past him.

"Let go." Abigail tried to yank herself free, but King Arthur's hold was unyielding. "King, let go!"

"You can't go in there."

Abigail looked at him like he slapped her. A dozen questions sputtered against her tongue, but none made it past the barricade of her lips.

"There isn't a fire. You can't go in there."

King Arthur's statement made no sense to Abigail. She tried to free herself again, but her arm wouldn't listen. She became putty in his grip. The disaster around her slipped away until it was just her and King Arthur. His gold crown became the sun, his hold became the ground, his words became law.

"You can't go in there," King Arthur said again. "Restrain the mother."

"Yes, sir."

King Arthur was the leader of the Round Table Knights and co-founder of the Hero Relief Center, whatever he ordered had to be the best course of action. He released her arm, and Abigail intercepted the mother as she ran toward the collapsing building. It was difficult to hold her back. The mother squirmed and screamed inside Abigail's arms, thrashing against her chest and even biting her arm. Abigail held firm, obeying King Arthur's command, and waited for his next order.

At some point, the first responders did arrive and entered the building with Lancelot who covered them with his psychic shield. Slowly, they guided survivors out of the Dox-Con tower. Slowly, the mother settled in Abigail's arms while they waited. She, waiting for her son. Abigail, waiting for King Arthur who continuously glanced in her direction.

A firefighter exited the tower. He cradled a small body in his arms. The mother shrieked in Abigail's ear. The sound pierced every part of her and left her ears ringing as more screams erupted from the mother. Gerald's body didn't move as the firefighter lowered him onto a gurney. The firefighter and paramedic exchanged disapproving head shakes. The paramedic wheeled the gurney away from the tower, away from the growing triage of injured and to a new group plagued with body bags.

The shrieking turned to sobs.

"You didn't save him!" The mother's words were half made of snot and tears. "Why didn't you save him?!"

Abigail didn't know.

The mother turned away from the tower and beat her fists against Abigail's chest. Abigail didn't fight back. The hits were fueled by anger, not evil, and that somehow made them worse. Each hit shook loose a question that Abigail didn't know the answer to. *Why? Why? Why?* She stood still until the mother slumped against her and returned to her sobs. A paramedic approached, and Abigail had to peel the mother off her so she could be carted away. Abigail didn't see which group the mother would be joining. She looked okay physically, but Abigail knew little of the pain that would course through her body. She returned to King Arthur who was complimenting Lancelot on his apparent job well done.

"There you are," King Arthur said as a greeting when Abigail arrived. "Let's head back to HQ."

"To get our new assignments?" Lancelot asked eagerly.

Abigail gasped and gestured to the destruction around them. "Isn't this our assignment? People still need help."

Shaking his head, King Arthur said, "The city's first responders are here. They'll handle it."

"They need us!" Abigail snarled. "We need to do everything in our power to help."

"Don't question me, Avalon." King Arthur's voice could have frozen lakes but did little to cool down Abigail's flames. "With all the first responders here, the rest of San Arbor is vulnerable. I know what is best for us."

In the pit of her stomach, Abigail didn't believe him.

Chapter Five

When her patrol shift ended, Abigail didn't go to her office. The reports that needed filing could wait. Her statement regarding the carjacking she stopped could wait. Her costume that needed cleaning could wait. Abigail exited the elevator and marched to the closed office door of King Arthur. Despite her instincts, she exhaled deeply before knocking. Depleting her oxygen meant she wouldn't carelessly combust if her anger surged. It also meant she couldn't quickly defend herself.

"Come in." King Arthur sounded behind the door.

The hair on her arms raised, but Abigail still pushed the door open and entered the room. It looked as it always did: polished and proper. Lemon cleaner clung to the air. Every object had a place on the bookshelf or desk. It was cold. Abigail rubbed her hands over her arms, wincing when she hit the four purple bruises left from King Arthur's earlier grip. She immediately dropped her hands.

"I want to talk about earlier," she declared.

King Arthur raised an eyebrow but gestured to the sitting area of his office. Two striped love seats faced each other with an ornate coffee table between them. A bizarre prism made of several pieces of steel, copper, and glass sat at the center, casting a rainbow of light on the otherwise dark wooden surface. "Let's sit."

Abigail did as he requested, sitting opposite of her leader who didn't seem worried that she kept a hand on the pommel of her sword. "At the tower today, you didn't—"

"Coffee?" King Arthur interrupted. "Something to drink?"

Abigail didn't answer him. "At the tower you didn't let me go in with Lancelot. I want to know why."

"There wasn't a fire. There was no reason for you to be there."

"That's bullshit," Abigail snapped. "I could have done way more than hold back someone. I could have saved the boy if you had let me."

King Arthur grinned. "I didn't realize you took my orders so seriously."

Abigail struggled to find her footing. Her hand tightened around her sword. "You gave me the command."

"Which you obeyed," he reminded. "I can see your upset about the outcome of today, but deep down, you knew what was best for the situation. Or else, you would have acted differently."

"I don't see how any of that bettered the situation. All three of us could have done more." Abigail tried to recall the events, but the more she focused on them, the further away they became. The small moments she could recall felt like someone else's memories or watching a movie on a crappy television. Most of what she remembered was static.

Across from her, King Arthur's grin widened, spreading across his handsome face like an oil spill. Abigail felt like she had won a prize the way he looked at her. Almost like he was proud of her discovery. "You're catching on. We can do more."

Abigail gasped. "You did this because of Benton!"

"Yes." King Arthur's acceptance was as cold as the room. "Now, Benton can see how his proposed ordinance would work."

"You killed that boy."

"It is a shame that Benton's first responders couldn't reach him quickly enough, but, once we have full control of the city, things like that won't happen."

Full control of the city? "You're insane."

King Arthur's grin morphed into a glare. "Every decision I make is for our longevity. Unlike *your* treasonous acts last year. Don't think I've forgotten about Cinder."

Abigail's heart seized at his name. Anger was a comforting emotion compared to the darkness encroaching her vision. She leaned into her flames. Red sparks bit into her palm as she clenched her fist. "How could I forget when you constantly hold it over me."

King Arthur stood from the couch. Abigail hated that she flinched at his movement. Thankfully, she didn't think he saw her weakness as he rounded the couch. The distance he put between them was a clear indicator that he was finished with their conversation.

"You're a good hero, Abigail. San Arbor would be in bad shape if you left."

"Is that a threat?"

"Just a reminder that every hero's contract is up for debate each year." King Arthur held open the door. "Have a good evening."

Abigail tightened her jaw as she left, the door shutting promptly behind her, and unleashed a breath laced with sulfuric smoke once she was in the hallway. King Arthur's ideas were sick. She couldn't believe she played his game and became a show piece for his war against Benton. He could keep caring about their *longevity* all he wanted. Abigail would continue to be a good hero. If his word was law, then she would break it.

She stomped down the hallway to her office. The files and reports were still the last thing on her mind. She needed to let loose some steam or else she'd burn something to the ground. Once she passed the threshold of her office door, Abigail unsheathed her sword and ignited it with the fire leaping from her fingers. She cut down a floor lamp and set her next attack on one of the two chairs in front of her desk.

Lancelot paled on the other side of the flaming sword. He carefully removed himself from the chair, both hands up in surrender.

"What are you doing here?" Abigail lowered her sword, but it still burned wildly at her side.

"I thought we could do our reports together," he answered.

"Now's not the best time."

Despite the flames and weapon, Lancelot approached her. When Abigail didn't move, he took the invitation to touch her free hand. "You're hurt."

It was the understatement of the year, but Abigail only addressed the bruises Lancelot could see. "It's fine."

"When I came home with bruises, my mom always gave me a frozen spoon to put on them."

The fire began to calm against the steel of her blade. "She kept spoons in the freezer?"

He smiled. "I had a lot of bruises."

"From who?" she demanded, her cherry-red flames mirroring her panic.

"Easy, hero," Lancelot chuckled. "Mostly from myself, trying out my powers, or crashing my bike. The cold spoons didn't help much with skinned knees. I have some spoons in my office if you want one."

Abigail returned her sword to its sheath. Her flames extinguished in a smokey huff. "Don't bother, I wouldn't feel them much anyway."

"I'm here if you want to talk about today. No spoons required."

Abigail fell into one of the plush seats and Lancelot quickly sat in the other, leaning toward her as she tried to bury herself inside the cushions. About a dozen nasty things to say about King Arthur, only half of them true, begged to be said, but Abigail swallowed them down. Lancelot didn't need to be in the middle of them. He didn't need to become collateral damage if something were to implode. Lancelot was a good hero.

"I can't seem to wrap my head around today," she admitted. "I remember some pieces and others are blurry." Like following King Arthur so blindly that a kid was dead because of her inability to act.

"It was traumatic," Lancelot replied. "Your mind is probably blocking some parts to protect you."

"I didn't know you specialized in the brain."

"I watched a documentary on it." Lancelot blushed and rubbed his palms against his pant legs. "Do you want to go to dinner tonight? We can do something to get your mind off today. Even the best heroes can have a bad day."

Abigail shook her head. "I don't think I deserve a fun night out."

Lancelot deflated like a week-old balloon. "Okay, we'll just go home then."

"I'm not coming over tonight." Abigail interrupted Lancelot's coming protest. "I just want to be alone."

"I'll pick you up in the morning?"

Shaking her head, Abigail tried to smile. "Save your gas money. I can get back here just fine."

Abigail opted to sleep on the couch that night. She only entered the haunted bedroom to snatch a pillow and blanket, both thrown into the wash to help remove the woodsmoke smell, and her toiletries which she left at the kitchen sink. The bedroom door made a terrible shield against the remaining contents of the room. Too many times Abigail thought she heard Thomas' voice on the other side of it.

It had been a full year since the fire. It had only been a year since he was buried. Abigail thought the pain would be gone by now. Or at least subside enough for her to go about her days on her own. Her brain played tug of war with different memories. No matter which side was victorious, she would be the loser. She could either think about Thomas, the real memories with him and the proposed future they wanted, or the Dox-Con tower collapse. More pieces of that event slipped away. The details turned hazy and cliché. Abigail wasn't sure she was even there.

Only the sight of the dead kid and the anguish of the mother appeared in full focus.

Abigail rolled over on the couch and grabbed her phone from the floor. Before she finished typing Lancelot's number, she stopped herself. She needed to be alone. She needed to prove she could do this. Abigail *was* strong enough to sleep alone in her apartment. Backspacing the number, she punched in the closest Chinese takeout restaurant's number, deciding a full belly would help her sleep.

The momentary relief of human interaction when the delivery arrived was just a bonus.

Chapter Six

Having spent the entire night alone, Abigail arrived at work the next morning with a strange sense of accomplishment. She shouldn't feel this way just from sleeping by herself, especially after the darkness from the day before, but she gripped tightly onto the feeling in case someone tried snatching it away. She knew this tiny victory could be the snowball that rolled into a day full of bigger victories. She chose the public entrance of the HRC and smiled at the receptionist.

The tabloid magazine in Shannon's hand was as permanent a fixture of the lobby as were the five large portraits of the Round Table Knights hanging on the wall. Each picture was over six feet long and depicted the hero in a dramatic, black and white pose. Visitors could purchase more practical sizes of the posters at the gift shop. Thomas had wanted to get one of Avalon for his firehouse despite the complaints of his squad. Abigail shook her head, returning the memory to its locked box, and addressed Shannon a bit too loudly for the empty lobby.

"Morning Shannon. Anything good in there?"

Shannon peered over the top of the magazine; her gold eyeshadow matched her gold nails. "You usually don't care about what's printed in these things."

Shannon was right. Abigail hated the tall tales printed within the tabloid's pages that usually centered around the Knights and their perceived social and private lives. "Anything good *for you* in there?"

Shannon smiled, flipping around the magazine to show Abigail a grainy picture of a big-headed newborn baby. "There's an excellent piece concerning an alien baby born in Nevada."

Combustion

"That's ridiculous," Abigail chuckled. "It's probably just a mutation power that showed early."

As super-human abilities became more common place in the world, so did different classifications to understand and label them. Abigail was considered an elementalist for her control over an element. The other classifications included: mentalist, physicalist, phaser, and, newly classified, mutationist.

"But what if it's not?" Shannon comically raised an eyebrow, turning the magazine back around. "Super heroes exist, why couldn't aliens?"

"If they do, I know you'll be the first to tell me." Abigail knocked her knuckles against the top of the welcome desk. "I'll see you later."

Shannon muttered a farewell as Abigail hopped into an elevator headed to the upper floors. The eleventh floor was suspiciously quiet as Abigail entered the hallway lined with the offices of the Knights. She didn't think she was late, but quickly changed into her Avalon costume and took the stairs two at a time to the Round Table where her colleagues waited for the morning meeting.

"Morning," Lancelot smiled when Abigail took her seat next to him. "Are you feeling better?"

Abigail glanced at King Arthur who was too distracted by Excalibur to hear the question. She couldn't show any weakness, and Lancelot's inquiry was dangerously close to admittance.

"I'm feeling great." Abigail returned his smile. "How was your night?"

"A little lonely," he whispered, pretending to pout. It didn't pull a reaction from Abigail as he probably hoped it would. "Just did some errands and stuff. What about yours?"

Thankfully, the door opened and Abigail didn't have to come up with a lie to tell Lancelot as President Samuels entered the room with a mask-wearing guest.

The air simmered with electricity. Abigail straightened her back, fearing her poor posture would reflect badly on the company. She knew this hero, but only by his picture. His striking yellow and white suit was hard to forget despite him residing in a city halfway across the country. In the pictures she'd seen, he was smiling, sometimes even glowing to show off his powers, but now he looked at the Knights with somber eyes. It was clear he wasn't over the sudden deaths of his teammates.

"Everyone," President Samuels said, "I'm sure you're aware of who this is, but let me introduce you to Hero Enterprises' Beacon."

"It's a pleasure," Beacon said. "I've always been a fan of your cohesive theme."

King Arthur stood and offered Beacon his hand. "We're all sorry about your loss. How are things in Tennyson City?"

"That's actually the reason I've come here," Beacon answered after shaking King Arthur's hand.

"Beacon has a proposition for you." Samuels offered Beacon a seat before sitting down himself. He glanced at the Knights, then kept his eyes on Abigail as he said, "The HRC would support either decision you make."

Beacon pressed his hands against the granite tabletop. The brightness of his gloves clashed terribly with the muted colors of the room. He clashed terribly with the tightness of the team surrounding him. The Knights became a hungry, five-headed hydra as they waited for his proposition. Lancelot's bouncing leg kept brushing the side of Abigail's. She scooted slightly away from him and his nervous energy.

"Another member of my team was killed yesterday," Beacon started. "Rush was found beheaded in an alleyway."

Combustion

Merlin attacked the silence that encased the room after Beacon's statement. "We didn't hear about this."

"We haven't told anyone outside of Rush's family."

"Was he killed the same way as The Swordfish and The Guppy?" asked Lancelot.

Abigail glared at him and his lack of compassion. King Arthur raised his hand to reestablish order before addressing Beacon, touching his shoulder as he did.

"This can't be easy. Our condolences, again."

"Rush's autopsy report also showed he was under the influence of illegal substances. There aren't many drugs that would affect his fast metabolism. And the ones that could are extremely difficult to get a hold of." Beacon shrugged out of King Arthur's hand. "There's something vile in my city, and I'm here to ask for your help."

"When do we leave?" Lancelot's leg bounced in double time, his nerves evolving into excitement. "Excalibur can cut down anyone you need him to."

Beacon's mouth twitched into a smile before he said, "I'm asking for your help because I hope we can handle this without a lot of violence."

"What are you asking of us?" Excalibur inquired.

"I've read through the reports of how a few years ago you took down a gang that planned to overtake your city. I was impressed with how quiet that was. I fear my citizens will panic even more if things get too . . . loud."

"Most of that was Avalon's plan." King Arthur's statement surprised Abigail. He beamed at her as if yesterday's conversation never happened. "She's the one who pieced it all together. Her quick thinking probably stopped a major gang war."

Abigail blushed under her mask but couldn't defend the statement as President Samuels addressed her. "Beacon is hoping you'll use that quick thinking in his city. And, I'm hoping you'll stop whatever is in Tennyson City from coming to San Arbor."

"What makes you think it'll come here?" Excalibur asked.

"Besides Reckenburg, we have the next largest hero company," Merlin suggested, earning an approving nod from Beacon. "If this villain is wiping out heroes, we'd be next on the list."

"What are you asking?" Abigail repeated Excalibur's earlier question, snatching Beacon's stare and refusing to let go. Seven people sat at this table, but this conversation was only between her and him.

"We believe a group has formed and is responsible for the attacks. I'm asking you to infiltrate them and help Hero Enterprises take them out," Beacon said simply. "My team is too recognizable to do it ourselves. We need an outsider."

Lancelot jumped to Abigail's unwanted aid. "Avalon is as recognizable as anyone! Name someone else with a flaming sword. She'll be found out as soon as she arrives."

"The sword is Avalon's schtick," Abigail defended herself. She wanted to slap Lancelot for assuming she couldn't hold her own but opted for the civil approach. "Before the HRC, I only used my flames. Staying undercover wouldn't be an issue."

"You should stick to range moves," Excalibur said. "I know you used to specialize in hand-to-hand."

Abigail nodded. "Good idea."

Lancelot grabbed her arm, gripping around the healing bruises from yesterday and he let go with widened eyes. Abigail glowered at him, and as he turned to King Arthur, she feared his next statement. She feared he would say something to belittle her and her skills. She feared he would reveal her weakness.

"Why can't King use his powers and stop the villains at their next attack?" Lancelot asked.

Combustion

It seemed to surprise everyone but Beacon. "That's what I initially wanted, but the group's attacks are too area based to be targeted by King Arthur. Besides, I won't wait until another hero is hurt."

"But you want to send Avalon in like a chew toy?"

Red sparks jumped around Abigail's fingers, and it was hard not to use them on her partner. "That's enough, Lancelot. I'll do it."

Beacon smiled. "Excellent! Thank you, Avalon."

"Beacon and I will work out the details of your arrival," President Samuels explained. "We'll also need to plan an explanation for your absence here."

"How long will I be there?"

"I suspect a few months," answered Samuels.

"To do this right," Beacon added, "To truly destroy the rat's nest, we need to make sure you have time to get in deep and discover everything. This may only be one piece of a much larger puzzle."

"Avy, are you seriously thinking about this?" Lancelot asked.

"I'm not thinking, I'm going." This job was just the change Abigail needed. An excuse to get away from the ghosts in her apartment, to get out of King Arthur's terrible game, to make space between herself and Lancelot, to be a good hero. A hero saves people, and right now Abigail could save heroes.

"Thank you," Beacon said again. "I can breathe a little easier already."

Excalibur leaned across the table toward Abigail. "While they do all the boring paperwork, want to work on some new moves?"

Abigail smiled. Excalibur's energy was infectious, but more importantly his support meant everything. "If that's okay with Mr. Samuels, I'm game."

"That sounds like a fine idea," President Samuels said. "I'll find you when we have the details ready."

Chapter Seven

Replacing her Avalon costume with an HRC logo printed track suit didn't make Abigail feel as naked as leaving her sword in her office did. If the goal of the training session was to work on her ranged combat moves, then she had no use for her sword. Abigail chewed the inside of her cheek: she would have no use for her sword for the entire mission. When she first trained with the weapon, Abigail thought the prop would remain just that. She believed it would see more action inside endorsement videos than actual crime fighting. She had been wrong. She would need to grow accustomed to the missing weight on her side.

Abigail now had to believe her sword tutor then would offer her the same level of advice today.

Excalibur completed a complicated looking stretch as Abigail entered the training room attached to his office. After untwisting himself, he greeted her with a nod and, what she assumed was a grin as his face was hidden by his helmet. He lacked his own sword that usually hung at his hip, but the four walls around them were filled with other weapon options. He plucked a long staff from a rack and joined Abigail in the center of the room.

"What's the best range you have right now?" he asked, foregoing any unnecessary small talk.

Abigail demonstrated her Dragon's Breath, unleashing a cloud of blue fire from her mouth and relishing in the strength it roused within her. The flames shot several yards away from her, and she stopped the blast before it could burn anything.

"Impressive, but I don't think you should be using that."

Combustion

"Dragon's Breath might be more recognizable than a sword," Abigail wiped her mouth, drawing a line of soot across the back of her hand, "but it's the best range I have."

"For now," Excalibur corrected. "Try some things out. If we have to table the range attacks, we can work on bettering some new close combat moves."

Abigail crashed her knuckles together, showering the floor in red sparks. "You got it, boss."

Abigail was not impressed with her lack of a breakthrough after the first few hours of training. The fire balls she crafted and launched into the air retained their shape, heat, and power, but the moves were well documented as Avalon. Trying to imitate her old partner, Volcanic, and his awesome ability to shoot streams of flames from his fists ended in frustrating wisps atop her knuckles. The cherry-red flames became nothing more than an extra foot of reach for the hero.

Excalibur stayed silent in his corner, working through different techniques with the long staff. The weapon's movement ticked off the moments like a metronome and didn't help Abigail's waning patience. She exhaled heavily, the flames dropping off her skin and charring the floor.

"At this rate I might as well wear a T-shirt with 'Hi, my name is Avalon,' printed on it," Abigail huffed. The most she'd accomplished was singeing off her jacket's sleeves.

Excalibur chuckled. "May I make a suggestion?"

"Please."

Excalibur left his long staff leaning against the wall and approached Abagail, avoiding the warmer parts of the padded floor that still bubbled. "How much of your body can you coat with your flames?"

Abigail didn't know. She summoned her flames atop her fingers and commanded them up her hands, over her wrists, around her arms. She'd created small shields around her forearms before but hadn't sustained it longer than the attack. The flames continued to loop around her arms, over her shoulders and formed a chest plate. Another layer of fire dropped around her hips and sizzled against her thighs and backside.

"You kind of look like a gladiator," Excalibur said.

"I feel like that marshmallow man."

"Not like Avalon?"

She shook her head. "Not very much."

"This could be it then. Plus, you could shield your face to better protect your identity."

Abigail willed the flames to gather around her collar before stretching over her jaw and to her eyes forming a face plate. "Too bad we didn't think of this before. When I was your sidekick. We'd really match like this."

Excalibur chuckled and attempted to place his hand on Abigail's shoulder. At his hesitation, Abigail dropped her armor made of flames.

"You're going to be careful out there, right?"

"Aren't I always?"

Excalibur didn't answer, and Abigail was grateful. He squeezed her shoulder.

"I'll be careful," she promised. *I won't be reckless.*

Excalibur pulled Abigail into a tight hug that was more painful than comforting due to his armor. Despite the pointed metal pressing into her, Abigail returned the hug.

"I'll see you when I get back," she added to her list of promises after he released her.

Above them, a speaker crackled an order for Avalon to report to the Round Table.

"My little sidekick, off to take down a criminal underground on her own." Excalibur pretended to wipe a tear away from his helmet's eye socket. "You've made me proud."

Abigail smiled so wide it hurt her cheeks. She couldn't recall the last time a real smile felt like this. "Thank you, boss."

The Round Table contained more people than Abigail expected when she arrived. President Samuels sat between Beacon and King Arthur, all of whom Abigail expected to oversee the mission, but also at the table was Trevor Markov, head of marketing, someone from the data analyst team based on his badge color, and an unknown woman whose table space was dominated by two open notebooks. She clicked her pen rapidly, ready to take notes on the meeting.

Wanting to get comfortable with the hero she'd be working under, Abigail took the empty seat next to Beacon. She thought the forced proximity would breed familiarity in the short time they had before the mission started.

"Hey everyone." Abigail nodded toward Trevor, the data analyst, and the new girl before addressing Samuels. "I didn't think you guys would be ready this soon."

Samuels grinned. "We had a lot of brains on the project. There are still a few smaller details to figure out, but let's start with addressing the major points. Let me know when you have questions."

"Nothing is set in stone yet." King Arthur leaned around Samuels to speak directly to Abigail. "You can back out at any time."

"I won't."

It was the third promise Abigail made today, and it was the one she was most determined to keep. The others seated at the Round Table may have believed King Arthur's sincerity, but all Abigail heard was the challenge in his voice.

"Right." Samuels regained Abigail's attention. "Let's get started. Beacon?"

Beacon cleared his throat, and although he continued to address the room, the new girl noting down his statements, his kind eyes never left Abigail's. "The rest of Hero Enterprises won't know your real identity. They won't know that there's a hero undercover, either. I'll do what I can to keep you protected, but it will be important for you not to be caught. By us, or the police."

"That sounds simple enough," Abigail said. "Will I report directly to you then?"

Beacon shook his head. "Although I'll try to keep you protected, I cannot have any association with you. Inside or outside of a mask. We cannot risk anyone finding out who you are, or what the mission is."

"So, this is deep, deep undercover." A ball tightened inside Abigail's stomach. She had understood this was a solo mission, but she thought she'd at least have Hero Enterprises' support.

President Samuels nodded. "Yes, but you have a way to contact HE. Justin has developed a code for this."

Abigail eyed Justin: his name tag confirmed his identity. "This quickly?"

"Secret codes and languages have always been a hobby of mine," Justin answered. "I had a few already crafted that just needed tweaking. How do you feel about crossword puzzles?"

"I was never too good at them."

"That doesn't matter." Justin removed a newspaper from a backpack on the floor and handed it to Abigail. He next passed her a single sheet of paper containing a table of characters and the sounds they shouldn't make. "That's the cypher. You'll need to memorize it."

"And the paper?" Abigail looked at the Tennyson City Tribune. The lettering was far easier to understand than the intimidating cypher that could have been a cross between Russian, ancient Greek, and some fabled language from a fantasy novel. A few of the letters were upside down.

"The daily crossword puzzle is on the back of the entertainment section. You'll use the empty spaces to write your messages. If your words don't match the clues or are misspelled, then it won't matter, and if someone sees a finished puzzle, they won't bother picking it up."

"I don't think I'm following you," Abigail admitted.

Beacon took over the explanation. "There's a coffee shop in Tennyson City in the epicenter of the attacks. If it's near the base of the villains, as we suspect, then visiting there shouldn't be suspicious. You enter the shop, grab a snack and a paper, fill out the puzzle, and place it near the trash. After you leave, one of Hero Enterprises' staff will collect it with their coffee and bring it to my desk."

Abigail chewed the inside of her cheek thinking of how this plan could fail. "Will anyone question you getting a used paper?"

"Hero Enterprises is trying to go green. Recycling newspapers won't look out of place."

Abigail looked back at the cypher. "How long do I have to memorize this thing?"

"At least a few days," President Samuels answered. "We need time to arrange your departure from San Arbor, which Mr. Markov has thought of."

"I hope Avalon is ready for desk duty." Trevor Markov spoke with the ghost of an Eastern European accent. "We will be staging a call where you will injure yourself, I propose a broken leg. The call will be big and flashy and somewhere that can be heavily documented by civilians. The more who see you fall, the more believable your absence will be. We will also be prerecording several updates on your recovery to post while you're gone. It is genius."

"How am I going to fake break my leg?"

"Lancelot will help with that," Trevor answered. "He can make a fall look real without you hitting the ground."

Abigail sighed. "He's not too keen on me doing this whole thing, are you sure he'll work with you on this?" She feared he may actually let her fall in order to keep her trapped in her office with a real broken leg.

"Lancelot will do as he's told," King Arthur answered with a certainty that made Abigail's skin crawl.

She didn't ponder her body's reaction to his cryptic response. She turned to Beacon and Samuels. "Okay, what else?"

"Your new identity," President Samuels answered. "Costumes said they'd be here before we got this far in the meeting—"

President Samuels was interrupted as the door swung open, banging against the side wall, narrowly missing a hanging monitor. Forever a fan of dramatic entrances, Veronica Fang entered the Round Table with several members of the costume department at her heels. The pink jacket draping to her stilettos was flashier than any hero costume she had designed. Veronica sat at the head of the table and clapped her hands twice. Her three oddly dressed coworkers lined up behind her.

All three employees posed as if they were about to strut down a Paris runway. One was dressed as a baseball player. The baseball she prepared to pitch had orange streamers adhered to the surface that poorly resembled flames. Another wore a modified firefighter turnout coat resembling a professional wrestling outfit. The final woman squeezed herself in a sequined onesie with red and yellow feathers draping off the arms like a cowgirl jacket.

"My apologies for being late," Veronica said. "I hope we didn't miss our cue?"

"You're right on time actually," President Samuels answered. "Please begin."

Abigail wouldn't be surprised if Veronica had waited outside the door until the perfect opportunity for her entrance. If the costume designer had more time, Abigail was sure the entrance would have been accompanied with spotlights and music.

"Now, Avalon, please do keep in mind that the designs behind me are simply prototypes. After you've made your choice, the costume will be properly developed and fitted to you." Veronica snapped her long-nailed fingers and the baseball model stepped forward and alternated through several poses. "Meet Hot Shot. After her major league dreams were quashed, this fastball pitcher decided that a life of crime better suited her fast-paced lifestyle."

Abigail stopped Veronica's explanation with an unappreciative laugh. When the rest of the table didn't share the humor, Abigail sobered. "What is this?"

"A villainous identity for you," Veronica snapped, crossing her arms. "As requested by President Samuels."

Abigail addressed her boss, "I'm sorry sir. I'm sure this was well intended, but it won't work."

President Samuels nodded for her to continue.

"An established villain could threaten the group. I need to approach them as someone off the street. A nobody. If I were to go as someone like that," Abigail pointed at the three models, "The gang would look into the history, and when they find nothing older than a week prior, red flags are sure to go up."

"You'll what then?" Veronica continued to bite. "Waltz up to the villains wearing that?"

"No." Abigail didn't think she needed to confirm that she wouldn't be wearing Avalon's costume while undercover, but the way Veronica fumed at the table she wanted to be sure everyone knew. "I'll wear street clothes, something normal. Cut and dye my hair, too."

"I agree that keeping a low profile would be better," Beacon said. "But there should be some kind of history on you. Some crime reports at the very least."

Samuels nodded. "Justin, is that something you can do?"

"For sure," Justin said excitedly. "Tell me the crimes and where they occurred, and I'll get them into the proper systems."

"You'll still need an alias," Samuels said to Abigail. "One for your super ego, too."

"I'll come up with one."

"You should commit a crime when you first arrive." Beacon's statement surprised Abigail. "Something to get their attention."

"I don't like the sound of that."

"It's for the greater good," Samuels assured Abigail. "You know you'll need to get some dirt on your hands to make this believable. Once the mission is completed, any crimes will be removed from your record."

It wasn't the black mark on her record that worried her. It was the people she'd potentially put in danger because of her actions.

"Unless you don't think you're up for it." King Arthur's sardonic tone was lost to everyone in the room as he leaned behind Samuels and locked eyes with Abigail.

"Can you arrange an armored truck?" Abigail asked Beacon, her blood simmering from King Arthur's taunt. "A couple bags of cash ought to entice them to let me in. Load the bags with trackers too. We'll start building a map and track their movements and any prominent locations."

Beacon smiled. "I knew you were the right person for the job. I'll make sure one's on the road when you arrive."

"Those are our major takeaways from this meeting," President Samuels said to the room. "Grace, did you get everything?"

The employee with her notebooks nodded. "Everything's scribed."

"Excellent. Trevor, get the details finalized on the staged call so we can get this mission started. Avalon, be ready tomorrow to prerecord your absence videos and study that cypher."

"Yes sir." The coded language would be the least of her worries once she started the mission. Abigail would learn it backward and forward by the end of the week, and then the real fun could begin. Excited energy rushed through her system. She'd be able to do a lot of good for a lot of people. To her, it was the ultimate task for a hero.

Abigail was, and would always be, a damn good hero.

Chapter Eight

A stack of seven scripts sat on Abigail's desk when she arrived to work the next morning. As she dressed in her costume she also accidentally donned a green mask of jealousy. Today was supposed to be her patrol day, but the job was given to Lancelot so she could spend the day at the HRC's recording studio. Not only was it unfair, but Abigail couldn't chance her partner getting hurt on a call that was supposed to be hers. She gritted her teeth, assuring herself one day of torturous PR would be worth starting her mission in Tennyson City. She grabbed the scripts, popped down in her chair and read through them.

After marking the pages up with a red pen, changing a few of the cheesier lines to resemble something she'd actually see herself saying, Abigail took the elevator to the recording level. A leg cast and wheelchair waited for her on the sound stage. Trevor was serious about making this look real. Abigail figured she'd be filmed with her legs below a table. Something less extreme than what lay before her.

She dropped her scripts off with the director's assistant and found Trevor among the walkie-talkie wearing minions of the marketing and PR teams. They scuttled around like crabs avoiding the boiling water that was this side of hero work. Abigail loosened her collar and took a deep breath.

"Hey Mr. Markov," she greeted. "Where do you want me?"

"Avalon, why not get seated there and we'll get the cast on you. You've read through the scripts?" His accent heightened the second *a* of her name.

Abigail seated herself in the wheelchair and one of the staff attached the leg cast. A carefully hidden clasp made the prop look like a solid piece of plaster once on. Abigail wasn't sure if props had this on hand for a situation like this, or if a poor intern was kept up all night making it for her. "I made a few adjustments," Abigail answered. "Are you sure we need to record so many?"

"Of course. We need to buy you enough time to complete your mission. We have two other story lines to record after your fabled recovery in case you are not back yet. You'll get those scripts after lunch. The story lines have you learning how to walk after wearing the cast for so long and helping a village in India by delivering food and medicine."

"Why don't we actually do that?" Abigail asked, jerking in the chair to better see Trevor. The assistant making the final adjustments on the cast begged her to be still. "Why are we pretending to help when I actually can?"

Trevor looked up from his clipboard. "That is a good idea. Good for The Round Table Knight's universal numbers."

Abigail's eyes widened. "It's good for the people in the village!"

Trevor's face softened, and it looked like he finally heard Abigail. "Okay. We'll arrange for a real shipment of medicine and food to be sent to a village and save the story line for when you Knights can go and hand out another supply run. Sound better?"

"Extremely. Thank you." It was absurd she needed to explain how to help people while inside a *hero company*, but she kept her annoyance hidden.

Trevor nodded, his nose back on the clipboard. "We'll need a new back up story line. Cameron? Get brainstorming."

Someone shouted, 'yes sir!' behind Abigail.

"I think two will be plenty," she tried to assure Trevor. The hope she had of getting out early and reclaiming her patrol shift was fading.

"Nonsense. We will record three. Better to be safe than sorry in this business. Besides, we have you booked all day. It will be fun."

"So much fun," Abigail grumbled.

Trevor smiled at her, then quickly frowned as his eyes dipped to her arm where the ghost of a bruise still clung onto Abigail's skin. "We need makeup, center stage!"

As a layer of foundation covered the bruise, Abigail imagined the makeup covering the entire grip King Arthur still had on her and this company.

"That's a wrap, Avalon!" shouted the director behind the glaring stage lights that blinded Abigail for the last five hours.

Abigail's knees cracked as she finally stood from the chair she'd been in, and she did several toe touches before leaping off the stage. No one attempted to adjust her costume, hand her a new script, or push her toward another set so she snuck to the exit before Trevor decided they needed a fourth and fifth story line.

The hallway outside the studio bled orange from the sunset burning on the other side of the windows, staining San Arbor in similar shades. She'd been trapped inside the studio all day. Useless to her city, dishonoring her powers, wasting her day. Abigail leaned her forehead against the glass, and the cool surface offered her little relief as her unnaturally warm body heated the glass.

Tomorrow the fake call, she reminded herself. *Friday, Tennyson City.*

No more heroes would die once she was there. No more civilians would be in danger once she arrived. When the threat there was eliminated then her own city would be safer. It was an easy trade off to lose her patrol day to the greedy claws of commercials for that outcome.

"Hey Avy! I didn't think they'd ever let you go." Lancelot's reflection joined Abigail's in the window. His polished teeth chomped through several downtown buildings.

"How was patrol?" Abigail turned away from the cityscape, leaning on the wall to face him.

"Don't worry. You didn't miss anything," he answered. "A little car accident that needed some heavy mental lifting, and a water line break at an elementary school. I was mostly there just as a precaution. The whole school did smell like sewage though."

Abigail sighed. "That's good."

"The sewage smell?" Lancelot scrunched his nose together.

Abigail chuckled and swatted his shoulder. "No, not the smell. That San Arbor is okay."

"Of course, it is Avy. She won't burn down one day without you."

"What about several?" Abigail regretted her comment. Lancelot's face dropped and it was clear her attempt at a joke did not take.

"Excalibur and I prepped the location for the call tomorrow," he admitted softly.

"You're going to catch me, right?" Her fear of him sabotaging her mission hadn't dissipated like she hoped it would.

"I'll always catch you." Lancelot's somber mood evaporated, leaving behind two bright suns. The one fading on the outside of the window, and the one growing in his smile.

Abigail faced the dying sun, knowing if she stared at it, she'd face fewer complications than her other option. Lancelot had always had her back. In his time as her sidekick to their time as equals, Abigail never feared his commitment to her or the Hero Relief Center. She refused to think she was wrong to worry about him, but she did recognize the bitter taste it left in her mouth. Lancelot was a good hero, and that wouldn't change while she was gone. Her gaze slid from the skyline to the lawn outside of the HRC. King Arthur's crown caught and reflected a beam of light, shooting it across a female figure. Abigail squinted her eyes but didn't recognize her.

"Who's with King?" The question slipped out.

Lancelot's body pressed against hers as he looked out the window. "That's Camellia Diaz, the president of Dox-Con."

"What are they talking about?"

"I think she came by to thank him, thank us, for being at the accident."

After their silent exchange, the Dox-Con president entered a car and left the HRC property. King Arthur waited several minutes before returning to the building.

"We should go out tonight."

"What?" Abigail asked him, turning around.

"We should go out tonight," he repeated. "You and me."

"I don't know Lance. I still have preparations to make before Tennyson."

"Please Abigail?" he whispered her name. "We won't see each other for, like, months. Let me give you a fun night in San Arbor before you go."

Saying "no" to Lancelot sometimes felt like kicking a puppy: an act of cruelty on something that just wanted to love you.

"Okay," she gave in with a sigh. "What are you thinking?"

Lancelot grinned. "The place we had our first date!"

Abigail's face blanked, and as the emotion drained away so did Lancelot's smile.

"You don't remember, do you?"

"It's not that." Abigail tried to recover. "I just don't know what you considered our first date to be."

"What do you think it is?"

Abigail doubted it was the first night she stumbled to his doorstep, shaking from the cold rain and her pain, or the first night she took advantage of his affection toward her and used him to forget herself for a few hours, or the first morning she bolted from his apartment before he woke. Feeling guilty and ashamed, she doubted it was the night she returned.

"That fusion place downtown," he filled the silence. "With the egg roll burritos."

"That's what I was thinking," she lied. "Dinner with you sounds great."

Lancelot's smile returned tenfold. "Awesome! Let's get changed and I'll meet you at the car."

The eight minute drive was filled with Lancelot's idle chatter about the car accident he helped clean up earlier that day. Abigail listened mindlessly, nodding when she needed and returning his animated facial expressions when he looked at her at stop lights. Guilt nauseated her as they neared the restaurant, and Abigail realized she couldn't recall any of the details Lancelot supplied about the crash.

She tried to lie to herself. The cypher kept her distracted. She should be focused on that, not going to dinner with anyone. But Abigail's subconscious was getting just as sick of her lies as she was of King Arthurs'.

It wasn't just the last eight minutes that she'd abused Lancelot's friendship, either. In the last year, how often had she used him without a second thought? The answer that came to her sickened Abigail. Lancelot wasn't hers to use. He was her partner, and it was time they returned to that status. She hoped in her absence his not-so-secret crush would evaporate.

"Here we are." Lancelot parked his car a few buildings down from the restaurant. He grabbed a fist full of change from the cup holder before exiting.

"Did you ever bring Monica here?" Abigail asked as she joined him on the sidewalk.

Pink dusted his nose as it usually did whenever the Channel 9 reporter was brought up. "Lancelot brought her take out from here once. We never moved passed the secret identity phase."

"That's the smartest thing," Abigail replied. "It should be the last thing you reveal to someone."

"You don't have to tell me twice. I still can't believe you told me your . . ." he trailed off as they neared the front door. "I knew you almost two years before you told me."

"You were so quick to tell me yours."

"Honestly, I thought you found out when you kept calling me Lance outside the office."

"It was your nickname," Abigail defended with a laugh, following the hostess to their table. "I had no idea it was actually your name."

Lancelot accepted a menu from the hostess, thanked her, and she left with their drink orders. "I bet you can understand why getting into the Knights was a big deal for me. My mom said I was destined for the team. My name already so close to an actual knight of legend."

"But that Lancelot betrayed his King Arthur."

Lancelot's eyes widened as if Abigail had accused him of the adultery committed by Lancelot du Lac. "I never read the actual stories."

"Well, there's no Guinevere on the team so I think you're safe."

"Why didn't anyone tell me I picked the worst knight?"

Abigail pulled back her menu as the waitress set their drinks down. She gave her food order before answering Lancelot. "He was actually one of the most skilled knights. Plus, I bet Samuels loved your name idea."

Lancelot smiled. "He did. I think that's why I got the job so easily."

"Not your powers?" Abigail playfully raised an eyebrow.

"Oh, I'm sure they came in handy, too," Lancelot chuckled then composed himself. "While you're gone, is there anyone I need to cover for?"

"What do you mean?"

"Is there anyone in the city that will wonder where you've gone? Any friends that will try to contact you?"

Abigail scratched the back of her head. "My only friends are at the HRC."

"That can't be right," Lancelot gasped. "How long have you been in San Arbor?"

"Not too long. At least six Christmases." Abigail had gotten a live tree her first year in San Arbor and still felt like she was cleaning needles out of her carpet."

"And we're your only friends?" Lancelot didn't seem to believe her.

Abigail shrugged. "What can I say? I found the best friends inside work so why bother looking elsewhere."

"It sounds lonely." Lancelot's comment stung more than he probably intended it to.

"It's the safest option." Abigail paused and smiled at the waitress as she delivered their food. The bizarre mixture of Asian spices and Mexican heat shouldn't have smelled as wonderful as it did. Abigail's stomach gurgled before she finished her explanation. "If someone connected who I was, then they could be targeted. Either by a villain or the media. Not to mention, if someone else made the connection then my friend could be used to hurt me. It's a situation I don't want to put anyone in."

"What if someone willingly wanted to be in that position?" Lancelot slurped up a noodle.

"I wouldn't give them the chance."

"What are you telling your parents?"

"About my *career* or my *business trip*?"

"Both? I can't wrap my head around you not telling them anything. Don't you think lying to them hurts them more than knowing?"

"I'd rather they be alive and lied to than be killed because of me," Abigail snapped.

Silence fell over their table interrupted only by the sounds of food consumption, which only seemed to make the silence worse. Abigail sighed.

"I think they do know, in a way. They always knew I wanted to be a hero, especially when I got my powers, so working a vague corporate job in the same city as The Round Table Knights? I'm sure they've pieced it together. As for the trip, I'm telling them I'm going overseas to open a new branch so communication will be difficult."

"Want me to keep an eye on them?"

"That would be nice, thank you." Abigail didn't mean to fall victim to Lancelot's puppy-dog eyes, but after her earlier bite she was glad to give him this victory. "There's a plant in my apartment that you could water, too."

"Let's bring it over to my place tonight! I'll probably forget about it if I'm not staring at it," he laughed.

That gave Abigail hope. Perhaps his affection would wane if he wasn't staring at her, too.

"You're going to do great, by the way." Lancelot's statement surprised her.

Abigail cautiously replied, "What changed your mind? Earlier it seemed like I was the least qualified for the job."

"I may have overreacted," he admitted. "The Knights are like my family and seeing one of them go away was scary."

"You offered up King pretty quick."

Combustion

"I may also have some bias toward you," Lancelot blushed. "But I mean it. You're going to do great. Tennyson City is lucky to have you."

"I'm coming back, Lance." Abigail reached across the table to hold his hand, despite her better judgement. "San Arbor is my home. The Knights are my team."

Chapter Nine

Abigail was used to running into burning buildings. Her fireproof body made her the perfect candidate for the job. Running across rooftops was another beast, however, and kept the hero second guessing every step that brought her closer to the edge of the building. The man she chased leapt off the building and crashed onto a fire escape. His backpack rattled with each movement, allowing Abigail to follow him without a line of sight. She slid onto the fire escape, dropping off the ladder into a roll that let her bounce back into a sprint. Running through the crowded street, the man tugged civilians off the sidewalk creating a mess of bodies for her to navigate through.

Abigail shouted apologies and helped a few people regain their balance but kept her eyes on the criminal, now scurrying up an awning and using a flagpole to return to the rooftops. Abigail summoned flames to her boots and rocketed herself to his level. A flurry of flashing cameras caught her ascent. She continued her chase. The edge of the roof grew closer.

"Ready in three . . . two . . . one . . ." Lancelot counted down in her earpiece as his icy psychic touch wrapped around her.

In an excellent display of athleticism that Abigail didn't possess, she soared across the alley between two buildings. She ran after the criminal as if she had leapt off a single step rather than crossing eight feet of air.

Of course, this chase was staged. This street chosen for the flat level of the roofs and popularity for outdoor lunches and midday shoppers. The *criminal* running ahead of Abigail was a criminal informant for the police who needed a reason to return to jail. The backpack of stolen goods was a collection of TV remotes and bike chains.

Combustion

"Two more jumps before we're there," Lancelot sounded in her earpiece. He lowered himself from the sky to fly beside Abigail. "You scared?"

"No way." She chanced looking at him, offering him a quick grin before returning her attention to the roof. "I know you won't let me fall."

Lancelot nodded and returned to his aerial position before counting down the next jump. Abigail launched herself off the roof, soared forward, and continued her sprint after somersaulting into her landing. A new surge of power edged her on, the feeling spurred on by the promise of freedom after two more base jumps. The idea of leaving San Arbor did scare her, but the thrill of her new mission in Tennyson City devoured that fear. Plus, she knew she was leaving her city in capable hands. Excalibur would protect her home.

And so would Lancelot. He had become a good hero, just like she knew he could when they first worked together.

"Final jump in three, two, one . . ."

Abigail sailed across the alleyway. The new roof she stood on was on the corner of two busy streets and the sounds of traffic, both automotive and commuter, blared around her. Her *criminal* clutched his backpack to his chest and slowly backed away from her. For a pretend chase atop an empty roof, he performed like he was on a stage.

"You won't get me!" shouted the man. "I know these streets better than you."

Abigail laughed. If she had a script for this event, this would have been redlined out. "Hand over the bag and I'll go easy on you."

Abigail's hair whipped around her. Loose debris lifted from the ground. She looked around for Lancelot but didn't find him or his cold mental touch. The windstorm picked up again and was accompanied by the deafening *whoosh-whoosh-whoosh* of a helicopter. Above her, the vehicle marked with the red Channel 9 logo hovered closer.

"Right on time." Abigail could barely hear Lancelot through her earpiece.

"I wasn't expecting this," she replied.

"Samuels leaked the chase to social media for better coverage. Ready?"

"Now or never."

Abigail knocked her knuckles together, sparks showering off her hands, and followed her target off the side of the building. As planned, the man pulled a grappling hook from his bag and fired it across the open air where it hooked into a building on the opposite side of the busy street. The criminal informant sailed across the air and vanished into an open window. Without a grappling hook, Abigail powered herself forward with a burst of flames concentrated at her feet. Her flames sputtered and her body dropped. She thought she'd be okay with the plan, but everything inside of her screamed to fight back. To summon her flames, to grow wings, to defy gravity. Abigail clamped her jaw shut and fell. Lancelot's cold touch wrapped around her waist, but she didn't slow down. She felt like a puppet, her limbs waving wildly without her control. The parked car was suddenly too close. She thought she was about to die.

They hadn't planned for Abigail to scream, but the reaction tore through her lungs before the sound was overpowered by shattering windows.

"You okay?" Lancelot shrilled in her ear. "Avalon!"

Under the dark smoke rising from the flattened car, Abigail produced a handful of red capsules the size of Tylenol pills and tossed them onto her left leg. Upon impact, the capsules, an invention from Merlin, filled the area with a red, blood-like substance. Abigail patted her chest and face with more of the chemical compound and twisted herself into a broken shape and moaned as the first civilian arrived. Their camera phone captured the damaged hero before their own eyes registered it.

More people surrounded the dented car and ogled Abigail like a zoo animal. She kept moaning, reaching down to her blood-soaked body, and screaming terribly as her hands brushed her would-be broken leg. She smashed her head against the car's roof to distract herself from the pain like she'd seen action stars do in movies. The self-inflicted attack hurt more than the entire fall. Even though she squeezed her eyes shut, the flashes of cameras still broke through. She tried reaching out to the closest person, a middle-aged woman in a crop top, and begged her to help.

Her camera phone clicked as a response.

"Avalon!" Lancelot shouted somewhere beyond the crowd. "Make a path! Avalon!" He pushed through the mob and clasped her hand that still reached out for the woman. "I've got you."

Abigail lost track of the number of times she felt his psychic hold today, but once again its icy tendrils wrapped around her and she was lifted from the car. It was easy to look broken in his hold, her arms falling limp and her head lolling to the side. She feigned unconsciousness, listening to Lancelot directing the crowd to give him space before rising in flight. The cacophony of panicked civilians covered the trick the heroes played.

After several silent minutes, Abigail opened one eye. He had replaced his mental hold for a physical one, but his arms were just as cold as his mind. Lancelot watched Abigail, his face unhappy and sad.

"Did it not work?" Abigail squirmed, which only made him tighten his hold around her.

"Easy," he instructed, talking through their earpieces, so she could hear him over the wind. "I don't want to drop you."

"Did it work?" she asked again.

"They bought it."

"Then why do you look like your goldfish just died?"

A smile tried forming on his mouth, but Lancelot didn't allow it to stay. "You don't look good."

Abigail glared. "Thanks. It's not like I fell 20 stories or something."

"I almost forgot it was pretend," he admitted. "When I got there, I thought you really were hurt. That I hadn't caught you."

Abigail regretted her hostility. "You caught me, just like you promised. I'm okay."

Lancelot didn't respond. The HRC loomed into view and Abigail knew the hospital wing would be waiting for her. A media van sped below them already wanting the first scoop covering the fallen Avalon. Abigail tucked her head into Lancelot's chest in case they had a telescopic lens trained on her.

"If it looked good enough to trick you," she whispered, "Then I say we pulled it off."

Lancelot touched down on the extended section of the roof reserved for helicopters and heroes with the ability of flight. He set Abigail on a waiting gurney. She returned to her previous unmoving state until they were behind the media free walls of the HRC. The scrubbed employee wheeled her into a windowless room and left without a word. At the sound of the door shutting, Abigail perked up and tore a tissue out of the box on the bedside table and dabbed the fake blood off her face.

After four tissues refused to clean herself up, Lancelot rummaged through the cabinets of medical supplies and found a box of hand wipes and set them on the edge of Abigail's gurney.

"Nice find." Abigail ripped into the wipes and scrubbed her hands and face with them. The white material turned red as the cleaning solution broke down Merlin's chemical bonds.

"Now I can really see that you're okay," Lancelot smiled.

Abigail, assuming she properly cleaned her face, balled up the red stained wipes and tossed them and the tissues into a waste basket. She stretched her legs over the edge of the gurney and then got to the floor to do a jumping jack for good measure.

"I couldn't imagine what it would be like to actually break my leg," she commented.

"Let's not find out," Lancelot said. "If you broke it in Tennyson City, I wouldn't be able to sign your cast."

Abigail returned to the edge of the gurney. Lancelot not being able to sign her cast would be the least of her worries if she got badly injured. She was certain that an organization capable of taking out heroes wouldn't hesitate to cut any dead weight off their own team. The door opened before she voiced that opinion.

"Excellent work." President Samuels greeted them. Mitch was at his heels holding a bag marked with the nearby drug store logo. "Even I thought the plan had gone south. You gave me a heart attack; I can only guess how Abigail here was feeling."

"I didn't doubt Lancelot," she reassured both her boss and partner. "I trust him."

"King Arthur is giving a heartfelt statement downstairs to the media," Samuels said.

"This soon?" Lancelot asked.

"Better to give the dogs their bone before they try sneaking in."

The bitterness tainting Samuel's words seeped into Abigail's own. "I still think we should have spiked the windowsills."

Samuels laughed and it broke the tension that tried suffocating the room. From his tailored suit jacket, the handkerchief and cufflinks a matching blue, he handed Abigail an envelope. She peered under the flap and found a ticket for the Jolt Station train depot.

"I'm ready to go." She folded the flap back down, securing her ticket inside.

"Not yet." Mitch moved out from behind President Samuels and offered his bag to her.

She carefully accepted the gift. It could have been full of angry scorpions based on the friendship they accumulated in Abigail's time at the Hero Relief Center. Thankfully, the bag only contained a box of red hair dye and scissors.

"To help with your new identity," he grumbled.

"Red's my favorite color." Abigail fought the urge to hug the grumpy assistant. Under all of his ill moods and complaints, he really did care. "Thank you."

"Speaking of your identity," Samuels cut in. "Have you decided on your new name?"

"I have." Abigail looked all three of them in the eyes before answering. "I've chosen Wildfire."

Chapter Ten

Adjusting her headphones, Abigail was again surprised by the lack of hair tangling in her fingers. The blonde curls she had admired since middle school were gone. Hastily chopped away with drug store scissors to form a sharp pixie cut and drenched in garnet red hair dye. The reflection she caught of herself in the train's window caused her to flinch. She barely recognized herself.

The nine-hour train ride was nearing its end. The stretching farmland outside slowly gained dimension as hills grew into cliffs, and farmland turned to sand and arid plants. Abigail spent most of the trip trying to nap, but her seat wasn't padded enough to stop all the bumps from the track. She chose to spend the remaining hour scrolling through the news feed on the modified phone President Samuels supplied. The device was normal in every way, except for the broken clock that always read 18:21.

Despite her appearance, Abigail easily recognized the hero flooding the articles and video clips. Avalon's "deadly dive" captured not only San Arbor but several surrounding cities and landed her the top story on the United Heroes website, covering every name brand hero in the nation. *Avalon crashed down 23 stories into a car, breaking her leg, injuring her spine and lacerating the hero in various places,* read one of the articles accompanied with a photo provided by the HRC of Abigail laid up in a hospital bed. *In a statement made by Hero Relief Center's King Arthur, Avalon will be out of commission until her injuries heal. The company is unsure how long it could take, but assured San Arbor citizens that being down a hero would not hinder their ability to serve the city. At the time of reporting, Avalon, The Dragon Slayer, was unavailable for comment.*

The next story included cell phone footage of the fall. Abigail winced at the sound her body made on impact. From the video's angle, she watched the car's windows burst as her body crashed onto the hood, the car collapsing under her. A human body would not have caused such a level of destruction. Lancelot's psychic force flattened the car a second before Abigail made contact. It looked gruesome, her limbs spilling over the car, the fake blood dripping through the under carriage mixing with oil and gasoline. On the video, people shouted just before running to the car. Abigail clicked out of the footage and other waiting news stories about her. She didn't want the reminder that her own citizens would rather film her death than offer her help.

That nasty taste still hadn't left her mouth.

She stored her belongings and watched Tennyson City rise out of the landscape. The arid plants broke away into subdivisions and highways. Silver buildings of Tennyson City's downtown shimmered in and out of focus like heat mirages. Beyond them, the ocean crashed onto rocky beaches. Abigail thought she was looking through a time machine. This metropolis seemed so futuristic compared to her humble city. The last nine hours could have transplanted her to Mars for all she knew with this bright and shining city set in the middle of a wasteland.

It was beautiful. It was new. It was a city that needed saving, and that was just what Abigail was going to do. No matter her appearance or pretend identity, Abigail knew her truth. Reaching under her shirt, she squeezed the remains of her engagement ring. She would save these heroes.

Tennyson City's Grand Mark Station was streamlined compared to Jolt Station. Instead of the octagon fingers stretching into six different banks with waiting trains, Grand Mark Station was a single, long bay where four different tracks made port under the vast skylight-filled dome. People entered and exited trains in outfits made colorful in comparison to the stark white of the station. It felt like a wild artist had unleashed several dozen paint buckets onto an empty canvas. Abigail's red hair went unnoticed as she traversed between a woman sporting green and blue pig tails.

Outside the station, modern buildings containing more glass than steel decorated Tennyson City. Beams of sunlight filtered in every direction and brightened the city. Muted plum and rose-colored plants grew inside colorful planters on street corners. San Arbor had been dominated by tall trees that shaded the city. These plants offered zero relief aside from their simple beauty, and made the sidewalk feel ten times hotter. Abigail didn't mind that though. She inhaled deeply, felt fire course under her skin, and tasted the salt from the ocean.

She hoped between sneaking into a villainous crime organization and hiding her true identity she'd be able to see the ocean while here.

Abigail took off down the street with an excited step. Shops lined the bottom floors of the corporate buildings, and somewhere a restaurant was preparing for lunch based on the spicy smells filling the air. She didn't know where she was going, and that was okay. The best way to get to know a city was to get lost in it. As she turned corners, she logged the street names into her memory and practiced recoding their names through the cypher.

By the eleventh street it was getting easier.

By the twelfth street, Abigail finally gave in to the delicious smell of food and ducked into the first establishment selling portable options. Two street tacos and a pair of comically large sunglasses in the shape of margarita glasses later, Abigail returned to the street and found the starting piece of her mission. She devoured her tacos, donned her improvised mask, and approached the grey armored truck. The license plate read 1821.

She crouched behind one of the colorful potted plants and watched the employee store his dolly in the back then join the driver in the truck's cab. Once the door shut, Abigail sprang forward and leapt onto the step bumper, using her fingers to burn small hand holds into the exterior and climb onto the truck's roof. The truck lurched forward and merged into traffic without anyone noticing the stowaway.

Too easy, Abigail thought, almost appalled at her realization. She hoped this truck was purposely put on the street for her today, and Tennyson City's other money moving vehicles were better enforced. She peered over the cab. Too engrossed with their own personal bubbles, other commuters didn't notice her atop the truck. She waited for the truck to slow at a stop light before moving forward. The stop was short lived, and the truck sped through a sharp turn. Abigail's grip slipped off the smooth surface and she flailed in the direction of the turn, slamming into the side of the truck. Her arm burned as she held herself up by four fingers. Tennyson City passed by tinged in green due to her novelty margarita sunglasses.

The truck bounced forward, making holding on more difficult. Abigail inhaled deeply, mentally preparing herself, and twisted her body to the right so she could rotate around. Her chest slammed into the truck and knocked loose her stored oxygen. Gritting her teeth, she pulled herself back onto the roof.

As she prepared to melt through the truck's roof, Abigail felt eyes on her.

Abigail peered over the truck. Everyone seemed too involved with their problems, a text message, a difficult level on a handheld game, an unruly child, to notice her, but someone wearing a dark hoodie stared at her. She couldn't see his face, but she couldn't deny the eerie feeling tiptoeing across her skin. She pressed herself closer to the top of the truck and the stranger vanished after the next turn.

Forcing the creepy-crawly feeling away, she heated her hands, and pressed them against the roof until a hole formed. Abigail dropped in, her boots crunching the cooling metal like icicles. The truck was almost empty. Only three bags of cash were left on the shelving units lining either side of the truck. She had no way of checking which bags had the trackers without opening them, and as the truck slowed down, she didn't have the time to check. Abigail shouldered two of the duffle bags and hauled herself out of the hole.

Where the sole of a boot kicked her back inside.

The duffle bags broke her fall, but she didn't have much time to be grateful as someone else dropped into the truck with her. The silver Hero Enterprises arm band gleamed against the hero's tiger striped body suit. Her cat ears twitched atop her dark hair, and her tail swished behind her. Bastet, one of Tennyson City's main heroes, loomed over Abigail with pointed claws and teeth glinting in the dim light.

"If you need funds, might I suggest applying at the prison's commissary," Bastet glared behind the grease paint of her mask, "because it's where you'll be staying for a while."

Abigail propped herself up on her elbows and eyed Bastet, mentally running through her notes. Bastet had the agility and cat-like reflexes as her name advertised but was mostly reserved for covert operations since she lacked physical strength. In a fight, Abigail could take her. The truck came to a full stop, and one of the cab doors slammed shut.

"I'm not in the market for a new career," she returned Bastet's banter. *When I talk to villains in San Arbor, do I sound as pretentious as this?*

Abigail grabbed the shelving unit's legs and used them to propel her into Bastet. They crashed against the back of the truck. Bastet wedged an arm free from Abigail's hold and elbowed her in the nose. Blood trailed down Abigail's mouth. She swallowed down the sulfuric taste of her emerging blue flame and head-butted Bastet instead. She needed to get away from the hero, not burn her. The truck door opened, and they both tumbled onto the sidewalk. Several people shouted around them. Dazed from the head-butt and the fall, Abigail scrambled awkwardly to her feet. Bastet elegantly spun upright while delivering a solid kick into Abigail's stomach. She stumbled back and summoned her fire armor but stopped when she smelled the duffle bags burning.

She needed the money. She needed to escape. She gritted her teeth. She needed to run. It wasn't the most heroic plan of action, but she wasn't a hero right now.

Abigail created fireballs in her hands and launched both at Bastet who nimbly dodged each by leaping into the air. Abigail grinned; she hadn't expected to be on this side of the age-old training drill. She launched a fireball at Bastet's feet who expectedly leapt up to avoid the impact but collided with the second, well-timed fireball Abigail tossed higher. Bastet frantically swatted at her chest to put out the flames.

"What's wrong?" Abigail asked, a smirk playing at the corners of her mouth. "I thought cats were only scared of water?"

Bastet glared at her and stepped forward. Abigail shot more fireballs between them, kicking up dust and smoke.

In the opaque debris, Bastet hacked through the dense smoke and swatted at anything she saw move within. Abigail dodged the hero's claws and tried to flee the area before Bastet regained her bearings. Following her heavy footfalls, Bastet chased Abigail through the smoke. In the chaos, one of the truck drivers appeared between them and was an easy target for Bastet's blind attacks.

"Move!" Abigail turned on her heel and pulled the driver out of the way. Bastet's claws raked through her shirt and tore into her arm, but it was better than them tearing through the driver's face. She pushed the pain away, ignoring how quickly her shirt absorbed the blood, and readied herself for the next attack.

Bastet ran the back of her hand over her eyes trying to clear them of the smoke. Abigail was done with this pointless endeavor, she needed to leave before she, or someone else, was seriously hurt. Abigail heel-kicked Bastet as hard as she could, sending the hero to the ground, and took off down the street.

She ducked into the first alley she crossed and searched for her next move. The backpack and duffle bags weighed her down and limited her options. She looked for fire escapes to ascend, manhole covers to fall into, dumpsters to hide in but only found potted plants. She continued running, sticking to the shadows, and hoping that as she got lost inside Tennyson City, she'd become lost to Bastet and Hero Enterprises.

Blood trickled down her arm and despite her best efforts to cover it with her hand, it left a trail for someone to follow. Abigail slid behind a parked car, its wiper holding down several parking tickets, and ripped apart the hem of her shirt to tie around her slashed arm. The tightness caused the injury to scream, but the pressure stopped the bleeding. Abigail pushed herself off the ground and continued on.

She turned down an alley stained red with bricks. The rough exterior of the buildings was extremely off-putting compared to the sleek steel around her. She ran until the alley dead-ended into a brick wall several stories tall. Her labored breath filled her ears, and the taste of rust filled her mouth. Behind her, someone approached. Their footsteps bounced around the confined space. She reached for the sword she no longer wielded and faced her opponent.

Chapter Eleven

"Don't attack," requested the stranger. The hooded man from the sidewalk stepped into the lone light produced by the red *exit* sign hanging above a back door.

"Why shouldn't I?" Abigail summoned a pair of flaming brass knuckles to encase her hands.

"Because I didn't attack you." The man slowly pushed his hood away from his face. Three pairs of eyes blinked at Abigail. The pair above and below his human brown eyes were a kaleidoscope of colors resembling those of a fly.

Exposing his face was not the sign she needed to power down.

"Show me your arm," demanded Abigail.

The man sighed, but did as she asked, rolling both of his sleeves over his arms, revealing there wasn't a Hero Enterprises armband on either. "I'm not one of *them*."

Venom dripped from his statement.

"Who are you then?" Abigail lowered her arms but didn't stop the fire burning across her knuckles. More red shadows danced across the brick walls.

He shook his head. "You're not in the position to be asking questions."

Abigail's fire grew momentarily with her anger. She wasn't used to being on this side of the interrogation. She exhaled and calmed both herself and her flames. Crossing her arms, she waited for him to continue.

"Who are you?" he mirrored her question.

"They call me Wildfire."

"What do you call yourself?"

"Wildfire," she growled.

The man raised his hands with a chuckle. "Okay, okay. Listen, Wildfire, you can't just come into our turf and stir up trouble without getting some trouble back. Understand?"

"I didn't realize Tennyson City was under your control," Abigail said. "Don't the heroes keep things in check? The remaining ones anyway."

The man spat when Abigail said heroes. "They won't be a problem for long."

She feigned a gasp. "Did you have something to do with The Swordfish and The Guppy?"

He grinned, his bug eyes shimmering with colors.

"You're the reason I came here!" Abigail's stomach soured as she pretended to be excited but didn't discredit her luck that brought them together. "I want to join you."

Bug Eyes laughed and it sounded more like a swarm of buzzing wings than a real laugh. "We're not recruiting."

"I'm not asking." Abigail shifted one of the stolen duffle bags at her side. "I have my tuition right here."

"You stole that for me?"

Abigail smiled. "Impressed? I saw you watching from the sidewalk."

"I saw Bastet nail you right in the jaw."

"I got away," she countered. "Next time I face that cat she won't get away so easily."

"Give me your *tuition* and I'll pass your audition tape to the boss."

"Where's the guarantee you'll keep your word? That you'll let me join you."

His buzzing laugh returned. "I never gave you my word. There is no guarantee."

Abigail tightened her hands around the duffle bag's straps. "Then you're not getting this."

"You said you stole it for us, was that a lie?"

"No, but—"

"You have no leverage here, girl." Bug Eyes took a few steps forward. "Hand over the cash and if we want you on the team, we'll find you."

Fire laced up her arms. "Think you can take it?"

"Picking fights with me won't help your cause."

Abigail tried a new angle, hoping he still had the heart of a man instead of an insect. "You're just going to leave me out here? What if Bastet comes back?"

"Thought you said you could handle her next time?" He gestured his hand toward the bag.

This wasn't how Abigail planned this interaction to go down but getting the tracker into Bug Eyes' hands would be a small victory for her. She had to hope he'd take it to their hideout. Abigail dismissed her flames. She pulled one duffle bag off her shoulder and tossed it toward him. Before doing the same with the other, she grabbed a tightly wound stack of twenties from the bag.

Bug Eyes raised an eyebrow at her.

"A girl's got to eat," she casually said, pocketing the money.

Bug Eyes retrieved both duffles from the ground and wrapped their handles around his fists. From the slits on the back of his hoodie, long, dragonfly-shaped wings emerged. Abigail leapt back at their sudden appearance. This made Bug Eyes chuckle again. The wings beat at his sides before he took off into the sky and flew away.

Abigail lost sight of him as he soared above the towering buildings. She didn't move for several minutes until she was sure she was alone in the alley. She gritted her teeth. Her plan was now in the hands of some bug-eyed villain who may or may not be involved with the gang she needed to find. He had told her to wait. Two things she was not good at: waiting and following orders from a villain.

She retrieved the money from her pocket. Only $500 to live on, and if she based Tennyson City on its expensive street tacos, it wouldn't last long. She combed through each bill looking for the tracker. If her bills were marked with it, then she could use it to track the others. If the tracker even worked like that. If she even knew how to reverse engineer the device. If she had grabbed a bag that contained a tracker at all.

Abigail unleashed a frustrated breath tangled with smoke. This was not going well. She tore off her margarita sunglasses and stashed them in her backpack. She eased out of her T-shirt and used the cleaner parts to wrap around her injured arms. She'd need to find something to clean the cuts properly. After dressing in a sweatshirt, Abigail retraced her messy steps to the main streets of Tennyson City. She'd continue to familiarize herself with the city, find out where the shadows hid, follow her own leads, and if she ran into Bug Eyes or Bastet, she'd prove she belonged here.

The sunny day morphed into a glaring twilight. The neon lights and traffic signals bounced around the mirrored windows and coated Tennyson City in a sickening color wheel. Moving away from the bright downtown, Abigail followed a new light. It called to her in a familiar way: fire. She didn't smell the toxic smoke of a house fire or hear the screams and sirens marking it as dangerous. She approached the light and inside the growing darkness of night, the trash can fire took shape. As did the three individuals around it.

Abigail smiled and raised her palms as a sign of peace.

The man in the center, his hair looking like an oil spill as the light danced over the grease that kept it away from his face, nodded her over. The woman on his left scooted closer to him as Abigail joined them, tucking herself under his arm for protection. The final member of their group didn't acknowledge her. His milky eyes watched the fire eat away the trash.

Abigail hovered her fingers above the flames. "I didn't think a city in the desert would get this cold at night. Does it get worse in the winter?"

"About the same," the oil slick hair man said. "You're not from around here."

"Came in this morning."

The milky-eyed man muttered something, but Abigail couldn't make it out. He shifted his weight away from her and muttered again.

"Tan's right," said Oil Slick. "There's probably a hundred other places you'd be better off."

Abigail glanced at Tan, curious at how anyone understood him. "Why's that?"

"Tennyson City's not safe."

"It's the safest city in the world, or so I read."

"Safest for people like them." The woman's words were as sharp as her fingernails. She pointed past Abigail toward the main streets. "Beasts only hunt things that won't be missed."

"Aren't there heroes that—"

The trio's laughter cut Abigail off.

"No one trusts those people," Oil Slick said. "They're more likely to hurt us than help."

Abigail prickled. *Of course, they would think that.* "Why?"

The woman sighed dramatically. "If they actually did their jobs then there wouldn't be so many dealers on the streets."

"Or they'd at least find the labs cutting the stuff." Oil Slick nodded at Tan. "Tan, tell her about your cousin that got a bad batch and died on the spot. His heart just about beat out of his chest, brook like four ribs."

Abigail was thankful Oil Slick gave the abridged version first because she still couldn't make out any of Tan's muttering.

"That's unfortunate, I'm sorry for your loss," Abigail told Tan, then looked back at the other two. "Is there anything else I should watch out for?"

"Monsters," grumbled the woman.

Oil Slick shook his head. "I told you to stop that, there's no monsters eating people. People are just dying."

"Something's getting them," the woman defended, but didn't press her opinion.

"You should watch out for Bastet," said Oil Slick. "Keep yourself out of her way and she should leave you alone."

"What's up with Bastet?" Abigail crossed her arms to hide the bloody rags clinging to her.

"Ruthless." Tan said clearly. He lifted his gaze away from the fire. Four faded claw marks cut down the length of his face, over each eye.

"Bastet'll cut up anyone to get what she wants," Oil Slick explained. "Best not catch yourself on the business end of her claws."

Abigail's forearms burned where she had been scratched earlier. "I won't."

It was difficult to tell night had fallen over Tennyson City. The buildings that tossed the sunlight around did the very same to the streetlights. Abigail almost reached for her sunglasses as she continued her exploration, dodging the ever-present pedestrians. She'd been walking for hours but knew she'd hardly seen half the city. Despite her desires, she turned away from the signs pointing toward the bay and trekked away from expensive waterfront and downtown rentals that would eat away her meager cash reserves.

She dipped between tall buildings, their metal exteriors trying, and failing, to assault her with their cooling touch, and was surprised to find a quiet section of the city. Since she'd gotten off the train, noise filled every moment. Bits of conversations, rattling of cars, shuffling of the aired plants. Noise plagued Tennyson City.

Except for this dark, one-way road.

A dumpster acted as a sentinel halfway down the street, making the route hardly wide enough to support a vehicle. The imposing buildings on either side of the street produced deep shadows. Something about this dark street made her uneasy. The feeling of an icy finger ran down the length of her spine. Abigail spun around expecting to find Bastet ready to finish their fight, but the street was empty.

Abigail swallowed her fears and entered the street, using a tiny fireball atop her finger for light. The red glow barely pierced the darkness.

Something slithered under the dumpster and Abigail jumped away from the potential venomous snake. She shined her light toward the dumpster's short legs and found a yellow strip of plastic instead. Both sides had been torn but she recognized the thick black printing. San Arbor had them too.

Crime Scene

Abigail wound the tape into a ball and tossed it into the dumpster. Despite the heavy air and eerie silence, no rat popped out like she had expected. After a few more steps, something reflected the fire's light. Abigail knelt and ran her finger along a wire strung between the buildings. When she lifted her finger, a thin line of blood broke through her skin.

Abigail tried to burn through the wire, but it remained taut. Her flames didn't even dull the razor edge of it. The wire was so thin someone could get seriously hurt walking through it. If it was neck level, the wire could easily slice someone's head off with the correct force.

The correct speed . . .

Abigail leapt away from the wire and gasped. The haunting air about this street suddenly made since. The cut atop her finger pulsed as Abigail worked through the damning evidence.

The Swordfish and her sidekick The Guppy were both found strung up with wires. Rush was found shredded apart by an unknown weapon.

This abandoned street, marked with crime scene tape and a forgotten trap, was where Rush was murdered. Abigail's stomach seethed and the remainder of her street tacos ended up on the ground.

"Guess you really are a fan."

Abigail summoned flames up both her arms before straightening up and finding Bug Eyes across from her. The fire wasn't hot enough to burn through her sweatshirt, but she could increase the temperature without hesitation if she needed. His dragonfly wings laid against his back, the longest part hanging below his knees. In the fire light, the membranes looked like stained glass.

"This is where it happened?" Abigail asked, already knowing the answer but needing confirmation for her report.

Bug Eyes shrugged. "The boss liked your audition tape. Sent me to come get you."

Abigail's stomach churned again, but nothing else came up. "Good."

"Not so fast." Bug Eyes raised a hand to stop Abigail's advancement down the street. "There's a condition."

Abigail crossed her arms and waited.

Bug Eyes pulled out a thick metal necklace from the front pocket of his hoodie. Abigail recognized it. San Arbor had them too. Power dampener collars. "I can either put this on you, or you can, but you're not leaving this street without it."

Abigail glanced around the street, looking for the subtle flash of light the wire had emitted. She didn't see any, but that didn't mean there weren't more strung around her. Looking into Bug Eyes' four insectoid eyes, she felt like a fly trapped in a spider web.

"Hand it over." Abigail refused to let Bug Eyes near her. She was still waiting to catch a glimpse of bug-like mandibles hidden in his mouth.

As soon as she attached the collar around her neck, the fire along Abigail's arms vanished. She snapped her fingers, but no flame sparked. For the first time in a very long time, Abigail felt cold.

"Now what?"

"Follow me." Bug Eyes retreated down the street, and Abigail made sure to follow his steps exactly.

They didn't go far. Up the murder street, down a similarly empty alleyway, over a manhole cover which Abigail was certain they'd climb into and came to the backdoor of a business. A deli by the smell of spoiled meat lingering in the air. Bug Eyes knocked against the door in a rhythmic pattern, but instead of it opening, the cellar beside the door snapped open.

He gestured for Abigail to take the old wooden stairs first. She didn't try arguing with him. The entire trip he'd been silent. Abigail doubted he'd open up now. She tried summoning flames to her hand to light the way, but nothing happened. Her fingers twitched with a phantom sensation. Abigail clenched her fist several times before the feeling went away. She descended into the cellar blindly.

After she reached the dirt floor, Bug Eyes dropped beside her. His wings vibrated against his back for several seconds before laying flat. The added air current caused Abigail's hair to slap her eyes. The cellar door shut above them, a single naked light bulb turned on, and Abigail readied to defend herself.

"Here she is, Warden." Bug Eyes addressed the other occupant in the basement.

"Your name's Warden?" Abigail asked.

Warden made San Arbor's Majestic's main linebacker look like a toddler. The white suit he wore must have been a custom job because Abigail doubted anyone sold something along the size of XXXXL in a store. The man's fists were easily the size of toaster ovens, and if the sheer force of his punch wouldn't be enough to take out his target, then the golden rings on each finger would cause serious damage.

"Executioner was already taken."

Abigail didn't want to know how powerful Executioner was if this man was afraid to take the moniker.

"Let's talk." Warden stepped aside to reveal a card table behind him. A large pile of cash sat atop it.

Abigail glanced between Warden and Bug Eyes before taking a seat at the table. She kept her back straight and planted each foot against the ground. She couldn't show any signs of fear or anxiety by fidgeting. Neither of the other two sat down, opting to stand next to the table. The power dampener weighed heavy around Abigail's neck.

"Odo says this was your haul?" Warden addressed the money.

"That's correct. I planned to nab more, but when I reached the truck it was mostly empty."

"What were you planning to buy?"

"Nothing, just wanted to impress you," Abigail smiled.

"Yes, because your stats aren't too impressive."

Abigail bristled at his comment. Bug Eyes handed him a tablet and Warden scrolled over the screen with his sausage sized fingers.

"Assault, armed robbery, unlawful wielding of powers, seems most of your arrests were because of theft."

Abigail cocked her head until she connected the dots. He was reading her fabricated police record. She tried to compose her momentary confusion. "It took me a few tries to get it right."

"You think you're *right* enough now?"

"I got the money, didn't I? And went toe-to-toe with Bastet." Abigail hadn't had many job interviews, but this was by far the most bizarre. "I'm right enough for whatever is going on here."

Warden handed the tablet back to Bug Eyes. "What is it that you think is going on here?"

"You're eliminating the heroes."

"Sure, but why?"

"That's easy," Abigail said. "To become top dogs of Tennyson City. Anyone would be crazy to not want a piece of that pie."

Warden didn't confirm if her guess was right. "This team was hand-picked. Why would I jeopardize that by adding a stranger?"

Abigail leveled her gaze with his. "Because a stranger figured it out. The Swordfish and Guppy and now Rush were all taken out with the same tools. By the same people. If I can figure that out, it won't be long before someone else does. You need someone fresh."

"And she would help our numbers," Bug Eyes whispered, resulting in Warden smacking the back of his head.

"Take the collar off." Warden slid a small key across the table toward Abigail. "Burn the money."

Abigail, halfway with inserting the key, stared at Warden. "What? Why?"

He smirked. "We're not in this business for the money."

Combustion

This was a test. One she needed to pass, but in doing so she'd destroy the tracker and the first part of her mission. She finished unlocking the collar. The contraption fell to the ground with a thud. She chewed the inside of her cheek. It was a necessary loss. Abigail produced a flame atop her finger, heat radiated through her blood as her powers returned, and tossed the fire onto the cash. The cherry-red flame morphed to a sickly yellow as the chemicals inside the bills corrupted the flame.

"Odo, take her to the others," Warden commanded after the money burned. The smoke turned his voice scratchy, and the black fumes clung to his suit without proper ventilation.

Breathing in the putrid smoke was easier than talking to Warden. Abigail happily followed Odo out of the cellar.

Chapter Twelve

"Who are the others?" Abigail demanded, after following Bug Eyes out of the cellar. Warden remained in the center of the room watching them leave, his arms somehow able to cross over his chest without bursting through his suit now stained with soot. She hoped that didn't mean she lost any points with her new boss.

"I thought you had us all figured out?" Bug Eyes looked over his shoulder at Abigail, an amused expression on his face.

"Not all of it," she grumbled. "Your name's Odo, then?"

"You got a problem with that?"

"It's better than Bug Eyes."

"Bug Eyes?" he asked. His expression darkened like he stepped in dog poop.

"It's what I'd call you."

"Odonata."

"Bless you?" Abigail wasn't sure what he said.

Odo sighed, pulling his hand down his face in pure frustration. "My codename is Odonata. You know, like the classification of dragonflies?"

"I was never good in biology," Abigail admitted. "Where are we going?"

Odo led her down several more side streets whose lights had either burnt out or were purposely tampered with. Abigail inhaled deeply, catching the strongest odor of fish she'd smelled since her fourth-grade field trip to the aquarium, and found comfort in the warmth of her flames ready to come alive if she called.

"You'll see," Odo answered her question.

"What's the next move?"

"You'll see."

"What should I—"

"You should be quiet." Odo interrupted. "Warden may have let you in, but you're far from being one of us. If you even make it past the training."

Abigail smirked. "Training won't be a problem."

Odo laughed. "You'll be thinking differently before the week's even up."

Doubt it. "Why'd you join?"

"Not one of us," Odo repeated in a sing song voice.

"But you vouched for me. You must believe I'd be helpful in some way."

"Helpful, sure. But not a friend." Odo stopped outside a closed restaurant where various window posters advertised hand rolled sushi. He unlocked the door and ushered Abigail forward. "Home sweet home."

Abigail could tell instantly the restaurant was a front. The exterior of the multi-story building was huge, but the restaurant barely had room for a counter and two tables. A glass paneled refrigerator housing several brands of bottled soft drinks bathed the tiled floor in blue light. Two doors stood on either side of the sushi counter. One was padlocked while the other was marked by a fading sign reading *kitchen staff only*.

"I thought it would be bigger." Abigail peered through the dome cover of the counter. The rolled sushi looked fake, and the restaurant surprisingly didn't smell as much like fish as she'd assumed it would.

"Down here." Odo yanked open the kitchen door and Abigail followed him down a set of stairs. "This is where you'll stay."

"Do I get my own room?" Abigail was more concerned with counting the steps and judging how far she was below the surface. When the stairs ended at another door, she'd guessed they were at least five stories below street level.

"Something like that."

Odo opened the door to a wide room made entirely of subway tiles. A green tarp poorly covered a gaping hole at the back of the room, and cold subterranean air soaked the old subway turnaround. A handful of bunk beds sat in a corner of the room while an assortment of gym equipment sat opposite it. A tiny kitchenette was constructed in the center. Two generators supplied power to a fridge and stove. A wooden table had a black and red checkered tablecloth that rustled in the ever-present breeze.

Abigail hadn't thought their evil lair would be the penthouse of a nice hotel, but she didn't think it'd be inside a cave either. She hoped there was a bathroom hidden somewhere among the items. The metal bunkbeds rattled as someone leapt out of a top bunk and Abigail tightened a fist in case she needed to defend herself.

"Odonata!" A blue haired woman greeted as she joined them at the door. She looked a couple of years younger than Abigail, and the blue of her hair continued to her skin and clothing. "We thought . . . well we weren't sure what we thought, but we're glad you're back."

"We thought you were caught," added a male voice from the home gym. He set a weight bar on the ground, slung a towel around his neck, and stood beside the blue girl.

"Tech would have told you if I was," Odo replied.

"I would!" agreed another voice from the bunk beds. Abigail didn't see him, but the soft glow of a computer screen marked his position on a lower bunk.

"I was with Warden," Odo answered their unspoken question about his whereabouts. "Vetting this new kid."

Combustion

Abigail hadn't been called *kid* in a very long time, and she refused to let it stick. "My name's Wildfire."

"I guess that means she passed," the guy from the gym said. "I'm Stretch. Tech's over there," he pointed toward the bunk beds, "and this is Cold Snap."

"Still working on the name," the blue girl blushed, and extended her hand for Abigail to shake.

"Nice to meet—" Abigail dropped Cold Snap's hand with a shout. Both girls rubbed their hands like they had been shocked. Steam raised from Cold Snap's reddened fingers.

Stretch pulled Cold Snap behind him and snapped at Abigail, "What did you do to her?"

"Me?" Abigail turned her hand and revealed a collection of red blisters across her palm. "What did she do to me?"

"Fire and ice reaction," Tech explained from his bunk. "Frost bite."

Abigail looked between her injured hand to Cold Snap. "You have ice powers."

"And you have fire," she smiled. "How cool."

Odo and Stretch groaned, and Abigail guessed they'd grown tired of ice puns.

"I'm usually not this warm on contact," Abigail offered an awkward apology. "I didn't mean to hurt you."

Cold Snap turned her hand over showing it was almost back to solid blue. "Don't worry about me."

Odo shoved Abigail a step forward so he could shut the door. "I suggest you get some sleep. Your training starts first thing in the morning."

Abigail assumed the training was more tests. Tests to prove her loyalty, her alliance, her powers, her usefulness. Regardless of what the tasks were, she'd excel in them. She had to. "Which bunk is mine?"

"You can share with me!" Cold Snap reached for Abigail's arm but stopped short of touching her. "Oops. Follow me."

Abigail did so. The dingy black and white floor tiles squeaked under Cold Snap's black combat boots. They were scuffed and worn, whatever traction they once had eroded away. When they arrived at the bunk beds, Cold Snap leaned against the metal support beams of one and pointed behind her.

"I've got the top one already, but the bottom one's all yours."

Abigail removed her backpack and tossed it onto the mattress outfitted with a pillow and blanket. "I didn't know we'd all be living together like this. I promise I don't snore."

Cold Snap giggled as she climbed onto her bunk. "I don't either. Candy?"

The red string of licorice almost slapped Abigail in the face as Cold Snap handed a piece out to her. The end closest to Cold Snap's hand had frosted over. Abigail accepted it and crawled onto her mattress.

"You look different." Tech said from the bottom bunk next to Abigail's. His bunk was closed off in a netting of ethernet cables humming with energy. Random orange lights ran the length of the thin cables before disappearing.

"How so?" Abigail kept her voice stable and focused on trying to find Tech behind the netting. Had her cover been blown already? She inhaled deeply through her nose until sulfur filled her mouth.

A laptop shoved out of the netting followed by a pale face layered in red and brown freckles. A few shimmered the same orange as the lights around him. On the screen was a police report complete with a black and white photo of Abigail. She didn't remember taking the mug shot, the data under the picture wasn't familiar either. Abigail touched her now short hair to make sure it hadn't grown to the length shown in the report.

"I thought you'd have black hair."

"I don't remember the original color," Abigail lied. "I've dyed it so many times."

Cold Snap's head appeared over the edge of her bed, hanging upside down. "It didn't change colors with your power?"

Abigail shook her head. "Did yours?"

"Turned this snowy blue the day I manifested them. I always wondered if other elemental powers changed hair too."

"Not that I've seen. Are we the only ones with elemental abilities?"

"So far," Cold Snap answered. "Odo has his dragonfly mutations, Stretch can, well, he can stretch his limbs, and Tech is the internet."

"The whole world wide web?" Abigail asked.

"I can connect to it," Tech said.

"The world's best hacker," Cold Snap complimented.

"Marie Barret." Abigail's cheeks flushed as Tech said her alias for the mission. "Villain name: Wildfire. Location: Unknown. Abilities: fire summoning, control of flames, martial combat. Documented crimes—"

Abigail stopped him. "You're the one who pulled my files for the Warden."

"World's best," Tech reminded.

"Don't even try to keep any secrets. One time, Tech even hacked my diary," Cold Snap chuckled and pulled herself back into her bunk.

"It was an easy lock," Tech said before returning inside the netting.

Abigail tried to laugh along with them, but the sound was hollow. She was one big secret. She made a plan to destroy her burner phone the moment she was away from them. If there was even a chance of Tech accessing the truth, she had to remove it. Abigail settled onto the thin mattress, folded her pillow twice and tried to sleep. Instead of counting sheep, she recoded everyone's name through the cypher. Warden. Odonata. Stretch. Tech. Cold Snap.

This small group of villains were the ones capable of killing heroes. The people Abigail would have to take out. It would be up to them to decide if they came willing when the law came, or if Abigail would be responsible for their removal.

She didn't sleep that night.

Chapter Thirteen

The hideout contained a constant state of noise which made sleeping difficult. Not that Abigail found falling asleep in a snake's nest easy to begin with. Wind banged against the poorly covered subway tunnel and violently shook the tarp covering the hole. It sounded like a caged beast trying to escape. It didn't ease Abigail's feelings of being trapped. The bunks on either side of her moaned as their occupants moved in their sleep. After too many hours, the creaking of mattress strings morphed into white noise and Abigail finally captured the comfort of sleep.

It did not last long.

A cold, wet rag dropped onto her face, snapping Abigail out of bed and ready to fight. The red flames across her fists illuminated her foes. Odo and Stretch eyed her, Stretch holding a half-empty water bottle.

"Get up, sleeping beauty," Odo instructed. Without his hoodie, his dragonfly wings expanded fully behind him. Her fire reflected inside their clear membranes like stunning stained-glass windows from an ancient church. His compound eyes did the same, absorbing the cherry-red hue and casting it aside. If Odo was on display at a church, this depiction would be of the devil.

"I am up." Abigail wiped her hand across her face, relieved when the dampness was indeed water. "What do you want? What's going on?"

"Time to start your training," Odo answered.

"It's the middle of the night." Abigail didn't actually know what the time was, but she hoped there was still time to sleep, if these two would leave her be.

"Almost morning," Stretch said off-handedly.

"I thought you said you liked training."

Abigail gritted her teeth listening to Odo's taunt. "Let's get started."

Stretch grinned. "Let me take you to my gym. I want to see if you have what it takes."

Abigail followed Stretch to the center of the hideout. His blue and white tracksuit matched the cracking rubber mats on the floor. His steps navigated through the cracks and uneven seams with familiar ease. If Tech's domain was the digital codes of the internet, then this was Stretch's. At least he didn't smell like a gym rat. "What it takes?"

"Takes to survive," Odo chuckled before taking to the air and sitting at the table to watch.

The barbell bench and stack of plates didn't give off the intense stakes Odo laid out. Abigail had trained under San Arbor's number one hero. Whatever these villains had for her wouldn't compare to Volcanic's training.

She sanded her hands together. "Let's do this."

Stretch extended his arms over the bench and picked up a plate from the pile. Seven feet away. His grin didn't change as his arms returned to their normal length, and he handed her the plate marked 45.

"Explains the name," she commented and took the plate.

Stretch retrieved a second weight and dropped it into Abigail's arms. The clang of the metal plates rang through the hideout. Abigail widened her stance to better support the weight.

Stretch jerked his head to the left. Abigail was surprised his neck didn't stretch away from his torso. "Get running."

"To where?"

"Until I say stop."

Abigail hugged the plates to her chest, silently apologized to her bare feet, and started her first lap around the hideout.

Sweat dripped between her shoulder blades and streaked against her arms, neck, and face as Abigail completed her seventh lap. She'd lost feeling in her feet on lap five. The numbness was a better feeling than the grainy texture of the floor. The cold air against her damp body felt constrictive. Abigail pushed her flames to the surface of her skin and evaporated the sweat. Her lungs burned, and the heat was comforting. Rounding the fourth corner, she locked eyes with Stretch and pushed forward to complete the next lap quicker than the last.

After the tenth one, Stretch cut off her route by extending his arm to the opposite wall to create a barricade. Abigail skidded to a stop so she wouldn't run through his arm making it a gory victory banner. She set the two 45-pound plates on the ground and forced her arms to straighten. The muscles ached and protested. Stamped into each of her upper arms was the indentation of the weight's brand name. The slashes she received from Bastet pulsed under the poorly constructed T-shirt bandage.

She forced her breath, labored and hot, through her nose, so her judges wouldn't see her panting.

Stretch, from his position in the center of the hideout, collected the plates and returned them to the stack, but not before completing a series of very extended curls. He examined the plates thoroughly with a frown as if Abigail had insulted them with her sweat and fingerprints.

Abigail crossed her arms and approached Odo. "Did I pass your test?"

"Wasn't my test," he answered.

"Yours isn't a flying contest, is it?"

Odo almost smiled. Abigail counted it as a small victory. "Don't have a way to get around in the air?"

Abigail chose not to answer. Keeping her rocketing ability to herself could prove handy. These villains didn't need to know everything she was capable of.

"Your endurance is fine," Odo continued, "But what about your strength?"

Abigail stifled a laugh. "What do you want me to hit? I don't see any sandbags or anything."

Odo did not hide his laughter. "You only wish we had the luxury of a punching bag. Come this way."

Abigail followed him toward the covered hole of the turnaround. The whine of the wind grew loud and annoying. "Seems like something you could put in a work order for."

"The hole?"

"The lack of equipment."

"People like us are used to that unfairness. Shouldn't you know that?"

"I just thought being with an organization, things would be more . . ." Abigail stumbled. "Organized."

"This isn't some mob movie." Odo pulled back the tarp and revealed an inky black expanse. "This is real life."

Abigail summoned a spark of light to her finger, but it did little to illuminate the unfinished tunnel. Exposed rock faces bubbled from the walls and ceiling. Discarded rail tracks disappeared into the shadows. Water dripped from somewhere unseen. "What are we doing here?"

"Pick a rock and start punching."

"That's barbaric." Abigail positioned herself in front of a slab of earth on her left. "I could break my hand."

"Tuck your thumb," was Odo's only advice.

The tiny spark on her finger grew to cover Abigail's knuckles and she inhaled deeply to grow the covering into a boxing glove. She readied her stance, left foot back and a slight bend in her front knee, and slammed her fist into the rock.

She grinned as the rock shifted under her fist. This section of the turnaround was full of sandstone. The soft rock must be the reason for the tunnel's abandonment. Tennyson City couldn't risk a cave in on their public transportation system. She assaulted the rock until a divot formed. She dropped her fire, and the sudden coldness of the tunnel stung her raw knuckles.

"Good enough?" she asked Odo.

"I mainly wanted to see if you'd do it." Odo grinned and it reminded Abigail of her little brother: prideful and annoying. "Why don't you heal that?"

"My hands? They'll scab up."

"I meant your arm. The scratches from Bastet."

Glancing down, Abigail noticed one of the wounds bled through the T-shirt. "I don't have healing."

"Can't you seal them up or something with the fire?"

"Cauterize?" Abigail shivered saying the word. "I'm immune to my own flames."

"Just *your* own?" Odo questioned.

Abigail caught the implication; he was fishing for her weakness. "All fires."

There had only been one to burn her and it was gone.

"You're done," Odo concluded their training portion and led the way back into the hideout.

An exposed waterline dripped down one of the walls furthest from the bunks. The bucket catching the water was almost full. The work lights dangling from wires flickered and swayed as movement above them disrupted their connections. Abigail hoped it was some train above them and not a rat burrowing through the ceiling. Dust from shifting rocks gathered on the top of the kitchen table. Abigail couldn't help but wipe it off as they passed.

Abigail hadn't realized she'd taken the Round Table for granted. Despite most of the sillier things inside the Hero Relief Center, it was still a state-of-the-art facility for heroes. She was impressed that these people were able to take out heroes with similar assets while calling this place home.

Stretch was not alone on his rubber mat. Cold Snap handled a barbell and, under the guidance of Stretch, moved through a series of arm motions. After she completed the circuit, Cold Snap lowered the weight and smiled at Abigail. Despite her icy presence, the greeting was warm and genuine.

"I didn't want to interrupt," Cold Snap said to Odo, "but Stretch said it was fine to come over."

"I bet he did." Odo narrowed his eyes at Stretch.

"Nothing wrong with all of us getting stronger." When Odo didn't argue, Stretch added to Cold Snap, "Since you're warmed up, how about I be your sparring partner?"

The girl glanced at Odo and Abigail. "I thought you were supposed to be training Wildfire?"

Abigail sat on the weight bench. "I don't mind sitting this round out. For a minute."

"Don't get comfortable," Odo warned but sat next to her. He tucked his wings around himself so they wouldn't touch her. Abigail appreciated the kind gesture, whether it was intended for her or not.

"I'm taking you down," Stretch said as he and Cold Snap readied themselves.

"You wish you could get your hands on me." There was a playfulness to Cold Snap's challenge that made Stretch grin, his lips turning up further than humanly possible.

Combustion

The way Stretch looked at Cold Snap, Abigail assumed he did wish that.

The pair circled each other. Cold Snap crossed her feet as she stepped, making herself unbalanced and Stretched leaned forward ready to take advantage of the girl's poor form. Abigail watched their fight with pity. Cold Snap didn't last once Stretch advanced. His stretching ability kept him safely out of Cold Snap's reach while he playfully tugged at her hair. Cold Snap huffed and rushed toward him, but a simple sidestep caused her to run into the pile of weights. She cursed, rubbed her stubbed toe, and returned to the fight.

"Go low," Abigail said as she passed the bench.

Odo cocked his head, but Abigail nodded back to the fight and they both saw the powerful hit Cold Snap landed against Stretch's chest as she sprang up inside of his reach. She shrieked in victory.

"That's cheating," Stretch accused.

"Aren't we villains?" she asked.

"We still have a code," Odo said. "But good call."

Abigail grinned at the compliment.

"Okay then," said Stretch, "You're next."

Abigail happily obliged, Cold Snap trading her places on the mat.

Maneuvering around Stretch's arms proved to be more difficult than Abigail expected. They whipped around him like thin tree branches in a windstorm. Where Cold Snap was only teased, Stretch tormented Abigail with strikes to her ribs and the sides of her head. She kept her arms up so most of the blows came across her forearms. She tried to get inside, but Stretch had learned from Cold Snap and kept Abigail a good distance away.

"Get him, Wildfire!" Cold Snap cheered from the side.

Stretch's right arm came down in a strike, and Abigail snatched it before he made contact. His other arm arched down, and Abigail took a blow to her shoulder in order to grab it too. With both arms trapped, Abigail head-butted him in the nose. When she released his noodle-like arms, Stretch tripped over a barbell and collapsed to the ground.

Despite cheering for Abigail a moment ago, Cold Snap leaped from her seat and knelt beside Stretch to assess his bloody nose. Left to be her own nurse, Abigail unwrapped the T-shirt pieces off her arm and grimaced at the open wounds.

"There's antiseptic under the sink." Odo's six eyes knitted together looking at the injury. "Maybe a dish towel too."

"I have the rest of the T-shirt I can use," Abigail replied. "Thanks, though."

Odo nodded, then returned to his commander role. "Cold Snap?"

"Yeah?" she asked, helping Stretch up.

Abigail didn't think she hit him with enough force to require any help to stand, but Stretch leaned on Cold Snap like his leg might give out at any moment. Neither seemed to mind.

"I want Wildfire to train you."

"Right now?" Cold Snap asked.

"The sooner the better. After she cleans up her arm."

"And breakfast," Cold Snap decided.

"What's for breakfast?" Abigail asked.

"Whatever is left over from upstairs."

Abigail wrinkled her nose, and Cold Snap laughed. "The tempura's not awful if you refry it."

Chapter Fourteen

The scent of overpriced coffee, slightly burnt bagels, and tangy orange juice was a nice improvement from the subway turnaround's cold dirt smell. The overpriced coffee and burnt bagel were also a nice improvement from the provided food in the hideout. The sushi restaurant was definitely a front, and all the uneaten food was shuffled downstairs for the villains to consume. Abigail was sure if she was forced to eat one more sour California roll she'd blow the whole undercover gig. She slowly picked at her blueberry bagel, savoring the flavor, and continued filling in the crossword puzzle on the back of The Tennyson City Tribune.

She counted off empty spaces in a row to fit her coded report. The combination of letters made absolutely no sense. Especially when two lanes intersected and shared letters. To anyone else it looked like Abigail had dumped a bowl of alphabet soup on the page. To the four people who knew the code it would be answers needed to take down the villainous organization. This week's puzzle looked much like last week's when Abigail completed it. The information she could provide was a disappointing amount for her two weeks inside the subway turnaround.

I'm still earning their trust. Abigail reminded herself as she tossed her garbage into the bin and set the completed paper back on the shelf for the next person to read. She hadn't seen any employee from Hero Enterprises collect the paper, but she had to believe her messages were getting to Beacon.

Once she finished with the message, she was instructed to leave. She had done so the first time, but now Abigail lingered by the bin.

Should she make sure the paper gets collected? Was there a better spot for her to place it? Was she at the wrong coffee shop?

"Do you need anything, ma'am?"

Abigail glanced around and caught the eyes of the young woman at the bakery counter who smiled and repeated her question.

"Yeah." Abigail approached the counter, accepting the reason to linger a little longer. "Can I get a dozen of those to go?"

The young woman piled an assortment of doughnuts into a striped box adorned with the shop's logo. If she needed to gain the trust of her new teammates to gather more information, she'd stoop as low as bribing. She was sure a few of them were as sick of sushi rolls as she was.

Abigail exchanged the box with a few dollar bills. "Thank you."

She stole a final look at the paper and found it still in its place. She had to believe it was getting to the proper channels. Abigail forced herself out of the bakery. As much as her red hair kept her true identity hidden, it made her fake one easy to spot in the crowd. She didn't want anyone catching on to her routine visits here, nor did she want Bastet to recognize her from the truck heist. The margarita glasses hadn't been the best mask.

Abigail would have her rematch when she was ready.

Returning to Simply Sushi became easier, as was navigating this section of Tennyson City. Several of the citizens became their own landmarks and helped guide Abigail back to the hideout. She turned a corner, jogged across a street, and met the first sentinel.

"Morning Jefferson," Abigail greeted the man whose salt-and-pepper hair turned into his beard somewhere halfway down his wrinkled face. "Want a doughnut?"

Jefferson's eyes brightened and he accepted the pastry Abigail held out for him. "Mighty grateful for you, Marie."

Abigail still hadn't grown used to her fake name. "It's the least I can do."

Jefferson bit into the doughnut, prompting the jelly interior to erupt from the bottom. Abigail handed him a napkin.

"Are there any shelters or agencies you'd want to go to? I don't mind helping you get to one."

Jefferson shook his head. "Shelters are dangerous. At least out here I can see my attacker coming. I can put up a fight if I need to."

"Are there many attacks this time of day?"

"Anytime of day."

"But the heroes?" Abigail asked. "I thought this was the safest city?"

Jefferson licked one of his fingers clean of the sugar coating from the doughnut. "Those heroes don't see everything."

Abigail stopped herself from frowning. She handed him a second doughnut. "Be careful out here, Jefferson. I'll see you next time."

"I'd be mighty grateful if next time I could get a cup of joe to go with the breakfast."

Abigail grinned. "Sure thing."

Abigail turned the next corner and lost Jefferson behind the colorful awnings of an organic food store. Despite the itch to do real hero work, Abigail knew she needed to complete her mission. Gather enough evidence to squash the entire operation. Once Hero Enterprises could stop looking over their shoulders at every call, the heroes of Tennyson City could focus on helping the fearful citizens.

Before making the final turn to Simply Sushi, Abigail prepared another doughnut delivery for the pigeon lady who usually commandeered a bus bench with four or five gray birds at her side. The bench was empty this morning though. Of both the lady and the birds. Only a handful of small feathers skittered on the ground. Abigail could only hope the pigeon lady had finally got on the bus that morning. She swallowed down Jefferson's paranoia of monster attacks and entered Simply Sushi.

The restaurant lobby was empty except for the chef behind the counter who Abigail still hadn't learned the name of. She assumed he was hired for his knife skills unrelated to cutting fish. She still gave him a head nod in greeting before disappearing down the long stairs to the subway turnaround. Despite the ever-present fire in her veins, Abigail still felt the dip in temperature the lower she went.

"You're late," Odo barked as Abigail entered the hideout.

"They're fresh." Abigail lifted the box of doughnuts in a peace offering.

Tech arrived on her heels as if he had developed super speed in her absence and claimed two pastries before Abigail set the box on the table. His fingertips flashed orange just like his freckles.

"You hooked into something right now?" Abigail asked him. In the two weeks she'd learned he only turned orange while accessing the internet. His eyes darted around the hideout, but she knew instead of the sparse furniture Tech was gazing at the world wide web.

"Soccer scores," Tech answered before returning to his nest.

"Apparently there's a big game in Milan right now." Cold Snap plucked a pink frosted doughnut from the box, pink sprinkles stuck to her lips as she took a bite. In the two weeks Abigail learned Cold Snap had a weakness for anything sweet.

"Tech should be looking into our next target," growled Stretch, reaching his impossibly long arm into the box and selected a doughnut at random. He pulled it back to him while he continued curling a weight at his seat at the bench. In the two weeks, Abigail learned Stretch was a gym rat with a soft spot for Cold Snap.

Combustion

All these things were documented inside her coded reports, but none of it seemed to matter. The little information she was gathering wouldn't save anyone.

"What's the next target?" Abigail asked, hopeful to know something useful.

"Not one of us." Odo's sing-song voice reminded her.

Abigail almost slammed the lid of the doughnut box shut before he could claim one.

In the two weeks Abigail had learned very little of their next job.

"How can I be useful if you don't tell me anything?" she challenged.

"I guess you'll have to keep proving your usefulness," Odo said. "You and Cold on the mat, now. She needs the combat training."

"Sure sure, Odo." Cold Snap dusted her fingers off on the tablecloth and headed to the rubber mat reserved for sparring. "Go easy on me today, Wildfire. My back is still achy from that toss yesterday."

"I'll try."

Abigail met Cold Snap on the mat and eyed the girl's scabbed knuckles. The ugly brown marks were healing, but with their daily sparring it would take weeks for them to completely recover. "Do you want gloves?"

"We don't have any."

Abigail shook her head. "Try this."

Cherry-red fire erupted atop Abigail's hand and morphed into boxing gloves encasing her knuckles.

Cold Snap's eyes widened at the display, and she mouthed *wow*. She mirrored Abigail's stance, raised her fist and tiny ice crystals formed over her knuckles. It was barely a dusting of frost before she unleashed a tired sigh.

"You'll get there," Abigail encouraged. "If you want to use your powers that way."

"It could come in handy," Cold Snap said. "I bet my punches would be way more hardcore if I could hit people with a block of ice."

Abigail chuckled at her enthusiasm and dispelled her fire. "We'll stick to normal fighting until then."

"Okey dokey." Cold Snap lowered herself into a better fighting stance, all of her weight on her back foot.

Abigail tossed her first punch toward Cold Snap who blocked easily before extending her own punch forward. It was sloppy compared to Abigail's, hovering in the air for too long, and she knocked it out of the way, stepped around Cold Snap, trapped her other arm across her chest and knocked Cold Snap to the ground with a bump to her hip.

Abigail helped Cold Snap back to her feet, their connected hands releasing a puff of steamy frost. The sensation had lessened from pain to annoyance after the first few days.

"I didn't see that coming," Cold Snap said.

"Most people don't." Abigail readied herself for their next round. "Bring your punches back faster, or else I'll grab your arm and snap it."

Cold Snap didn't respond. Her face paled even more than it already was. Abigail almost regretted her threat, but knew it was better the poor fighting happened here than with someone who actually would break her arm.

Sparks crackled along her fists. Abigail should be teaching Cold Snap the wrong moves. She shouldn't be bettering a villain's skill. She should be purposefully injuring the girl to weaken her.

A frozen fist sailed across the side of Abigail's face. Cold Snap's gasp of surprises mirrored Abigail's feelings. She hadn't been focusing on the fight.

Wiping the back of her hand across her mouth, Abigail happily found no blood or chipped teeth. "Good hit, but don't let up after."

Abigail closed in and smacked the side of Cold Snap's head. In the girl's daze, Abigail delivered two solid body shots before tapping her knuckles in a pretend uppercut against Cold Snap's jaw.

"Don't stop until they're down, got it."

Cold Snap rubbed her left ear where Abigail had slapped it.

Abigail dropped to the ground and swept Cold Snap's front leg out from under her causing her to tumble to the ground like an oversized Jenga tower. "Never assume your opponent is done, either."

Cold Snap reached forward attempting to grab Abigail's ankles with nails strengthened by ice, but a quick hop backward left too great a space between them.

"Not bad," complimented a voice Abigail hadn't heard since her first day in Tennyson City. Warden stepped onto the mat. The cavernous tunnel became small with him inside. His large shoes indented the foam pieces with each step. "I didn't expect you to possess a strong combat background."

Abigail let the insult roll off her. "I had a good teacher."

"I would say so," sneered Warden. "Odo?"

"Yeah boss?" Odo fluttered to Warden's side, his dragonfly wings casting rainbows of light around the hideout in the process.

"It's time for our next hit." Warden's announcement sent a chill far greater than Cold Snap could ever produce down Abigail's spine.

Chapter Fifteen

"You're taking out Bastet?" Abigail gasped after Warden explained the assignment. His statement didn't sound real. Someone could've announced they were leaving to pick up their dry cleaning with more urgency than his simple words. A hero's life so easily dismissed as if they didn't matter. Abigail tried to shake off her chill but failed.

"*You're* killing Bastet," Warden corrected, nodding toward her and the rest of the villains around her.

Behind him, Odo mouthed *one of us* with a smile. The low light turned his six eyes into nightmarish portals as they reflected the surrounding shadows.

"Are we using the slip n' slide like we did with Rush?" asked Cold Snap.

Abigail's stomach twisted at the carnival name used to describe the decapitation of the hero. She took a deep breath, focused on the dampness of the air that pierced her nose, and steadied herself. She needed the details in order to save Bastet. Nothing bad would happen to the hero so long as Abigail stayed on task.

"When?" she asked, praying she could make another coffee run before it.

"Curb your enthusiasm," Warden answered. "There's prep work first. Tech?"

With a laptop under each arm, Tech emerged from his ethernet nest and commandeered the table, opting to sit atop the checkered tablecloth rather than a chair.

Warden produced a folded piece of paper from his pocket and handed it to Tech. "We need these supplies. Find them."

Tech's rapid-fire typing came as his reply.

"How are we going to kill Bastet?" The sentence was vile in Abigail's mouth. Even pretending to be part of this horrendous act was horrible, but without solid details, she could never warn Beacon and the others in time.

"A couple of solid blows ought to do the trick." Stretch boxed the apparent moves he'd use in the fight. His skills were more advanced than Cold Snap's. Abigail knew he wouldn't fall for her simple take downs.

"Scared you won't keep your word?" Odo asked Abigail. She hated how his compound eyes locked onto her fear and pulled it to the center of the room. Thankfully, the real reason for her fear wasn't what he saw.

Abigail crossed her arms. "Bastet won't be easy to fight."

"You had such bravado earlier," Odo challenged.

"Sonic sounds," Tech chimed from the table, revealing the shopping list. "We're going to use a sonic boom device."

"What for?" Cold Snap asked.

"Bastet's greatest asset is her advanced hearing," Warden explained. "We eliminate that, and the playing field is leveled."

"What about her tail?" Stretch asked. "Her agility and balance come from that."

"Cut it off."

Stretch nodded at Warden's command.

"Found it," Tech said. "A device capable of producing a sonic blast of 200 decibels is being held inside the Wittman Research Lab. Basement Level 4. Storage facility."

"Are we getting ear protection?" asked Cold Snap. "To use during the attack?"

"Already found them," answered Tech.

"Get what you need," Warden instructed. "I want this sonic boom device tonight. We can't move forward without it."

A resounding chorus of "yes, sir!" sounded around the room. Everyone was eager to begin except Abigail.

Running a mission with this group of villains was different than operating with the Round Table Knights. The biggest difference was the lack of communication. No one wore an earpiece. There wasn't even a walkie-talkie between them. Abigail's headspace was completely quiet. She felt completely alone despite Stretch standing beside her. If anything were to go wrong with the other teams at their positions no one would know. There would be no warning.

Abigail chewed the inside of her cheek. This feeling was vulnerability. She felt expendable. Perhaps they all did. Perhaps this was how the dead heroes felt just before disaster.

"Let's go." Stretch nudged her with his arm and they walked to the front entrance of the Wittman Research Lab.

The modest four-story facility housed several research studies and a handful of rentable lab spaces that, according to Tech's snooping, paid for a majority of the building's utilities. Most of the research conducted was for new cosmetic products, drug trials, and an occasional college thesis project that required more space than the local university could provide. Wittman Research Lab appeared to be an average place for science.

Except for the seven sub levels not advertised and only marked on blueprints hidden so deep in the web that Tech required a full thirteen minutes to find the reports. The young techno-wizard had not been pleased with himself.

The automatic front doors opened as Abigail and Stretch neared them. The next set of doors required a badge which both Abigail and

Stretch produced from the lab coats they wore. Tech made the badges. Odo found the coats. Abigail assumed she and Stretch were given this portion of the mission because they would blend in with the normal looking employees. Her red hair was hidden beneath a ball cap sporting the lab's logo.

With the knowledge supplied by the public blueprints of the lab, Abigail and Stretch walked the first floor with pretend purpose. As they came across other people, exchanging polite smiles, Abigail looked at the badges hanging off their lanyards. She needed to find one with a red barcode. The green stripe on hers and Stretch's only accessed the main doors. A red badge would allow access to the basement floors.

Stretch turned down a hallway on their left with such speed his coat flapped in a flourish, and Abigail hurried behind him. It wasn't the coveted red badge he stopped at, however. Abigail crossed her arms as Stretch examined a vending machine.

"Seriously?" she hissed.

"Just keep watch." Stretch elongated his arm, reaching inside the machine to steal a protein bar and a pack of gummy candy .

"We're supposed to be looking for a red badge." Abigail couldn't believe she was reminding a villain to commit a crime.

"You're such a stick in the mud." Stretch bit into his bar and slipped the gummies into his lab coat pocket.

Abigail rolled her eyes.

"Did they restock the chips yet?"

Abigail stiffened like a board. She hadn't heard anyone approach. She slowly turned around with a bright smile and addressed the stranger, "Looks like it."

"Nice. Last week they were all out and I had to drive half away across town to . . ."

Abigail stopped listening to his story. Hanging off the right side of his coat's collar was his name badge ending with a red bar code. Stretch stepped away from the machine and caught Abigail's signal about the badge. He nodded and gave her his own code: keep him distracted.

". . . I should have bought more for the experiment."

"What kind of experiment?" Abigail asked a bit too eagerly, leaning against the wall on his left side.

The man squared his shoulders a bit more. "I'm testing the effects of the artificial orange coloration of these chips on rodents. Once these trials are done, I can apply the results to human nature."

"You're not hurting the animals, are you?"

He chuckled. "Maybe just their beach bodies. The chemicals are harmless, but the effects of the dye could show in hair follicles. If my theory is correct, I'll have orange rats in a week."

"How fascinating," lied Abigail.

"I could show you my work, if you want. That lab's just upstairs."

"Maybe next time," Stretch answered coming around to stand between them. "We have our own job to finish."

"It was nice meeting you." Abigail turned away from the man before he offered another rat visitation. Once they were further down the hallway, she whispered, "Please tell me you have it?"

"Easy." Stretch spun the badge's clip around his pointer finger.

"Excellent." Abigail hurried back through the main section of the floor and toward the south side of the building. This late in the evening, most of the employees had already left, which made the next part of their plan easier. Abigail and Stretch entered a stairwell leading to the upper four levels and one emergency door to the outside. The red light above the door wasn't on. It was the only form of communication with the secondary team.

Combustion

Using her fake badge, Abigail opened the door for Cold Snap and Odo to enter the building. Dark hoods hid their faces and Cold Snap wore gloves to hide her blue hands.

"Tech's circling the facility," Odo informed. "Did you secure the badge?"

"Right here." Stretch continued spinning the badge around his finger, gaining an approving smile from Cold Snap. "But I still don't understand why Tech couldn't make us one of the special ones."

Sighing, Odo explained it for a second time. "The red encryption changes too frequently to chance us having the right code."

"Guess Tech can't do *everything*."

"He did well enough." Abigail shocked herself by defending the cybercriminal.

Odo took the lead out of the stairwell. "Move quickly."

Abigail resisted the urge to do the opposite. She resisted pulling the fire alarm as they passed one. She resisted yelling to get someone's attention and sabotaging the plan. She had to keep her cover even though she knew ruining this part of the operation would keep Bastet and the other heroes safe. She knew her orders. She had to see this through to the end. She had to see how big this was. She knew she'd be able to warn Beacon before the hit happened.

They reached the two elevators, and Stretch swiped the red badge to call the one accessing the basement levels. The five of them piled inside quickly while Cold Snap pressed the door closed button repeatedly before selecting B4 on the panel.

"Will Scott be down here?" she asked, examining the badge still dangling from Stretch's fingers.

Abigail hadn't asked the scientist's name while they talked at the vending machine, but she assumed Rat Man was the man in question.

113

"He said he had a lab upstairs and was conducting his experiment there. He shouldn't notice we took the badge."

"When we leave make sure you ditch it somewhere on the main floor," Odo told Stretch.

Stretch nodded and slipped the badge into his coat pocket.

The elevator door opened without any fanfare, and the group of villains stepped into the dimly lit hallway. Abigail called a small fire atop her finger and led the way. With the new light, the hallway morphed into its true form. The floor contained row after row of containers. Each the size of a self-storage pod with a clear front, but instead of old furniture, dusty gym equipment, or bagged clothes, Abigail wasn't sure what she saw inside these containers.

"How will we know when we find it?" Cold Snap asked, mirroring Abigail's thoughts.

"What's a sonic boom device even look like?" added Stretch.

"If Tech's right," Odo answered them, "It'll be in bay 19-4."

Cold Snap pointed at the metal sign hanging atop the container on her left. "Here's 1-7."

"The 19 must be the row," Abigail said, growing her flame and taking the lead. "Fourth container in row 19."

She still couldn't tell what mysterious things were inside the containers. Some were filled with wooden crates marked with biohazard waste, others contained long chairs that looked like they belonged in a dentist's office, others were completely empty, and some only contained smudgy handprints on the inside of the glass.

"Help."

The voice was small, almost a whisper, and unrecognizable. Abigail looked over her shoulder, but nothing looked out of place. Cold Snap grinned when they made eye contact.

"Please."

Combustion

Abigail whipped her head around. "Who's saying that?"

"Saying what?" Cold Snap asked.

"You don't hear anything?" Abigail asked, her voice raising. "It's a kid, asking for help."

"Keep your cool, new girl," Odo interrupted. "You can't be losing your head on your first mission."

"You must be hearing things," Cold Snap said with more kindness than Odo.

"Maybe." Abigail turned around and continued down the rows. She knew about phantom sensations. She knew some people with missing limbs would still feel the missing part itch. Or think her phone was vibrating against her leg when it wasn't in her pocket. She wondered if this was the phantom sensation for heroes: a ghost asking for help.

Abigail grew her fire a third time as they entered the final row and came to the container marked with 19-4. She would never have guessed the thing inside was a sonic boom device. A cordless hair dryer resembling something out of a space-themed western sat atop a pedestal. A lime green six-pointed star logo was stamped on the handle.

"Is that it?" Stretch asked.

Abigail thought the same thing. The item didn't look capable of producing anything more than a cheesy sound effect.

"It has to be," Odo answered. "Cold Snap, do your thing."

Cold Snap laid her hands on the container's clear surface. Frost snaked out from under her fingertips and caused spiderweb cracks along the glass. "This is going to take a few minutes."

"Someone, please help me."

The phantom voice sounded again, this time more urgently. Abigail refused to ignore it. She walked further down the row. When the voice didn't sound again, when she didn't see anyone down the row, Abigail almost believed it to be a figment of her imagination.

She was glad she didn't.

"Help!" The voice was accompanied by a small hand smacking against the glass of the last container.

A girl dressed in rags banged her tiny hand against the glass again. Abigail lowered herself and the flame to better see inside. The girl flinched away from the fire, shielding her eyes from the light. Abigail extinguished the flame. In part to help comfort the girl, in part to comfort herself. The light illuminated the girl's sunken cheek bones in a way that made her look like a skeleton.

"Who are you?" Abigail asked. "Why are you in here?"

"I'm Courtney." Her voice barely penetrated through the glass. "I don't know why they put me here."

"They?" Abigail didn't need Courtney's full story, she just needed to keep the girl talking. To keep the girl from becoming the corpse she looked like. Abigail frantically looked around for a lock but didn't see any way into the container.

An alarm above them wailed, bathing the floor in rotating red light.

"Wildfire!" someone shouted down the row. "We need to leave."

"Please!" Courtney yelled, banging her hands against the glass. "Please don't leave me."

"I won't. Get away from the glass." Abigail's fists ignited and she bashed them into the glass.

A hero saves people, and she was not going to lose another kid.

The glass shattered, pieces melting under Abigail's intense heat, and Abigail ushered the girl forward. "Are you the only one?"

Courtney nodded her head. "The only one left alive."

The fire on Abigail's arms raged, growing tall and whipping above her head.

"Wildfire!" Cold Snap's combat boots slapped against the concrete floor as she approached. "We have to leave. Like, yesterday. The whole building is going to know we're here."

"I'm not leaving her," Abigail growled, tucking Courtney behind her.

Cold Snap raised her hands. Abigail's fire paled her skin even more than it usually was. The villain smiled, her white teeth a peace offering. "I wouldn't want you to. Bring her, too."

Through the wailing alarm and shouting of the others, Abigail heard the stomping of boots. She dismissed her fire, plucked Courtney into her arms and ran down the row with Cold Snap.

Chapter Sixteen

Abigail slid into the aisle and immediately turned back, slamming against Cold Snap. A hornet's nest of red dots filled the floor where she stood a moment before as armed guards tried to locate them. The wall of mysterious containers became Abigail's only cover, but they wouldn't help once the guards came down this row.

Abigail finally understood the expression "shooting fish in a barrel."

"Did the others make it out?" Abigail asked, repositioning Courtney to her left hip so the girl wouldn't be in a guard's direct line of fire.

"Odo can fly and Stretch probably stepped over the top of these." Cold Snap pointed at the nearest container.

"Why didn't you go with them?" Abigail's concern came out as a snarl.

"I wanted to get you. When the alarm started and you weren't behind me, I went to find you. You're my teammate and—"

Abigail stopped her. "Thanks for getting me but let me return the favor."

"You have a way out?" Cold Snap asked, equal parts hopeful and panicked.

"We're going to make one. I need you to lay ice on the floor ahead of us."

Cold Snap widened her stance like she did during their combat training before performing a serious move. Tiny frozen crystals materialized on her outstretched hands and grew into six-inch talons of pure ice. Courtney shivered against Abigail as the temperature around them plummeted. Cold Snap flicked her wrists, shooting the ice talons into the floor of the aisle. A bullet shot into one but didn't shatter the structure. The armed guards approached faster. Their footsteps ricocheting off the containers.

"Get ready to run," Abigail said. "Go straight to the elevator and don't stop."

With her free hand, Abigail morphed a huge fire ball to life and tossed it at the ice. A terrible hissing filled the room just before a burst of steam erupted. Abigail ran ahead first, pausing to toss several fireballs down the aisle for additional cover before taking off after Cold Snap. Gunfire chased after her.

Through the flashing red alarm lights and wisps of heavy steam, the elevator glowed like a lighthouse on the other side of the floor. Its doors stood wide open. Abigail ran faster. The gunshots grew louder. The light inside the elevator shattered as a bullet connected with it. Abigail prayed the door would stay open long enough for her to reach it.

The last 20 yards widened into an infinite expanse as Abigail zigzagged to avoid stray bullets emerging from the steam. The malnourished girl in her arms grew three times heavier as the elevator neared. Abigail's thighs burned. She wanted to rocket to the elevator. She wanted to summon all her flames to the soles of her feet. But she couldn't. Doing so would evaporate the steam and remove their cover if Cold Snap was still hidden inside.

Miraculously, the elevator door remained opened the entire time, and Abigail slammed herself inside.

Kneeling below the control panel, Cold Snap released the "door open" button and pressed the button marked with a star.

"I told you not to wait," Abigail panted, her back pressed against the elevator wall. Several bullets banged against the outside of the door.

Cold Snap grinned in response.

"There's probably a whole swarm of guards waiting for this elevator to open."

"I think together we can beat them back." Cold Snap stood.

Abigail did not want to beat any guard back who was simply doing their job of being a hero and stopping the bad guys. Like she should be doing. She raised from her crouch and tucked Courtney's face into her arm. The less the girl saw, the better.

"Stay on that side of the door," Abigail ordered. "Don't come out until I do. And keep your eyes down."

The door chimed open just as Abigail finished her instructions. She didn't look to see if her theory was correct. One second of hesitation could mean her death. She shot a blinding flash of fire from her free hand into the hallway. Shadows disappeared as light filled every available space in the hallway and elevator. When the fire left her arm, Abigail grabbed Cold Snap's hand and pulled her to the stairwell, her icy fingers easy to ignore under the threat of gun fire.

Once they were through the door, Abigail released Cold Snap's hand and melted the doorknob. She did the same with the exterior knob for security.

A car horn blared, and Abigail leapt about a foot into the air, gripping tightly onto Courtney. Adrenaline pulsed behind her ears in deafening waves.

"Come on." Abigail had to read Cold Snap's lips as she spoke. "That's our cue."

A gray electrical repair van idled across the street. The side panel door slid open as Abigail and Cold Snap approached. Odo and Tech grabbed their arms and hauled them inside. Stretch slammed on the gas pedal, and the van lurched forward. Abigail found momentary comfort as the van sped away from the Wittman Research Lab. They'd all gotten out. The comfort dissolved when Abigail locked eyes with Odo. His compound eyes looked at her, at Courtney, and at the sonic boom device all at the same time. It was as unnerving as feeling tiny spider legs crawling up her arms.

"She was inside one of the containers," Abigail answered his unspoken question. "I wasn't going to leave her."

Odo's six eyes blinked slowly, and the effect didn't help the spider leg feeling. "We can't keep her."

"I agree." Abigail wasn't about to let an innocent child anywhere near this gang of murderers. "Courtney, do you have a place to go?"

The girl pulled herself out of the crook in Abigail's neck. Her face was smeared with tears and snot. Abigail used her sleeve to clean her up.

"I stay at the Northbend Community Home sometimes," she answered, her voice frail.

"You don't have any family?" Cold Snap wedged herself next to Abigail. The back of the van was small to begin with; adding four adults and a plethora of Tech's equipment didn't help any.

"Sometimes my aunt watches me." Courtney fiddled with one of the strings of Abigail's hoodie. "You can take me anywhere, as long as it's not back there."

"We should take her to a hospital." Cold Snap said to Abigail.

"Too public," Odo shot down her idea. "We're *fleeing* an active crime scene, remember?"

Tech snickered beside him, his glowing orange freckles hidden behind a computer screen. "I'm sending them on a goose chase, don't worry about them. The false reports I'm sending will take them to the beach."

Tech's plan impressed Abigail. She could breathe a little better knowing a troop of armed guards wouldn't be chasing them down right away. "Courtney, how did you get there? You said there were others?"

The girl wrapped and unwrapped Abigail's hoodie strings around her tiny fingers. She didn't look away from her hands. "Someone just took me off the street. Like they do in movies. Someone put a bag over my head and tossed me in a car. I woke up inside that cage with some other people. People would take us sometimes, the ones they took never came back. One lady had a bird, but they didn't take the bird when they took her. I tried to keep the bird alive but . . ."

Abigail hugged Courtney and the girl shook in her arms. "What did the people look like?"

"I don't know. They always wore black masks and suits."

Abigail shot a hot breath out of her nose; her blood was boiling. She glared at Odo and the other villains. These abductions could've been stopped if Hero Enterprises wasn't dealing with these criminals. She'd include the details of Courtney in her next report. Beacon could better explore the research lab and stop whatever was happening.

"She's going to a hospital," Abigail told Odo.

He sighed, dragging a hand down his face. "We'll stop a block away from one."

"She was nabbed walking alone!" Cold Snap reminded.

"I'm protecting *our* investment!" Snapped Odo.

"I'm protecting this girl," Abigail growled, sulfur filling her mouth despite her efforts to keep her Dragon's Breath dormant.

From the square window that connected the cab to the back, Stretch hollered, "There's a 24 hour urgent care clinic coming up."

Tech's fingers flew across his keyboard. "There's no cameras."

"Fine." Odo pinned Abigail with his compound eyes, all 48 sections drilling into her. "But don't stop the van."

Abigail cupped Courtney's chin so she'd look at her. It felt like she held a Halloween decoration. All she felt was bone. "Stay at the clinic. Someone will help you. I promise."

Courtney nodded.

The van slowed and Stretch announced their arrival. Cold Snap pulled open the side panel and Abigail helped Courtney to the edge. The girl hesitated and stared at the sidewalk passing by. Abigail didn't want to test Odo's hospitality. She waited for the upcoming median filled with soft looking grass and pushed Courtney into it. The side panel snapped shut before Abigail saw if Courtney landed okay.

"Thanks," she told Odo.

"No more detours," Odo addressed them all. "Warden's waiting."

Warden waited for them under an awning outside a restaurant. People with a smaller frame could have disappeared within the shadows, but Warden's imposing silhouette dominated the darkness. The soft glow of a cigarette danced between his hand and mouth. The tiny ember glinted across the golden rings clinging to each finger. He dropped the cigarette and snuffed it with the heel of his boot as Abigail exited the van behind the rest of his crew. She rolled up the sleeve of her left arm so it matched the length of the right where it was seared off at the elbow from her stunt outside the elevator.

Once outside of the cramped electrical van, Abigail took stock of herself and her team. Aside from a scrape atop her knee and a tender spot on her hip she knew would bruise, Abigail was fine. Cold Snap's bottom lip was cut down the center and bloody, but her cold body must help keep the swelling down. Stretch and Tech didn't seem affected by the chase. Abigail lingered on Odo, though. His left wing wasn't collapsed against his back like the right one. It rustled together like a paper fan with each step. The membrane around the edges didn't shimmer like she'd seen it do before. The clear membrane was shattered. Torn apart by gun shots.

"Took longer than I expected." Warden didn't waste time with small talk or any notion of concern, faked or genuine. "Do you have it?"

Odo handed him the hairdryer-shaped device, wincing when his damaged wing knocked against the other. "We had a small complication, but everything's okay. Tech finished scrubbing the security footage before we got here."

"The only thing they'll see is a group of gray blobs," Tech added, his orange freckles glowing as softly as the cigarette ember had. "Superimposed an ice cream truck over our van, too."

Abigail was once again impressed by Tech's talent and attention to detail. At this rate, she would have an entire book of things to look for when she returned to the HRC. If she could figure out how Tech completed his miracles, maybe someone at the HRC could reverse it and create a program to rid a recording of scrubbed images.

Perhaps, after everything was done, Abigail could convince Tech to work off his societal debt at the HRC and help heroes.

Warden examined the sonic boom device as delicately as he could with his massive hands. He took aim at the building across the street. The seconds were agonizing as Abigail waited to see if he would test the device, but Warden didn't pull the trigger. He stuck it inside the interior of his coat next to a pistol.

"The boss will be pleased."

Abigail whipped her head from the almost destroyed building to Warden. "You're not our boss?"

Her cheeks pinked at the outburst, and she clamped her mouth shut. The laughter that came from Odo only darkened her features.

"I'm *your* boss, yes." Warden didn't elaborate, then addressed the others, "Go back to the hideout and wait for me. The hit on Bastet is set for tomorrow night."

Chapter Seventeen

Abigail pulled on a pair of wool socks while still under the thin blanket of her bunk. The hideout was dark except for occasional orange flashes of Tech's Ethernet netting to her right. He was either dreaming, the lights flickering in a similar manner as a dog's legs might twitch, or some program ran without his supervision. Around her, the mixture of deep breathing and snoring of the sleeping villains kept her company. No one said much when they made it back last night, and Abigail assumed most would still be asleep when she returned. Her feet were silent as she slipped off her bunk. She grabbed her shoes, planning to lace them up once she was out of the subterranean level, and tip-toed toward the door.

A hissing stopped her. She peered over her shoulder, expecting Warden's terrifying features to merge out of the shadows, but saw Odo bracing himself against the kitchen table instead. Despite his dominating bug features, she couldn't deny the very human emotion of pain etched across his face. Abigail left the door and joined him. The white-knuckle grip Odo had on the table didn't lessen as she took a seat.

"You okay?" she asked.

Odo shook his head *no*. The movement caused him to wince.

"What's wrong? What's happening to you?"

Odo didn't answer. He held onto the table with such force Abigail was certain he'd crack the wood. The plastic tablecloth tore under his grip. She ignited her fingers. The fire bathed Odo in blood red shadows and highlighted the tear in his left wing. The small rip Abigail saw earlier had extended up the membrane for almost two feet. A dark liquid oozed around the edges.

Abigail gasped. "This looks bad."

Through gritted teeth, Odo remarked, "Imagine how it feels."

"What can I do to help?"

"Nothing. It has to heal on its own." His statement was interrupted by another painful wince and his wings shuddered.

Abigail kneeled to better see the injury. The dark ooze slowly pulled the two sides of the membrane together like slimy stitches. At the bottom, where the bullet initially struck him, the wing rebuilt itself.

"Incredible."

Abigail's compliment was lost as Odo shook again. She wasn't sure what a half dragonfly man needed for comfort, but she searched the small kitchenette until she produced something that could help. A glass of water, damp washrag, pack of fun-sized chocolate candies, a half empty bottle of aspirin. She set it all within arm's reach of Odo and pushed a chair closer to him.

Odo reached for the aspirin bottle, but a convulsion caused him to smack it to the ground. Abigail retrieved it from where it rolled under the table and shook two tiny pills into her hand. She shook out a third. She offered them and the water to him. Odo didn't look happy, a mixture of the pain and the acceptance of her help, but he swallowed down both.

"Why are you up this early?" he asked.

"Wanted to get some coffee." Abigail helped ease him into the chair. "Didn't think I'd have time today after everyone was up. With the hit happening and all."

"Think you're ready?"

"To kill a hero?"

Abigail didn't like the direction of their conversation, but she was glad Odo was making coherent sentences. He released the tabletop and gripped the washrag instead. Water dripped between his fingers.

Combustion

Abigail could use his vulnerability to get more information before making her report.

"They die like the rest of us."

"Why do you do it?" Abigail gestured around the hideout. "Why'd you join Warden?"

He sighed. "One day I just got tired of getting the short end of things. You try to do what's expected of you, go to school, get a good job, buy a house in the suburbs, but no one wants someone with *bug eyes*. They built this society and this is the role I was expected to play, I guess."

Odo's words rattled inside Abigail's head, pulling ghosts of past feelings she couldn't completely recall. It was a sensation of Deja vu except she didn't have any of the five senses to remember. She swallowed down the strange feeling.

"Did Warden or his boss recruit you?"

"Warden does all the recruiting," Odo answered, clinching his teeth as his wings shivered. "No one's met the boss."

"But you take all his orders?"

"They haven't let us down, so why question it? Whoever is calling the shots is clever. I trust them."

"Do you know the full plan for Bastet yet?"

"Why? Nervous?"

Abigail caught the momentary grin from Odo before the darkness of the room or his pain snatched it. "A little bit."

"Warden will tell us everything we need to know, don't worry."

"Will you be able to go like this?" The mending ability of Odo's wings was impressive, but even if they were healed before the mission, would he be strong enough to go toe-to-toe with a hero like Bastet?

"I'll be there no matter what." Odo's hands loosened around the washrag. Whether he pretended to be better or he actually was, Abigail couldn't tell. She hoped the aspirin had kicked in. "Are you still getting coffee?"

"That's my plan. Want something special?"

Abigail took Odo's order, surprisingly caramel flavored for someone so harsh, and finally slipped out of the hideout. Once she was outside of Simply Sushi, she ran to the coffee shop. She wanted to run straight to Beacon to warn him directly. She couldn't trust their crossword messages with something this heavy, but she didn't have a choice. She agreed to the cypher, she agreed to the mission's terms, she knew the risks, Beacon knew the risks too.

The barista jerked his attention to the door when Abigail ran inside, the force of her entry slamming the door against the wall. Her face flushed and she commanded her legs to walk to the counter. She placed her order, half of it to go, between deep breaths and moved to the pickup counter. The top rack of papers was empty. Abigail's blood pressure spiked.

"Where's today's paper?" she asked the sleepy-eyed employee smearing cream cheese on a bagel across the counter from her.

"Must not have arrived yet."

"When does it get here?" Abigail rifled through the remaining papers from yesterday praying one might morph into the one she needed.

"Sometimes not until ten."

"That's ridiculous."

"Well, it is six a.m. on a Saturday."

Abigail gritted her teeth and yanked yesterday's paper from the rack. She accepted her bagel and coffee from the employee and retreated to a booth. The shop was mostly empty, those who did choose coffee over sleeping in on a weekend opted to take their breakfasts to go, but Abigail remained vigilant on keeping her crossword puzzle blocked from wondering eyes. She repeated her code in every available

Combustion

space: Attack on Bastet tonight. Using sonic boom to disorientate. Targeting tail. Unknown location. Someone in charge above Warden. Kidnapped kids at Wittman Research Lab.

By the time the squares were filled, the back of the Tennyson City Tribune looked like the writings of a deranged lunatic. Abigail felt like one as she crammed the message in one final time above the clues. She folded the paper back together and was tempted to scrawl *BEACON* across the top but capped her pen before she could.

If Beacon believed in the success of their communication, then she needed to as well.

Abigail picked apart her bagel. Whatever pieces actually found their way into her mouth didn't sit well in her stomach. Tonight, she would pretend to kill a hero. It didn't matter how much focus she placed on the pretending part. After tonight, Abigail wasn't sure she'd be able to look at herself again.

For the greater good, she reminded herself. *Besides, Bastet will be fine. I'll be there to protect her if she doesn't get the message.*

"Marie?" the barista called. "To go order for Marie?"

Abigail looked around the empty shop before realizing the order was for her. The paper stared up at her among the crumbs and spilt coffee on the table. Her time was up. She needed to return to the hideout before Odo got suspicious. Abigail still gathered her trash at a glacier's pace and loitered at the trash bin. Her to go orders cooled at the pickup counter. She double checked her cypher and refolded the paper, twice, before heading to the rack to return it.

"Excuse me," someone asked behind her. "Is that today's paper?"

"It's yesterday's," Abigail answered too defensively for a newspaper's date as she turned around. The Heroes Enterprise badge caught her attention before the rest of the man. His meek frame didn't look strong enough to withstand a gust of wind, and whatever style his hair had been in that morning was already a mess across his face. "But it has a lot of good articles!" Abigail handed him the paper.

"Thank you," the HE employee accepted the paper.

Abigail couldn't stop the grin that probably did label her as a lunatic from splitting her face in half. "You're welcome."

She plucked her order off the counter and left the shop with newly found relief. Despite tonight's attack looming over her.

The office building was quiet this late at night, which made sense. The wall clock read a quarter till ten so even the most diligent employee would have left by now. What didn't make sense was why the attack on Bastet was taking place at an office selling expensive yachts. Abigail could only suspect the hero wanted to acquire a boat without the media knowing. The others didn't seem as concerned with the location when Warden delivered their assignments two hours ago.

The eagerness they shared about the mission was alarming. She knew they were villains, but she hadn't realized how far they'd cross the moral line. If they had ever stood on the good side of it to begin with. Their willingness to murder made Abigail sick. The excitement about conducting the act made her head dizzy.

Twenty minutes before, the four of them picked the lock on a back door, waited for Tech to flash the van's lights to confirm the alarm was off, and infiltrated the office. Four sets of cubicles occupied this level and offered little entertainment while they waited. The temptation of partaking in an office supply battle waned as soon as Stretch suggested it.

"Almost time." Cold Snap whispered to Abigail as they hid below a desk. The hanging vines of an ivy plant dangled between them.

Their role was simple. Allegedly, the yacht meeting would end at 10:05, and Bastet would be led out of the main office and down this hallway. Abigail and Cold Snap were to cover the flank while Odo and Stretch incited a frontal attack. Without knowing the location when Abigail scribed her note that morning, she didn't know if Bastet was actually here. The ease of infiltrating the building didn't bode well for any extra security if she was.

The hope that the building was empty vanished when the overhead lights turned on. Footsteps and voices sounded at the far end of the office where a bend in a hallway kept their owners hidden. The cover didn't matter; Abigail recognized Bastet's voice. Even thanking someone for their time, the hero sounded just as mocking as she had when Abigail first faced her.

The temperature around Abigail dropped as Cold Snap formed a disk of ice in her palm. She angled it so they could see a reflection of Bastet and her business partner rounding the corner. Their mirrored bodies stretched and wobbled as if Abigail were looking through a carnival mirror. A teal headband wrapped tightly atop Bastet's head hid her cat ears, and her tail was most likely hidden beneath her grey pleated skirt. The business partner was still laughing at something she must have said. Assuming the steep price of a yacht, Abigail imagined he'd laugh at any bad joke to help move a sale along. Looming behind them was a third man unabashedly armed with a gleaming pistol on his hip.

It was just as Warden said. Three people but only one target. The deaths of the businessman and security guard should be avoided, but Warden said he understood if loose ends needed tying.

Abigail gritted her teeth. Why didn't Beacon keep Bastet at Hero Enterprises all night where she could be protected? Where two civilians couldn't get hurt in the crossfire?

The trio walked past Abigail and Cold Snap's hiding place unaware of the villains and continued blindly to Odo and Stretch. Abigail inserted tiny black velvet-covered spheres in her ears to lessen the effects of the sonic boom device and waited for Cold Snap to do the same. The technology of the ear protectors reminded her of the noise canceling earmuffs she was required to wear at a ribbon cutting ceremony at San Arbor's airfield. Normal conversation would pass through the sphere but anything louder than a gunshot would be silenced. After receiving Cold Snap's thumbs up, Abigail made a series of hand signs signifying she'd go after the gunman.

It wasn't that Abigail didn't think Cold Snap was capable of taking him out, she just didn't think she'd be capable of doing it without hurting him.

Her skull buzzed, a side effect of the sonic boom device activating, and Abigail leapt out of her hiding place and swept the gunman's feet out from under him with a solid strike against his shins. In his confusion, she snatched the gun from his side and aimed it at his head. His mustachioed face twisted into a snarl, but he remained on the ground.

The businessman dropped to his knees, both hands covering the sides of his head. His body shook with the assault of an unknown noise. Blood dripped from his ears. With a fist covered in ice, Cold Snap punched the back of his head and knocked him out.

Cold Snap smiled at Abigail, and Abigail recognized the familiar expression: excitement, pride, and victory. It mirrored her own thrill when she took down an opponent. Only Abigail's opponents were usually bad guys. Cold Snap's pride resonated sinister energy rather than justice. Abigail watched the businessman's chest until she was certain he was still breathing.

Their portion of the plan was completed, both civilians down, but Bastet remained standing, grinning at Abigail with a smile full of malice. Abigail didn't think Bastet had tiger fangs, but with the danger seeping in the air, she could've been fooled.

"Bank Robber." Bastet purred at Abigail as if she were greeting an old friend instead of an enemy. "I was hoping I'd see you again."

"Odo?" Cold Snap called, not looking away from the hero and gunman who weren't reacting to the sonic device like the businessman. "Any day now."

"It's not working!" Odo called back, smacking the palm of his hand against the sonic boom device's handle. A decorative vase shattered when the energy wave passed over it.

Bastet flicked her wrist and five sharp talons as dark as her eyes grew from her nails. She slipped one under her teal headband, slicing it apart to reveal her cat ears.

They were stuffed with a clay-like material.

The device had worked, it just hadn't affected Bastet.

Beacon had received Abigail's note in time.

"Swordfish and Rush underestimated you." Bastet unleashed the rest of her cat-like qualities, tearing off her skirt at the knee to give her tail better motion. "I won't make that mistake. Tonight, the hero killers die."

Arriving at Bastet's command, three more gunmen rounded the corner on Odo and Stretch's side. The two snapped into action, foregoing the sonic boom device for their own skills.

Ditching the pistol for something she was more comfortable with, Abigail ignited her flames into gauntlets over her arms and braced for Bastet's attack. The hero hesitated momentarily, but still sliced through the lukewarm flames and connected with Abigail's forearms. Abigail hadn't expected her temperature illusion to fail. Blood trickled between her fingers, and she gritted her teeth against the pain. Bastet stepped back. Abigail used the opening to kick her in the chest. Bastet staggered backwards but dropped to the floor ready to pounce. Her claws aimed at Abigail's jugular.

Bastet leapt forward quick as a lightening strike.

It happened on instinct. Her flames surging to protect their master. Fire blossomed across Abigail's chest, morphing into the suit of armor to cover herself. The fire engulfed her in a safe embrace that felt barely warmer than a pot of coffee. At the painful cries outside the flame armor, Abigail knew the fire was real on the other side. She forced the fire away from her face and found a scorched Bastet across from her. Bastet's long hair was singed into a jagged mess, her claws reduced to stubs, her face charred and blistered. Pieces of dark flesh fell to the ground.

One more hit like that, and the hero would be defeated.

By Abigail's own hands.

Hero killer.

The fire around her whipped into a confusing inferno until Abigail exhaled and the flames disappeared. Her bloody and soot-covered arms looked cleaner than how she currently felt.

Behind Bastet, Abigail caught Odo and Stretch staring at her, waiting for her to finish the job. A job she wouldn't do. A job she couldn't do.

"Wildfire!" Cold Snap yelped behind her. The sounds of shattering ice followed her cry.

Abigail broke the first rule of combat, she turned away from her opponent. The gunman held Cold Snap by the neck, crushing her against a wall. The woman's face was bluer than normal, and her glacier eyes bore into Abigail's, pleading for help.

Giving up her fight with Bastet, Abigail launched a flurry of blows at the gunman. He pulled Cold Snap off the wall and used her as a human shield. Abigail's fist wailed into Cold Snap, bloodying her nose, but her next hit sailed into the gunman's eye, and he dropped his hostage.

Combustion

Abigail caught Cold Snap and lowered her to the ground. The girl's face was stained red, and a terrible black bruise constricted around her neck. She couldn't protect the hero, and now she couldn't protect her teammate. Anger breathed new life into her, kindling her fire. Once back on her feet, she knocked her fists together, her knuckles catching fire, and stared down the gunman. He pointed a second pistol at her, but before he could pull the trigger, Abigail exhaled a mouthful of smoke that obscured the space between them. The sounds of other combat penetrated the smoke. She didn't know which side was winning. She advanced cautiously, listening for the gunman's movements, and caught the glint of his weapon through a shaft of light. Abigail tossed a fireball at the gun.

Even with the ear protectors, his agonizing screams tore through Abigail as the gunman's hand exploded with his weapon. She wished she hadn't thrown the fireball. She wished she didn't smell burning flesh. She wished she could take this whole night back. Under the cover of the smoke, Abigail found the gunman cradling the remainder of his arm. He tried to swat her away, but there was no strength left. Blood pooled beneath him.

"You're going to be okay." Abigail doubted he believed her; she barely believed herself.

She reached for him, but the gunman twisted away, crying out again as he rammed into an office chair. Before she developed her powers, Abigail knew one thing: she wanted to save people. She wanted to be a hero. She never imagined someone would deny her help. She never imagined someone would be afraid of her.

More blood crashed onto the floor in globs of scarlet. Even if the hand had survived the explosion, there would have been no time for a surgeon to reattach it. Abigail had to save this man.

"Let me help you," she snarled, yanking his arm to her.

Without his permission, Abigail cauterized the wound. The gunman screamed until he passed out. It was a terrible sound.

A cold hand gripped Abigail's shoulder. The smoke had lifted. She didn't realize the cover was gone. Cold Snap pulled her up.

"We have to go," Cold Snap said. "Like, right now."

The rest happened in slow motion. Odo used the sonic boom device to shatter a row of windows and fired it again at the wall behind Bastet, causing it to collapse around her and the one remaining guard. Odo flew out of the opening and Stretch waved Cold Snap and Abigail forward. His bare arms and chest were covered in slashes and blood had already seeped down his pant legs.

Cold Snap created an ice ramp down to the street level and Abigail melted it when the three of them were on the ground.

They had failed their mission.

Abigail should have been happy. Bastet wasn't killed, but seeing the damage done to her team and knowing the damage she caused to the heroes registered this victory as a defeat.

Chapter Eighteen

Ghosts filled Abigail's dreams the night after the failed mission, except it wasn't Thomas' face haunting her. Her nightmares replayed the horrific audios from the office building. She didn't know who designed the ear blockers, Tech acquired them before they left, but Abigail thought they all deserved a refund. The devices had stopped the sonic boom device but hadn't quelled any of the screams that refused to leave Abigail's subconscious. She kept hearing the businessman's piercing yowl as he bled out of his ears. Abigail guessed HE didn't supply him with the earphones their agents had. She kept hearing Bastet's cries as her skin melted away. She kept hearing the gunman shout in fear as she approached, his panicked screams as she seared what was left of his hand.

The pillow she wrapped around her ears did little to muffle the real-life moans and whimpers of Cold Snap and Stretch as they tried to rest in their bunks.

Cold Snap had grown mute when they piled into the getaway van. She created a cold compress to hold over her bruising throat and encased her other wrist in ice hoping to heal the sprain she also received from the gunman. Her chipper mood was non-existent. She hadn't even issued a good night before retreating to her bunk.

Abigail imagined it was worse for Stretch. He watched Cold Snap like a hawk, ready to aid her in any way he could, but could do nothing to ease her pain. And, besides the bottle of aspirin, there was nothing to ease the pain to his arms and chest carved up by Bastet's claws. Abigail helped Odo clean them with antiseptic wipes and covered the deepest of the cuts with Band-Aids.

A Girl Scout would've been better equipped.

Abigail rolled over in her bunk, gritting her teeth when the springs rattled too loudly. She knew this mission would be difficult, but not for this reason. She was prepared to commit thievery, crimes that had no real victims. She hadn't been prepared to sear away Bastet's skin or amputate a stranger's hand. She also hadn't been prepared to care about these criminals like she did.

They're hero killers, she told herself. *They would've killed Bastet tonight if I didn't warn them. They'll kill me too if they ever find out.*

They'd kill more heroes too if they weren't stopped. Abigail rolled over again, moving as slowly as possible to avoid making noise, and steeled her resolve.

Beacon told her this mission would likely take months to complete. To find the true leader and exterminate the entire gang like a pack of rats. Tonight had been successful according to her true goal. Injuring the villains was also a good thing. The longer they were out of commission the more time the heroes could spend doing their jobs.

Neither of these points helped Abigail sleep. The ghosts continued their haunting until morning.

Two days later and Cold Snap had graduated to speaking single word sentences. The words were hoarse and the bruising around her neck was still visible, but a playful energy had returned to her blue features. Odo managed to find proper disinfectant and bandages and was pretty sure he staved off any infections on Stretch. The group was in high spirits after the days of dark clouds looming over the hideout. It was a welcomed sensation that warranted a celebration, and Abigail happily offered to pick up a real breakfast that didn't include day old raw fish.

The cashier smiled at Abigail when she entered the coffee shop. She was learning the faces and names of the staff, and hoped they

Combustion

weren't doing the same with her. She was just a repeat customer, no one to be suspicious of. Abigail grabbed the day's newspaper before joining the line. The smell of ground coffee beans perked her senses while the familiar smell of doughnut glaze and heated sausage patties lured her into a comfort she hadn't realized the shop provided.

The cashier rang up her order, tagging the food as to-go, and poured black coffee into a ceramic mug for her in house consumption. Abigail settled into her usual booth and set to work filling out the crossword puzzle. The intimidating cypher had grown easy in its use, and she quickly filled the boxes in a bizarre pattern of sounds. She wanted to ask how the gunman was, but knew she'd never get a reply. Not to mention the question would take up too much valuable space on paper.

Around her, the coffee shop bustled into a frenzy of movement. A bus load of children piled into the dining room already half full of weekday diners. Their mindless chattered overpowered the soft pop soundtrack trying to give the room ambience. The barking of orders in the kitchen clashed with the digital chimes of the register. The plastic bench seat across Abigail crinkled as someone sat across from her.

"Writing anything good about me, doll?"

The air escaped Abigail's lungs. Her heart plummeted into her stomach. The noise of the coffee shop vanished. Her pen melted inside her hand. His voice called her home as it did every time before. He commandeered the bench seat, his arms stretching over the back, like it was a golden throne instead of cracking vinyl. The hood of his jacket tried to hide his face, but a crisscrossing of new burn scars clutched his twisted smile. The darkness caused his emerald eyes to gleam.

Cinder.

Thomas.

Alive.

Abigail unclenched her hand and the charred remains of the pen clattered to the table. Her mouth was too dry to form words. Her body too tense to move. Her mind too stunned to think.

With one finger, Cinder dragged the newspaper to his side of the table. The space between them incredibly intimate and incredibly vast at the same time. His eyes never left Abigail's, and their weight pinned her to the bench. He rolled the paper tightly and stuffed it inside his jacket where he removed a second paper and pencil. Cinder slid them both to Abigail along with a wave of woodsmoke-scented air. It knocked the returning senses out of Abigail's head, and a hundred emotions flooded her system until she felt like she'd combust under the pressure.

Disbelief. Infuriated. Powerless. Confusion. Nervousness. Everything swelled inside her, but at its center was hopefulness. A relief that he was alive. Abigail wanted to leap across the table and pull Thomas into her, refuse to let him go. Abigail also wanted to leap across the table and clobber Cinder for everything he'd put her through. The war inside her kept her still, but heat filled her veins in either anticipation or excitement.

Cinder tapped the pencil against the paper. "I need you to write a new message."

"Why would I?" Abigail finally found her voice and it was saturated with venom.

Cinder grinned, dangerous and hungry, and leaned across the table so only Abigail could hear him. "You and I are the only fireproof ones here. Do what I say, or I'll level this place."

Abigail looked around the dining room. Several tables were full of chattering kids who couldn't be older than eleven. Across the room, a mother coaxed her toddler to eat eggs. An elderly couple sat on the same side of a booth giggling and picking apart a chocolate covered doughnut. The employee who had made Abigail a dozen drinks dropped off a sandwich to a customer.

"What's it going to be?"

Abigail returned her gaze to Cinder. Wisps of smoke raised off his fingertips. She gripped the pencil, the wooden exterior splintering in her hold.

"What do you want me to write?"

"Tell Hero Enterprises you're taking a break," he answered. "That there's no new attack planned. Tell them you're moving locations." Cinder paused, glancing around the room before landing his gaze back on Abigail. Their sudden emerald assault left her breathless. "Tell them the whole operation is moving to a warehouse east of the train station. An empty one on Maddison Street. Tonight is the best night to strike. Before their security is set up."

Abigail wrote down his lies. The cyphered letters feeling dirty on the page. When the last square was filled, Cinder pulled the paper back to his side and compared it to the original one stashed in his coat.

"Don't trust me?" Abigail asked.

"It's hard to trust anyone." Apparently satisfied with the message, he burned the original paper in a flash of blue fire too quick for anyone to notice. "Except for me. You trusted my threat."

"I won't put these people's lives in jeopardy for you."

"You always were a good hero." Cinder's grin twitched momentarily before returning to its twisted form. He grabbed her hand, and the touch shocked Abigail. His touch was warm, alive, and sent the same flutter down her stomach as it always did. He hauled her to her feet before she realized it. "Don't make a scene," he whispered in her ear, his hood blocking his face from the other customers.

"My to-go order." Abigail tried pulling her wrist free of his grip, but Cinder held on too tight.

He rolled his eyes but plucked it off the counter as he dragged Abigail out of the coffee shop. The newspaper of lies waiting for the HE agent to collect. Outside, the blazing sun didn't hold a candle to the searing heat Abigail felt on her wrist from Cinder's touch. It burned more than the fire running through both their veins. The heat took the form of a spirit and plunged itself deep inside Abigail's mind, body, and soul. Every time she thought she grasped clarity of the situation, of her feelings, a blast of embers left her dazed.

Cinder could have dragged her across the street or halfway across Tennyson City before Abigail regained her senses. The stale air pumping through the city bus she sat in teased her short hair into a mess of frizz. She pressed her free hand against the window and focused on the cold glass. Beads of condensation formed an outline of her fingers in minutes, and she wiped her now damp hand on her pants.

She caught Cinder staring at her. She felt like a painting hanging in some foreign museum. She couldn't read him, and she desperately wanted to know what he was thinking. The way he looked at her, absorbed her image, made her wonder if he desperately wanted to know what she was thinking too.

Thomas Sanders had died over a year ago. Yet the emerald wastelands of his eyes currently filled Abigail's vision. They were just as she remembered. The same vastness she had willingly drowned in, the same vastness she had tried to salvage, the same vastness that filled her subconscious.

Abigail never knew how beautiful the color green was until she knew Cinder. Thomas. Whoever this person was who continued to hold her wrist despite there being nowhere for her to run. The bus collected its next group of passengers and lumbered on.

Neither of them looked away, but Cinder's expression morphed into his signature twisted grin and Abigail counted it a victory for her.

Combustion

She still retained her stoic features despite the butterflies trying to crawl from her stomach into her mouth. The metaphorical bugs changed between slimy worms and dainty Monarchs. Abigail dropped her gaze.

A snicker came from Cinder's lips as easily as a breath.

In his free hand, more of the wispy cigarette smoke lifted off his skin.

"You can stop with that," Abigail snapped, locking her gaze on him. The smoke easily ignored by the other passengers was a clear threat to their safety to Abigail. "I'm not going to cause a scene."

"I didn't think you would." His voiced rumbled lowly for only her to hear.

Abigail's response fizzled on her tongue. The air between them grew thin and it was hard for her to breathe. She expected that to happen while fighting fires, not riding a city bus. Silence enveloped them. The only proof he was actually there was the hand around her wrist. It continued to burn Abigail in ways she didn't understand. In ways she didn't want to explore. The white paper bag of breakfast sandwiches and doughnuts was laughable sitting between them. How normal they must have looked to strangers was laughable. Abigail wanted to laugh, she wanted to do something to unleash the bubbling emotions inside herself but was ultimately too scared to do anything.

Not for the passenger's sakes. She'd be able to save them.

There were a hundred things she wanted to say, wanted to know, but the very fact he was here silenced her. She feared making too much noise and scaring away this ghost.

The bus heaved itself to the curb and deposited Abigail and Cinder at the corner usually guarded by Jefferson, but it was empty. Abigail assumed that was for the best. She didn't know how to explain her current predicament. Cinder led them to the final block to Simply Sushi, not letting go of Abigail's wrist until they were inside the restaurant.

The moment he let go, the heat vanished and the cold that overcame it was almost painful. Abigail didn't leave his side. Cinder's presence had the same gravitational pull as a dying star. She shifted the bag of food from one hip to the other.

"Set that down." Cinder pointed to the door leading to the subterranean level before approaching the door on the other side of the counter.

Abigail did so and joined Cinder in time to see him open the series of locks with several keys he pulled from various pockets of his coat and pants. The door sprang open. Cinder stepped back and ushered Abigail forward.

She looked up the stairs before committing to the first step. The staircase was lit in hazy blue light from some window higher up. The thin carpet patterned to look like flowers thinned in the center from use. The scent of ash and woodsmoke saturated the small area. Abigail inhaled deeply, partly savoring the smell and partly to refill her oxygen tank, and ascended the stairs.

The door shut and bolted behind her, and Cinder was on her heels. Their closeness in the confined space became suffocating. Abigail forced her legs to move faster, to create distance, before she could act on the closeness. The stairs wrapped around the building three times before spilling onto a platform with a lone door. Abigail opened it and stepped into a loft.

Slats of sunlight fell through the skylights and illuminated half of the open space. The light highlighted sections of a desk, a bed, a tile encrusted bathroom, kitchenette accented in iron, and exposed brick walls that marked this loft a renter's paradise. Where the sunlight didn't illuminate, deep shadows devoured the normality and promised secrets only attainable by blood.

"You've been here the whole time?" Abigail accused Cinder, turning to face him.

Combustion

"Just got back, actually," he answered.

"Where have you been?"

His twisted grin cut his scarred face in half, and he looked a lot like the light-patched room he stood in. Half alive with light and half hidden in shadow. "I'll be asking the questions right now."

Abigail crossed her arms and waited.

Cinder made her wait longer. He circled the loft. Stripping out of his jacket and laying it across a kitchen stool. He flipped through a stack of mail on the counter, tossed half of it away, and set the other half on the large wooden desk. He fumbled through a few other pieces of the paper, burning the pieces he either didn't need or didn't approve of, and finally leaned against the desk to look at Abigail.

"I like that you used my name, Wildfire. When Warden told me he was thinking of hiring new blood I was upset that some lowlife was using it. Imagine my surprise when that lowlife turned out to be you."

Abigail's face heated at the compliment even though Cinder hadn't made one.

"I was also surprised to see you join this group, even more surprised at what you did the other night at the lab. I almost thought you were really on our side." Cinder raised a finger to silence her coming protest. "The letters you send, who gets them? Who knows you're here?"

"You don't expect me to answer that, do you?"

Cinder shrugged. "I expected you to lie."

Abigail glared at him and pierced her nails against the interior of her arms. The longer they were together, the more she wanted to touch him. She still hadn't decided in what manner: passion or rage.

"It doesn't matter, I'll find out soon enough." Cinder turned his back to examine more of the annoying documents on the desk. "You can go back downstairs."

Abigail dropped her arms. Rage and confusion fueled her remarks. "You want me to just go back to work? I'm going to continue—"

"I want you to work for me, now." Cinder slowly turned back to face Abigail with the precision of a tiger stalking its prey. "Keep following orders, keep writing to Beacon and his crew but now only what I say, and keep training Cold Snap. She needs a good role model."

Abigail finally laughed. A dry sounding chuckle that scratched her throat. "What makes you think I'll do any of that?"

"Because you're a good hero, Abigail." Cinder summoned his blue fire to his hands. Abigail felt the intense heat from where she stood. Despite her constant training, she still wasn't immune to his flames. The indigo embers were the only thing strong enough to burn her. It was clear neither of them forgot it. "If you deviate from my orders, or try to send word to Hero Enterprises, I'll do far worse than killing *heroes*. I'll attack civilians."

Chapter Nineteen

The takeout bag was gone when Abigail returned to the restaurant level. She doubted she'd be able to carry it to the hideout with Cinder's threat, with Cinder himself, weighing her down. Everything she knew was crumbling beneath her. She watched Thomas die. His body reduced to ashes. She cried inside his mother's arms. Descended into darkness to cope with his death. Now, her whole body shook at his return. Cinder's return. The villain's scarred face, his dark plans, his disregard for life, didn't belong to Thomas.

If Cinder was alive, then Abigail had to hope that Thomas was too. Buried somewhere below that crooked smile.

A hero saves people, and just as before, all Abigail wanted to save was him.

Entering the subterranean floor, Abigail was assaulted by a slap of cold air mixed with secondhand café smells. The takeout bag was ripped open at the table, the sandwiches and doughnuts distributed among the villains including Warden whose doughnut looked like a Cheerio in his grasp. The laughter among them should have warmed Abigail, especially Cold Snap's glee sailing over the other voices, but Abigail continued to drown in a sea of emeralds.

"Wildfire." Odo beckoned her over. The way he said her name was a broken Christmas light compared to the Eiffel Tower sensation Cinder caused when he said it. "You're just in time."

"In time for what?" she absently asked, auto pilot taking over.

"Your next assignment," Warden answered.

Abigail blinked several times at the big man. "I thought we were taking a few days off?"

Warden chuckled. "Who told you that?"

Abigail's cheeks flushed. Of course, this was part of Cinder's plan. Everything she wrote in today's crossword puzzle would be a lie. Her stomach twisted.

"They won't expect another attack so quickly," Cold Snap said.

"Are you even ready to go back out?" Real concern streaked through Abigail's question.

"She's fine," Warden answered. Cold Snap nodded in agreement.

"What's the plan?" Odo impatiently asked. His newly healed wings twitched with excitement. "I'm ready for a rematch."

"We're setting a trap inside a warehouse." Warden passed out blue sheets of paper to every other person. Abigail accepted hers, Cold Snap peering over her shoulder, and examined the blueprint. "Two teams. Odo, Stretch, and Tech, you're setting the warehouse with traps. We have word that HE is checking out this location. Cold Snap, Wildfire, you're going to Bastet's house. If she's there, take her out."

"We know where she lives?" Abigail blurted out.

"Tech just found out." Stretch extended his arms across the table and shook the boy's shoulders. "He really can find anything on his computer."

"Don't make tonight a repeat, understand?" Warden's tone didn't allow for any questions or wavering resolve. Tonight, Bastet would die.

Unless Abigail saved her.

Abigail continued studying the blueprint while she and Cold Snap hid outside the colonial style home just outside downtown. The manicured lawns around the home probably cost a fortune to keep green and happy. Abigail hadn't seen this much grass since she left San Arbor. Cars driving below twinkled like stars, and at this distance they were as silent as stars. The blueprint detailed the house having three main stories and a basement level chopped into several tiny rooms. There were a lot of rooms to hide in, to be ambushed from, but only two main doors for a clean exit. Abigail wasn't sure if the intense layout of the house was a blessing or a curse. She analyzed every inch of the blueprint, running through different scenarios and finding the best option to keep Bastet alive.

If she was even at the house. Abigail had to hope she was. If she went to the warehouse where the others were laying enough razor wire to wrap around the city, she wouldn't make it out alive. With all her mental planning, Abigail wasn't able to think about Cinder.

What his being alive meant.

What his being alive meant *to her*.

She exhaled the blooming thoughts of him, the memories of them, and forced her focus on the mission.

"You okay?" Cold Snap whispered beside her. "You're, like, really tense."

Abigail swapped her gaze from the blueprint to Cold Snap. The bruise around her neck had almost faded, but Abigail still saw how bad it was. How injured Cold Snap had been. Having caught her staring, Cold Snap rubbed her neck to hide the mark.

"I'm better, really I am."

"I should have rescued you sooner," Abigail admitted. "I won't let you out of my sight this time."

Cold Snap smiled. "Don't think I need your protection the whole time. I've been learning a lot from you. Too bad you don't have any ice powers, then you could really show me something *cool*."

Cold Snap giggled at her joke.

"I don't think our abilities are too different," Abigail said. "Besides the elemental thing, I think building control and strength would be the same."

"After this you have to teach me."

Cinder's voice crept into her head: *she needs a good role model.*

"Why not right now?" Abigail asked. "We still have some time."

The distraction would be nice for Abigail as memories tinged in blue flames burned around the edges of her mind.

Despite crouching inside a bush, Cold Snap readied a fighting stance.

"You can sit down for this." Abigail waited for Cold Snap to return to her rump and lit a tiny fire atop her pointer finger. It trailed down her knuckles, swirled into her palm, ran up the length of her arm and sizzled out at the crook of her elbow. "You try it."

Cold Snap raised her hand in front of her face and stared at her pointer finger, her tongue slipping over her upper lip. Ice crystals gathered atop the nail before bursting into a long claw jutting through the top of the bush.

Abigail summoned a tiny flame and sawed through the ice pick until it severed from Cold Snap's finger, falling between them.

"Maybe we won't train outside the enemy's house," Cold Snap said, embarrassed.

"Good idea."

Cold Snap picked up the ice pick and rolled it between her hands. "I never did properly thank you. For earlier. Thanks for saving me, I mean. I don't know if I would've made it out of there alive."

Abigail struggled with her response. The way Cold Snap fidgeted with the ice, she knew this was difficult. She didn't think something heartfelt would ease her anxiety. Abigail cracked a smile and gently knocked her fist against Cold Snap's knee. "I guess I'm your hero, now?"

"A hero only saves good people."

"That's not true," Abigail backpedaled. "You are a good person."

Combustion

Cold Snap snorted, not buying Abigail's statement, but finally looked away from the ice pick. "I would like it if you could teach me how to make those gloves over my hands. Like you do with your flames."

"Absolutely." Abigail didn't know if she could keep the promise. Helping a girl learn to control her powers *was* something Abigail wanted, but strengthening a villain was not something a hero did.

Ahead of them, the side yard became saturated in yellow as someone turned on a kitchen light. Through the window, Abigail saw a silhouette of a woman with cat ears moving about the kitchen, apparently making dinner.

"Yes!" Cold Snap cheered in a whisper. "We got her. Let's move."

Abigail grabbed Cold Snap's wrist, the difference in their body temperatures creating steam. "Wait." A slight panic filled Abigail which she swallowed down. "Let's circle the house and go upstairs. The kitchen has too many knives and things that could be used as weapons."

"Isn't that a good thing?"

"Not if Bastet and her quick feet use them on us."

"Oh, okay. Good idea."

Abigail's mental gears ground together as she adjusted her plan. By the time they reached the back door, Abigail had a solid, if somewhat-sloppy, plan. Once upstairs, Abigail would knock out Cold Snap from behind, warn Bastet of the attacks and developments, hoping the hero believed her enough to listen and pass the message to Beacon, and drag her friend back to their hideout.

"Locked." Cold Snap stepped away from the door for Abigail to confirm her statement.

Abigail gripped the knob and melted it, insides and all. The door swung open, and Abigail stepped inside the hall. According to the blueprint, the closest stairwell would be on her left. Bastet's home wasn't decorated with anything personal. Sepia-toned paint and framed photographs of jungle animals dominated the walls. Large fern plants lined the hallway every few feet and the space felt more jungle than colonial home. Identical lion statues stood guard on either side of the back staircase.

The second level contained more plants and the zig-zagging track lights cast dangerous shadows along the floor and walls. Abigail wasn't sure if the darting shadows or the looming plants hunted her more, but she felt watched. The hairs on the back of her neck stood on high alert. Her fingers sparked red in tune with her heart.

"I'm going to check in here." Cold Snap dipped into a cracked door before Abigail could protest.

Based on the blueprint, Abigail assumed this room had been a bedroom from the dimensions. She hadn't expected the baseball diamond sized closet they entered. The room filled with light as a motion sensor triggered at their entrance. Abigail froze inside the doorway, readying a strike, but nothing came after the lights. She joined Cold Snap who attempted to pull open a drawer of a jewelry box.

"Think your fire would work here?" Cold Snap asked.

"Lock's too small," Abigail lied. "I'd probably burn everything inside."

Cold Snap grinned mischievously. "I'm going to try and pick it."

"Why do you want to snoop in her stuff?"

"Bastet's done enough bad stuff to us; taking some jewelry is totally worth it." The hitch in Cold Snap's voice let Abigail know something darker dwelled inside the girl. Perhaps it was simple curiosity. Perhaps it was because she was a villain. "Besides, it's not like she'll be needing this stuff after tonight."

Combustion

Abigail stepped back from Cold Snap and her fatal attraction with murder. "I'm going to find us cover. Don't go far."

Abigail scanned the floor for a heavy object to use to knock out Cold Snap. She came across heeled boots, strappy sandals, an assortment of abandoned handbags piled atop each other, a mound of dirty laundry overflowing from a basket, and a doorknob half hidden between two fur coats.

This wasn't listed on the blueprint.

Abigail melted the lock like before. Using a small flame in her hand for light, she entered the room. Filing cabinets lined the personal office from wall to wall. Abigail tried opening one of the cabinets, but it was locked. She wiped off her fingerprints on the handle with the hem of her shirt and retreated for the door. Until something morbid caught her eye. Sitting on the desk was a tiny skull, avian in shape and about the size of a pigeon.

Drawn to the skull, Abigail approached the desk without realizing her feet had moved. A spread sheet sat beside it. Several pages stapled together formed a thick booklet. Abigail flipped open the first page and read over the shipping manifest. Everything in the spreadsheet was headed to a newly purchased plot of land off Tennyson City's coast later this week. The travel log stated the pickup of the cargo would be at the Wittman Research Lab. The list of cargo contained photos of each item.

Of each person.

Of their suggested price.

Abigail forgot to breathe.

The shipping manifest contained people. One of them being the Pigeon Lady. Hundreds of people being shipped away. Abigail flipped to the end of the document. This had to be a mistake. There had to be a dozen reasons this was in a secret office in Bastet's house. This was the case HE was working on. The hero brought her work home.

The document fell to the ground. The last page was signed off by the organizer. Amelia Little.

Bastet's real name.

Abigail scrambled to get the shipping manifest off the floor, bumping the desk and knocking the skull to the ground where it shattered.

Outside, Cold Snap screamed.

Abigail raced out of the private office and skidded to a stop among the fur coats and sequined party dresses. A man in tactical gear loomed over Cold Snap who was on the floor with a broken and bleeding nose. He advanced toward her with the butt of his rifle.

Flames licked up both of Abigail's arms. "Get away from her."

The man didn't listen. He slammed the rifle against the side of Cold Snap's head and knocked her across the floor. A rack of shirts fell on top of her body.

Abigail leapt at the man, yanking the gun from him and uppercutting his jaw with a burning fist. She separated the magazine from the gun, launched both behind her, and assaulted the man with rage-filled punches. The man grabbed her arms, wincing at the fire, and threw Abigail over his shoulder into the hallway. She landed hard on her back, the air expelling from her lungs and the fire extinguishing off her arms.

At the top of the stairs, a woman wearing costume cat ears shrieked and disappeared to the main level. Gritting her teeth, Abigail got to her feet. Bastet wasn't even here. She heard the click of the magazine reattaching to the rifle. She scrambled back to the closet, knowing few things were faster than a bullet. Flames accumulated at the soles of her shoes and shot Abigail into the man, knocking them both into a shoe rack.

Combustion

Heels and tiny buckles dug into Abigail's arms and legs. A foot-scented cloud enveloped her and made her eyes water. She crawled out of the pile. The back of an earring punctured her hand. As she emerged from the shoes, Cold Snap pulled herself out of the clothes rack across her. A thick icy fog oozed off her skin. Their eyes snapped together. Abigail tasted the panic in Cold Snap's eyes like she was being force fed maple syrup. Beside her, the assailant burst out of the shoes with his gun drawn.

Abigail dove to Cold Snap, but, without her rockets, she wasn't fast enough. The deafening boom from the rifle rang out before Abigail could reach her.

"Cold!" Abigail screamed, but Cold Snap didn't move. She only stared at Abigail, her hand slowly covering her fear-stricken face.

Abigail followed Cold Snap's gaze to her side where blood fell to the floor in loud glops. Abigail summoned fire to her hand and pressed it against her wound, but it didn't work. She was fireproof to her flames. Her fingers pressed into the missing section of her side where the bullet tore through her flesh.

She crashed to the floor. The last thing Abigail saw was Cold Snap running toward her before everything became dark and cold.

Chapter Twenty

When Abigail was five years old, she'd fallen into a snowbank. She didn't remember much about that trip with her family. A photo hung on the fridge of the four Turners dressed in winter gear outside the ski lodge, but it could have been a photo of any family at any snowy town. Abigail's tiny mind hadn't stored the memories of the long car ride there, of the hot chocolate served with every meal, of snowman making, or the sledding hill. What Abigail did remember was the cold. She remembered how it pierced her lips and nose as she struggled to breathe half buried in the snowbank. She remembered how bad her hands and feet hurt just before they numbed. She remembered the violent shaking of her legs as her body spasmed trying to warm itself.

A year later, she developed her fire powers and Abigail hadn't experienced so much as a shiver. The flames living inside her veins kept her warm, and she loved it.

She was cold now. Her body refused to move under her mental commands. She couldn't open her eyes. She couldn't hear anything. She could only feel the coldness holding her, clinging to her. The flames inside her suffocated. They were a wimpy candle flame in a snowstorm: Desperately hanging onto the feeble life that remained within. Abigail felt like she was dying. Taken out by the cold rather than the gunshot.

Abigail didn't think often of her own death. She didn't wonder what happened to her soul after she died, if anything were to happen. She wasn't faithless, but she didn't spend her waking life worrying about a potential sleeping life. If Abigail did picture a heaven, she would not picture a man with horn-rimmed glasses and a goatee manning the gates.

Except there weren't any gates and the man held a scalpel instead of a book filled with names. She blinked. The simple task took a long time to complete, but the man was still there when she opened her eyes again. Abigail didn't know where she was. Shadows encroached her vision and fog hazed over most of her senses.

It still felt like Abigail was submerged in an ice bath, the frigid water replacing the fluids in her body, but underneath the cold she felt a new sensation. One of pain. One of her skin ripping apart and something pressing deeply against her organs. She pulled away from the man, desperate to escape, but slammed against a wall before she got away. Blinding light cascaded in front of her vision as more pain gripped her core.

"Lay still." Goatee instructed. "I'm almost done."

Abigail twisted her fists inside the blanket under her as another painful wave blossomed at her side. Half her mind screamed for the cold to take her, to kill the pain, while the other half tried to relish in it. Feeling this ensured she was still alive. Her eyes darted around the room. She named each thing she saw to keep distracted. Couch. Brick wall. Bloody rags. Duffle bag. Bar stool. Cinder.

Cinder.

She didn't know how she missed him. He loomed over Goatee, shifting in and out of the shadows. He had one hand pressed against his mouth. His eyes shook in a way she'd never seen before. Smoke lifted off his shoulders. Blue sparks danced along his bare arms. He could combust. He would kill them.

"No." Abigail tried to speak, but her mouth was too dry to form the words. She continued to try, her head shaking back and forth attempting to shake loose the words. She needed to warn Goatee, she needed to get out of here, she needed her fire. Blood oozed from her hip. Her vision spotted. "No. No. No. No!"

Something sharp and small pierced the inside of her arm. Goatee injected a clear liquid into her vein from the needle biting her. Cinder jumped out from behind him. Abigail panicked.

Blue fire erupted around her and filled her vision before a sea of blackness drowned her.

Finally, she was warm.

Awareness came peacefully the second time around. There were no icebergs ramming inside Abigail. There was no excruciating tugging and pulling against her skin. Only a dull ache at her side proved an ordeal had occurred. Abigail shifted through the fragmented memories in her mind. She remembered breaking into Bastet's home. She remembered Cold Snap collapsing. She remembered a secret room. She remembered Goatee and a lack of pearly gates. Abigail remembered Cinder.

She shot forward and winced. Her consciousness attempted to shut down, to return to a peaceful state, but Abigail refused. All the fragmented memories bashed against the inside of her skull and pain seared at her side, feeling like a bike chain and kitchen knives grinding against her. A hand eased her back onto the bed.

"Easy," Goatee soothed. "You're in no position to be moving around like that."

Abigail blinked her eyes open as the pain at her side calmed down. She was in a bed, one that smelled like her own except she wasn't in her home. Nor had she slept in her bed in a long while. She watched Goatee fill a glass of water from the sink at the kitchenette and return to her bedside. She squeezed her eyes shut as one of the memories finally became clear. This was Cinder's loft.

The water glass tapped against her hand. "You need to rehydrate."

Combustion

Abigail wouldn't dispute that. The way her throat felt she wondered if the last thing she ate was a pile of sand. Abigail accepted the glass, eased herself up on an elbow and downed the drink. As she returned the glass, another memory struggled to re-form. Goatee's face was marred with a fresh burn. Abigail's stomach dropped.

Goatee took the glass and sat in the chair next to the bed, keeping the burned half of his face out of Abigail's line of sight. "I'm sure you have questions."

Abigail had a million but decided to start with the ones she figured he could answer. "Who are you?"

"Doctor Miles Hilgard," he answered. "I specialize in certain house calls."

"What happened to me?"

"You were shot. As for the how and why, I don't know, and you won't be telling me. I extracted the bullet and patched you up."

Abigail trailed her fingers to her side and flinched.

"Yes, that was where the bullet was. If you don't want it getting infected, you'll keep your fingers out of it."

Abigail blushed. "What happened to Cold Snap?"

"Cold Snap?" Hilgard echoed.

"My friend. She was with me when . . ." Abigail trailed off, trying to keep the doctor's request in mind. "Did she make it back?"

"I don't know. When I arrived, it was only you up here, but if she needed medical help, I'm sure I would have seen her."

"I'm sorry that I burned you," she whispered, ashamed she'd lost control again.

Hilgard turned so Abigail could see the burn. It ebbed and flowed over his wrinkling skin. "You didn't do this."

"But—," Abigail stopped herself. There were two people who could catch fire. "Cinder. But why?"

Abigail tried to get out of the bed, wanting to ready a counterattack for his return, but an unescapable sucker-punch of pain, nausea, and light headedness sent her back down.

Hilgard adjusted her pillows to help Abigail stay in a half laying, half sitting position. "You should stop trying to get up. You need a few days of rest."

"Why did Cinder attack you?" she demanded, eyes darting around the loft trying to pick him out of the shadows. If he was still here, Abigail needed to defend the doctor.

"It wasn't an attack. He'll heal it once he calms down, this isn't the first time he's done this."

"He hurts you a lot?" Abigail's attention snapped to the doctor.

"Not intentionally. The man's sick. He can't help it."

"What do you mean?" she asked slowly.

Hilgard took off his glasses and cleaned the lenses with his shirt. His eyes never left his diligent cleaning. "Cinder is, to put it simply, overheating. When his emotions flare up so does his internal temperature and his body expels the heat the only way it knows how."

Abigail didn't understand the grave tone in Hilgard's explanation. That wasn't anything new to her. She experienced it too.

"That doesn't sound like something he couldn't control."

"It wasn't at first. When I first saw him, the episodes were mild. He kept them internalized, which worsened the condition. It only took a few months for the internal damage to become permanent. He's burning hotter with each episode. The blasts are getting bigger. I'm afraid he's . . ."

Abigail wanted to rip the glasses out of the doctor's hands but fought against it. "What does that mean? Is Cinder dying?"

"I can't disclose the confidential information of my patients." Hilgard returned his glasses to his face.

"Bullshit," Abigail spat, but it didn't contain the malice she wanted it to. "You just told me all about him."

"If a man is dying," Hilgard stood from his seat, and searched inside his bag on the nightstand, "I think it's his decision who to tell."

"Then why say anything at all?"

"So you know the hazards of your similar ability. A doctor's precaution."

Abigail wasn't ungrateful for the doctor's warning, but keeping herself safe was the last of her priorities. "Where is he now?"

"Unsure." Hilgard retrieved a syringe from the bag. "This is for the pain. It will make you drowsy."

"I feel fine," Abigail protested.

"Because the first dose hasn't completely worn off."

"I don't need another one. You should save it for someone else. Maybe Cold Snap is hurt."

"Have you ever been shot?"

"First time."

"Trust me when I say you'll want this. I don't care how tough you want to pretend you are. I heard the screams when I first arrived. They were horrifying."

Abigail swallowed hard and rotated her arm for the doctor to have access to the inside of her elbow.

Chapter Twenty-One

The next time Abigail awoke, she was alone. The seat next to her was free of Dr. Hilgard. The loft was empty. She closed her eyes and listened. When she was confident the only noises were her breathing, she slowly left the bed. Returning to a vertical position was harder than Abigail remembered it being. A nebula of colors clouded her vision and left her momentarily blinded. Once her head stopped spinning, she eased herself to the edge of the mattress. The smallest amount of twisting added a painful pressure to her bandaged side. Abigail gritted her teeth and moved through the pain.

Abigail had run into more burning buildings than she could count. None of them had been as difficult as standing right now.

Once both feet were on the floor, Abigail grabbed the chair and hoisted herself the rest of the way up. A thousand needles pierced the heels of her feet as blood returned to the appendages. She gripped the chair until the fuzzy feeling subsided and she was able to move, albeit slowly, through the loft.

She wouldn't waste this opportunity to snoop.

She started with the desk. The papers that captivated Cinder during her first visit were still out. Abigail plucked one and growled at its contents: classified ads in a newspaper. Useless information to her. Most of the desk was useless. Simply covered in newspapers. Some issues from the Tennyson City Tribune, and other issues from cities nowhere close to here.

Abigail found a San Arbor Sun issued two weeks ago. The cover sported a colorful picture of King Arthur shaking hands with some woman dressed to the nines in corporate royalty.

HRC Leader King Arthur shakes the hand of Dox-Con President Camellia Diaz after the announcement of their partnership to expand power lines and cable lines in San Arbor, read the caption.

Abigail returned the paper to the messy desk. It appeared that King Arthur and San Arbor were moving along without her.

That's a good thing, Abigail reminded herself. *You don't have to worry about San Arbor.*

She just had to worry about this mission.

She continued her tour of the loft. It was sparsely decorated and contained few clues. Without the toothbrush and toothpaste tube on the bathroom sink, she could have believed no one lived here. The smell of woodsmoke clinging to every surface proved otherwise. Standing in front of the bathroom mirror, Abigail lifted her shirt to better see her injury. Due to the wrapping, it was hard to discern the real damage. A nasty purple and blue bruise peeked around the edges of the bandages above her hip.

She was tempted to touch the area but dropped her shirt before the temptation was too great. The doctor was probably right, poking around wouldn't help her heal, and she needed to be back to full strength before something bad happened. Abigail pulled her shirt down and frowned. *Manchester Public University* was stitched around a symbol of twin olive branches on the front. She didn't own this shirt, or the black workout shorts underneath.

Fire sparked atop her fingers at the violation of someone having undressed her.

Abigail moved to the kitchenette for a glass of water. She peered inside the fridge and found it as sparse as hers. A loaf of bread and stack of plastic wrapped cheese were the only occupants. Just seeing the food made her stomach rumble and she made a sandwich. With plans to grill it, Abigail discovered there wasn't a stove. She sighed and heated the sandwich between her hands.

The door rattled opened behind her, and Abigail dropped the sandwich, melted cheese oozing out onto the counter. Cinder closed the door with his foot, his eyes landing on hers like a heat seeking missile. Neither of them broke the eye contact as Cinder walked from the door to her, dropping a fist full of keys on his desk and taking a seat across her at the counter.

"You're up." A tinge of relief touched his observation.

"You changed me." Poison seeped through Abigail's.

Cinder smirked, grabbing the sandwich and ripping it in two crooked pieces. He set half back down in front of her and bit into the other one. "I asked Cold Snap to bring you some clean clothes. She did the changing."

The hostility fled her voice. "How is she?"

"Cold's fine, more worried about you."

"What happened? At the house, do you know what happened to us?"

Cinder nodded, finishing his half of the sandwich. "According to Cold, you two were attacked by a guard stationed inside Bastet's home. After you blacked out, Cold Snap carried you out of there and all the way here. If the bullet wasn't going to kill you, then her hypothermic touch would have. I didn't think you could get that cold."

Abigail ran her hands up her arms, leaving a trail of sparks to chase away the feeling his words brought on. Cold Snap carrying her helped piece together the coldness Abigail had felt. But Cinder's explanation did not explain the rest of the night.

"What happened with Bastet?"

"Killed. The warehouse trap worked."

Combustion

Abigail didn't feel like eating anymore and pushed the rest of her sandwich toward him. Cinder waited for her hand to return to her side of the counter before taking the food.

"I found documents inside a secret room in Bastet's house," Abigail said, slowly tracing the stone pattern of the counter with her eyes. "Documents claiming she's involved with moving people out of Tennyson City."

"Say it as it is, Abigail. Bastet was trafficking people."

"You knew?" Her attention snapped to Cinder. "Why didn't you say anything?"

"You wouldn't have believed me." His statement wasn't wrong, but it still left Abigail fuming. "You wouldn't have believed it until you saw it for yourself. These heroes aren't what you think they are. They're not like you, Abigail."

"What are you talking about? Tennyson City is the safest city in the country. Bastet may have been . . ." Abigail couldn't say it. "It doesn't mean the others are bad."

"Tennyson City is 'safe' because Hero Enterprises is running the crime. Swordfish and Guppy were controlling the ports, allowing shipments of guns and drugs inside for Rush to put into the hands of their goons and allowing Bastet to make her own sales overseas. The heroes aren't stopping the crime here, they are the criminals."

Abigail shook her head. "That's not possible."

"Do you have to see Bastet taking someone off the street for yourself before you believe me? It's not pretty, trust me. Those claws can shred vocal cords like rice paper."

"But why?"

Cinder shrugged. "Couldn't tell you. Maybe for the money. Probably for the power. When I was a villain, I did things to survive and eventually for my pride. But never something this . . . vile."

Abigail exhaled. "You're still a villain."

"And you're still a hero," he smirked. "It's why I sent you to her house. I knew you'd find the evidence."

"You have it?"

Cinder shrugged again, his strong shoulders moving inside the sleeves of his coat. "More or less."

"Evidence on Swordfish and Rush?" Heat rushed to her fingers in a knee buckling mixture of fear and enthusiasm. "Of their alleged crimes?"

"It's not alleged if it's true."

She crossed her arms at his interruption. "If what you're saying is true, how can it happen without people knowing about it?"

"The same way it's happening all over the country. And Abigail, people do know but they feel powerless to stop them. I'm not out here killing heroes; I'm here stopping monsters."

"I don't believe you." Abigail pushed off the counter. The force sent her backward, hitting her head against the refrigerator. Stars flashed in her vision, and she slid to the ground.

Cinder leapt over the island, crouching beside her, and checked the back of her head. "You're still so reckless."

His hands remained tangled in the back of her hair. His face remained inches from hers.

In the intimate space, Abigail finally said it. "You died."

As Abigail feared, he pulled away with a heavy sigh. "You shouldn't be out of bed. I know Hilgard told you to lay down for a while."

"In your bed?" Abigail used the refrigerator's door handle to pull herself up.

"Figured it would be more comfortable than the couch."

"Why not downstairs?"

"I wouldn't be able to keep an eye on you like I'd like."

Abigail hated the blush that rushed to her cheeks. "I got up because I was hungry, and you ate my sandwich."

Cinder laughed. "I'll make you a new one."

"I'm not staying here." Abigail's heart attempted to strangle her logical brain.

"If you can make it down the stairs, I won't stop you. You're not my prisoner."

Abigail swallowed the bitter laugh his statement caused. She wondered if he knew just how wrong he was. She wanted nothing more than to stay forever suspended inside this tiny kitchen making dumb grilled cheese sandwiches with him. The hazy light almost made this encounter feel like a dream. The unreal circumstances had to be a dream. But the hammering inside her head and pulsing at her side ensured she was awake.

She rounded the kitchen counter before she could say or do something she'd regret. The way her chest ached as the distance between her and Cinder grew caused a big part of herself to regret *this* decision. Abigail gripped the door for support and refused to let go until her other hand could grab the handrail outside. Her vision spotted more with each step. Her energy siphoned away quicker than a cracked gas tank. Her hand slipped off the handrail. Her body crashed onto the stairs.

Abigail released her frustration in a series of curses. She reached up for the handrail but grabbed Cinder's hand instead. He hoisted her into his arms. Abigail was enveloped in his woodsmoke scent and forgot where she was for a moment. She thought she was home. For a tiny moment that stretched endlessly in her mind this was Thomas carrying her across the threshold of their apartment after their wedding.

Cinder lowered her onto the bed, the falling lights highlighting the burn scars on his face. He tucked the bed's comforter around her and said, "You can try again tomorrow."

Abigail fought the sudden onset of drowsiness slamming into her but couldn't keep her eyes open. Between her fruitless exploration, appalling conversation, and painful tumble, Abigail had wasted all her energy. The pounding in her head lessened with her eyes shut, so she kept them closed. Only until the pain subsided, she told herself, only for a few minutes, only until she could stand again.

Abigail was asleep in seconds.

Abigail dreamt of a train platform stranded in a field of stargazer lilies. The sky above was splattered in white stars that mirrored the infinite flowers around her. She looked up and down the track for the train, but there was no sign of it. In the strange workings of dream time, the train suddenly appeared on the tracks moving away from the platform. It was moving away from Abigail with incredible speed. She leapt off the platform and chased after it. She needed to be on that train. Behind her, something grabbed her ankle and stopped her. Looking over her shoulder, Abigail saw the dead heroes of Hero Enterprises. Their faces were sunken and dark, dirt clung to their hair, and worms tunneled through their pale eyes and out their noses and mouths. They emerged from the ground and tried to pull her into them while the train sped away, its smoke covering the sky above. Abigail kicked at their rotted hands and freed herself. Desperation to reach the train overcame all rational thought. She ran down the tracks. The zombie heroes crawled faster than she could run. Their decaying hands pulled her down and covered her.

"Abigail!"

Combustion

Abigail bolted upright, sweat beading off her forehead and down the sides of her face. She frantically looked around the dark room. The flowers were gone. The dead heroes were gone. The train was gone.

"Abigail, it's okay." Cinder repeated. "You were dreaming."

Abigail inhaled a breath and lit a red flame atop her finger to chase away the encroaching darkness. The fire whipped wildly, matching her racing heart. Cinder's hand was on her arm, probably meant to be comforting, but Abigail stared at it until he removed it.

"What time is it?" she muttered, unsure why it was important. Perhaps it was just to hear his voice again. Perhaps it was to have some control over the situation. Just a piece of knowledge she could know was true.

Cinder took a seat next to the bed. "It's the middle of the night."

Abigail turned her flame toward him to better see his face. Dark bags fell under his eyes and some sort of patchy beard tried to grow around his burn scars. He clasped his hands together in his lap. Dark blue smoke danced above them. He slipped them inside the pockets of his jacket.

Abigail condensed her flame into a single ember. The light it produced barely illuminated his silhouette. In the darkness, Abigail felt brave.

"You died."

"I'm alive."

"How?"

Their words drifted around the loft as heavy spirits. Too dense to float out the skylights, too supple to sink below the floorboards.

Cinder sighed heavily, but finally answered. "When the Community Center was falling, after the final blast, I ran out the back and into the forest. Everyone was too distracted to see me leave. The forest was too smokey for anyone to track me. It was a clean escape."

"You didn't come back."

Cinder didn't answer.

"Why?"

"I saw an opportunity."

"To disappear?" Abigail said too loudly, and her ember burst into a flash of light.

When the darkness returned, so did Cinder's hollow voice. "An opportunity to try again."

"I don't understand."

"Sometimes I don't either."

"What *do* you understand?"

"That this world needs to change. There are heroes who are abusing their power and people are suffering. There are people with powers that don't look super, and they're being punished for it." Cinder pinned Abigail down with a heavy stare. The rumble in his voice was so intense it rattled Abigail's bones. "I will dismantle this hero world so that everyone can be equal."

"But if you get rid of the heroes, who will save people who actually need help?"

"There will still be *good* people in the world. People who can be heroes without superpowers, people who can do good without a mask."

Abigail drew her knees to her chest and regretted it. Her side spasmed at the sudden pressure causing her to yelp. Cinder leapt from his seat preparing to help in any way he could.

"I'm okay," Abigail hissed through clenched teeth, lowering her legs back to the bed.

"Hilgard has more of the painkiller, I'll call him."

Abigail grabbed Cinder's shirt sleeve before he got too far. "I don't want it. I don't want to fall asleep again."

Combustion

"The nightmares?" Cinder lowered himself back to the seat, scooting it closer to her.

"I don't want to miss any more time while blacked out," she answered. "I actually didn't mind this nightmare too much."

"Which ones do you mind?"

The tiny ember extinguished. "The ones with you. Thomas, Cinder, whoever, I loved you and thought you loved me, and I spent all this time thinking you were dead. I spent all this time unable to get over you, and now I find out you've been alive this whole time. Did I mean nothing to you?"

Cinder pulled his sleeve from Abigail's grasp and replaced it with his hand. Their fingers intertwined as naturally as breathing.

"I thought leaving you would be better for you."

"Bullshit."

"It's true. I thought I was . . . I don't know, I thought I was making you choose between me and something normal. I knew what you wanted, and even trying to be *him*, I knew I couldn't be what you wanted."

"I've always wanted you." Abigail squeezed his hand until her fingers numbed. "That hasn't changed." *It would never change.*

A chuckle as faint as a hummingbird's wings escaped his lips. "Maybe we could try this again."

"After you finish this war on evil heroes?"

"Yeah."

The world shifted, becoming unbalanced, and Abigail felt like she was free falling.

"Which one are you right now?" Abigail used her free hand and illuminated his face with a dancing flame. She searched his eyes for the truth. "Thomas or Cinder?"

"Can't I be both?"

"I could only trust one of you."

"That's a lie," Cinder smirked handsomely in the low light.

The truth stunned her. She knew he was right. He knew it too.

"You're putting labels on me," he continued, "Just like the hero world did. Villain or hero. Cinder or Thomas. I know you're better than them, doll."

He ran his free hand down the length of his face. Blue smoke poured out of his fingers, and he removed his scars.

"Call me Cinder. I wasn't able to get enough done as Thomas."

"I need you to tell me one more thing." Abigail wasn't going to let Cinder's chatty mood go to waste. They found their way back together, even evading death to do so, and she wasn't going to let something else threaten his life. "Hilgard said you had an illness."

Cinder tried to pull his hand free, but Abigail kept ahold of him. She wasn't his prisoner, but that didn't mean he wasn't hers for the next few minutes.

"What's happening to you?"

"I'm overheating," Cinder repeated the doctor's earlier diagnosis. "I have been for a while, ever since Volcanic's blast, but it's finally caught up with me."

"What does that mean?"

"It means if I'm not extremely careful, I'll unleash a killer heat wave."

"Careful how?"

Cinder sighed. "You sure do have a ton of questions tonight."

"I haven't seen you in a year."

"So, shouldn't you ask me about what happened in the year? Tried any new foods? If I'm seeing anyone? Picked up a new hobby?"

Abigail stared at him, refusing to let his deflection work.

Combustion

Cinder raised a hand in defeat and smoke drifted off his fingertips. "If I don't expel the heat then it builds up inside of me before bursting out. If I don't keep my cool," he paused for Abigail to laugh, but when she didn't, he continued, "It will seep out."

"Why did you lose 'your cool' with Dr. Hilgard?"

The blush that crept over Cinder's face was as cute as she remembered. How his face went from boyish to handsome with a twist of his smile reminded her of how infatuated she had been. Of how she was still infatuated with him.

"I thought he was hurting you. I wanted to protect you."

"You know I can protect myself," Abigail attempted to defend.

"You were shot."

Abigail grew tired of the reminder.

"How many bad heroes are left in Tennyson City?" she asked.

"Are you joining my cause?" Cinder's aura shifted from shy to smug. It was intoxicating. She didn't breathe it in.

"I'm looking at my options. I don't want any more of Tennyson's people getting hurt because of corrupt heroes."

"There's just one left."

"Who?"

"I'll tell you in the morning."

"Cinder—"

"You need your rest."

"Is this you protecting me again? Because I didn't ask for it."

He shrugged, rising from his chair, and escaping Abigail's grasp but not before sparking his fingers against hers. Her mind flashed back to a time when his lips did the same. "This is me wanting you to stay here one more night."

"You said I wasn't your prisoner," she reminded.

"You're still free to go." Cinder walked to the couch, tossing a wave over his shoulder.

Abigail grumbled, lowering herself back into the bed. She knew she was too weak to make it down the stairs without falling. She knew she needed the final pieces of information. She knew she didn't want to leave just yet, either.

Chapter Twenty-Two

Abigail reveled in the scratchy bedsheets as if they were made of the softest silk. She let her hazy mind, half drunk on sleep and dreams, run wild as she tried to stay unconscious. In the quiet minutes before the sleep dust burned away, Abigail imagined a life far away from the oceanfront city. Snowflakes drifted in front of massive chalet windows. Her legs tangled together with his. Their lips bruised from the night before. Her heart full of promises for the days to come. The constructed dream began to fizzle around the edges as outside noise infiltrated her headspace. Abigail held onto the image for as long as she could, but eventually her consciousness stole it away. She eased herself out of bed.

The entire loft burned orange with the rising sun. Abigail tapped a glowing corner of the nightstand to make sure the flames were strictly solar. After her confirmation, she searched the open layout for Cinder. His back was to her while he stood in the kitchen, clattering some poor dish ware together.

"What are you doing?" Abigail asked as she claimed a barstool across the counter. Her hip still ached but moving became easier.

"Making breakfast, what's it look like?" Cinder turned around, balancing two pans in either of his hands lit with blue flames. Bacon sizzled in one while scrambled eggs bubbled apart in the other. His wild black hair added to his appearance of a mad scientist more than a chef.

"It looks like a mess."

"How are you feeling?" Cinder ignored her criticism.

"Better. Sore but better." She watched smoke fall off his arms from wrist to elbow even though the fire remained inside his palms. "What about you?"

"Hungry."

"Can I help?" Abigail didn't like seeing so much smoke ooze from his body.

"You can toast bread." Cinder jerked his chin toward the loaf between them.

Abigail pulled the bag closer and retrieved a handful of slices. She used a lower temperature than him and slowly turned the bread from white squish to brown crisp.

"Have you thought more on my proposition?"

Abigail raised an eyebrow. "Proposition?"

"Will you join my cause?"

She watched the bread toast in her hands. She didn't need to think about his proposition. It was ridiculous. She was not going to help him kill heroes. No matter how corrupt they were, or he believed them to be.

"Why don't we take this evidence you have to the police?"

"We?" Cinder smirked, clearly pleased with her word choice.

Abigail tried to ignore him. "You have evidence, right? You take it to the police and have the bad heroes arrested."

"I would if I could. HE has the police bought, though." Cinder set his pans on a dishrag on the counter and dusted his hands over the sink. Ash drifted into the stainless-steel bottom. "And if they weren't, sending someone to arrest a super powered person wouldn't be safe for the person. Not to mention the law is blind in their favor. The heroes would make sure their crimes wouldn't stick. They'd make sure whoever brought in the evidence was eliminated."

Abigail finished her toasting. "I hate this."

"I do too. After fighting for so long not to be this villain, I have to be. To save people."

A hero saves people.

"I won't help you kill anyone," Abigail decided. "But I will help protect the people here."

"Like you're protecting my team?"

"I imagine they're good people too, since they're following your ideals."

Cinder chuckled, setting everything on Abigail's side of the counter before taking the seat next to her. He bumped their knees together in a secret language known only to them. "They all have their own reasons. None of them share my ideals."

Abigail gawked. "You hired real killers?"

"They do a good job." Cinder constructed sandwiches, folding each one inside a paper napkin. "And I can't hire them without being able to pay them."

"They're all here on their own?"

"You should ask Cold Snap why she joined me."

"Why won't you tell me?"

Cinder looked at her; as he spoke his breath fell across her lips. "It's not my secret to tell."

Abigail suddenly felt drunk by his proximity. "What secret will you tell me?"

"I'm glad you kept chasing me."

Cinder leaned in and Abigail was ready to drown in him. She fisted her hands into the sides of his jacket and pursed her lips. Cinder's never came. Instead, the pressure she expected came in the form of a breakfast sandwich pressing into her stomach. She opened her eyes to Cinder's twisted smile hanging handsomely off his mouth.

"You should go back to the hideout."

"With this?" Abigail snatched the sandwich.

"Unless there's something more you want?"

Abigail refused to give into his obvious bait. Her tomato-red face betrayed her on its own.

"I want to see the rest of your evidence." The stillness in her voice surprised Abigail. She assumed it'd be as shaky as her insides.

"Against Hero Enterprises?"

"Is there more?" His earlier statement of heroes elsewhere also allegedly abusing their powers floated to her mind.

"Could be."

"Cinder."

His eyes softened and the corner of his mouth quirked up. "I'll show you what I have."

He remained on his stool, taking a bite of the final constructed sandwich. He picked a piece of bread from between his front teeth with his nail.

"Well?" Abigail asked, seeing Cinder showed no motivation of supplying the evidence.

"Well, it's not here. I'll get all of it the next time I'm out."

"How long will that take?" Her earlier embarrassment may have left her, but the heat remaining simmered into a new, agitated life.

Cinder only shrugged, focusing on his breakfast.

Abigail removed herself from the counter, her hands leaving blackened prints where she pushed her chair away. Steam escaped her mouth along with an annoyed *huff*.

"I'll see you later, doll." Cinder's chuckle followed her all the way to the door.

Abigail stomped down the stairs breathless and hungry, burning the wrapped sandwich in her rage. She let the sooty remains stain the carpet. She hoped the smell of burnt eggs stained the air for weeks. She hoped all of his bacon burned. Abigail was too mad and embarrassed to be proud of her successful journey down the stairs. Being shot hadn't felt this bad. She slammed the door shut, rattling the drinks stored in the fridge inside Simply Sushi's lobby.

She hadn't expected to see anyone on this level of the hideout, least of all Warden. His massive form barely fit behind the sushi counter. He still wore a suit and washed blood out of his golden rings at the utility sink. She told herself it was from some poor fish that would serve as today's pretend special.

Warden ripped a paper towel out of the wall container and dried his hands before eyeing her over one gigantic shoulder.

Abigail's breath caught in her throat and her legs forgot their motor functions. She finally understood the terrified expression painted on the tiny mouse figures inside *Mouse Trap*. She had no idea if she was allowed up the stairs. She had no idea how much Warden already knew. She had no idea if he was going to grab the butcher's knife sitting next to the sink. She had no idea if Warden was going to finish the job the bullet hadn't.

"Seems you're feeling better."

"Sure am." Her voice dipped into the safety of her media persona, the one that lied the easiest.

"Good. Your next mission is coming up soon."

"How soon? Against who?" Abigail stumbled over her questions. "Where at?"

"As soon as the others get back with supplies." Warden tossed his paper towel away and approached Abigail. The plastic cage dropped closer on the tiny mouse. "They left this morning."

"It'll be nice to get this wrapped up. Not too many heroes left." Abigail tasted sulfur in the back of her throat.

"Then it will be time to decide what to do with you lot."

"We work so well together, might as well take us along for the next adventure." Abigail added a playful chuckle to the end of her statement, but it was all nerves. She stepped around Warden so there wasn't a wall directly behind her. Despite feeling better, she couldn't have any additional disadvantages if she needed to fight. This close, Warden's fists looked less like cinderblocks and more like wrecking balls.

"We'll see what the boss has to say."

"He's the boss," Abigail awkwardly agreed. "He told me to go back downstairs, so if you don't mind. I'll be taking my leave."

"Not going to that coffee shop today?"

Heat flushed her cheeks. An icy touch ran down the length of her spine. Warden's simple question was a heavy accusation.

"Not today." Abigail walked to the door leading down and quickly enclosed herself inside.

Abigail sucked down the cold air until she was sure every blood vessel had enough oxygen to combust. She exhaled the building sulfur in her mouth in a breath of blue smoke. The heat of it made her teeth tingle. She'd forgotten how breathing her Dragon's Breath made her feel, how it heated every piece inside her, how breathing it reminded her of the night she received the ability.

Remembering Cinder, of the intimacy they once had, made her stomp the rest of the way down to the subterranean level. She had more important things to think about than him and whether he still had any of those feelings for her. It had been a full year, and just because she spent the year refusing to let go of his ghosts didn't mean he hadn't exorcised her from his thoughts. *"Maybe we could try this again?" Yeah right.* That thought made her fingers shoot out red sparks in agitation. She shoved opened the door to the hideout and clenched her sparking hands into fists as Cold Snap looked up from the table.

Her chair crashed to the floor as Cold Snap ran to Abigail. She held her so tightly her hug felt like a vice grip. Abigail winced at the coldness of her skin and tried to push Cold Snap away from her still bandaged side.

"You're alive!"

"Maybe not if you keep doing this." Abigail wheezed out.

Cold Snap set her down, muttering an apology. "I knew you weren't *dead* dead after Cinder let me see you, but I still didn't know if you'd be okay. You lost so much blood and the bullet hole looked so deep. It was awful to see you like that."

Abigail cupped Cold Snap's shoulder and held her watery gaze. "I'm pretty sure I'm only alive because of you. Thank you."

Cold Snap blushed, the pink morphing to purple under the blue hue of her skin. "It was nothing. Just returning the favor."

"It was not nothing. You're *my* hero now, Cold. I owe you."

"Don't call me a hero, I was just doing what any reasonable person would do." Cold Snap said hero like it pained her.

"Why aren't you with Odo and them? Warden said everyone was getting supplies?" Abigail changed the subject.

"Boys only mission, I guess," Cold Snap shrugged. "They probably had to go somewhere where I'd stick out. I don't mind a day off to myself. It's even better now that you're here!"

Abigail didn't press that Odo had also gotten to go despite his sticking out. "What did you have in mind? On your day off?"

"Well, before you came in, I was counting colored candies, so I'm open to suggestions."

"What would you normally do?"

"Before I came here?"

Abigail nodded.

"I loved going to the mall," Cold Snap sighed. "Before I turned blue, it's all I ever did. That and roller skate."

A lightbulb lit in Abigail's head. "Let's move some of this furniture out of the way and make an ice rink. You can freeze the floors and we'll skate."

Cold Snap beamed. "That would be so much fun!"

Restricted to just the lighter things, Abigail helped clear the floor as much as she could but ultimately it was Cold Snap who did the heavy lifting. Abigail sat on the edge of the ice-covered floor and tied her sneakers' laces together. Switching into her own clothes, and having proper footwear on, made Abigail feel better than the drugs had.

"Hey Cold?" Abigail asked while Cold Snap tested the ice with a speedy skate around the edges. "Can I ask you something?"

"Sure." Cold Snap completed a spin in the center of the rink.

"Why did you join this team? What brought you here?"

Cold Snap's graceful movements stopped. She forced a smile that Abigail could tell was as fragile as the ice around them. "Oh, you know, probably the same reason you did."

Abigail eased herself onto the ice. "I doubt it."

The worn soles of her sneakers didn't stand a chance against the slick surface and as she kicked off toward Cold Snap, Abigail came dangerously close to kissing the ice. Cold Snap grabbed her hand before she could fall and hoisted Abigail back to her feet. Abigail grabbed Cold Snap's other hand, ignoring the discomfort their touch created, and used her for balance. The pair slowly rotated on the ice.

"You're a little out of your element."

"You could say that," Abigail replied.

"I've always loved the cold, even before getting my powers." The hideout spun around them as Cold Snap spoke. Her voice became as fragile as her smile. Abigail struggled to hear every word. "When it snowed, I'd play outside in it all day long. The other kids in the neighborhood would play with me too. We once built this huge igloo at the turnaround and had everyone's car stuck. That was a fun winter.

"The next winter is when I turned blue, and no one wanted to play with me anymore. It wasn't that they didn't still play, they just never let me join them. They would pile their bikes in front of the door so I couldn't get out. Things got worse as I got older. People teased me, which I could handle, and I was used to being alone, but when the bullies got physical, that was the worst."

"You didn't fight back?" Abigail interrupted.

"How could I?" Cold Snap asked desperately. "I couldn't control my powers as well back then. One wrong move and . . . well, one wrong move did happen and some kids got seriously hurt. They ran me out of town after a second one died. But it was an accident. Wildfire, I swear I didn't do it on purpose."

Cinder's thunderstorm voice sounded in her mind as he admitted to hiring killers.

"You killed the heroes here on purpose."

"Yeah, but they're not real heroes."

"Did Cinder tell you that?" Abigail asked. If Warden had been truthful with her, this was the first time the others would have met him.

"He confirmed it, that the Hero Enterprises people are actually evil, but I had my suspicions about that a while ago. The people here seemed so afraid of them."

"What else did he tell you guys?"

"Why he's taking them out. He told us that it doesn't change our end goal, but that we didn't have to conform to his belief. I feel like I'm on a first-string team right now."

"What's his belief?"

"He's going to even out the game," Cold Snap answered with a hopeful smile. "That there's a better world we can make. I believe him too."

"What does that even mean?"

Cold Snap's eyes widened for a moment as she thought. The hideout slowed down around them. "It means that people won't be so scared of people who look different. I bet if I didn't turn blue with my powers then the bullying wouldn't have started. I just want to be accepted, Wildfire. And I think if the divide between hero and villain is gone, then I will be. It always felt that if someone has powers then they have to be one or the other. I just want to be me, working at the mall and going on dates."

"You can't do that now?"

Cold Snap frowned. "Not looking like this. Not when people are scared of me."

"No one outside my family knew when I developed my powers. I didn't tell anyone at school, only the licensing board, and I only trained in the backyard where we had a tall privacy fence. I guess I was scared of my classmates finding out even though I loved my flames." Abigail tightened her hands around Cold Snap's; a layer of frost had formed over their knuckles and Abigail slowly melted it away. "I'm not afraid of you, Cold Snap."

"Maybe if I had a friend like you growing up, I wouldn't have fallen into this life of crime." Cold Snap laughed, stretching the last half of her statement like a song, and pushed away from Abigail to display a spin that would have knocked Abigail on her butt. "What about you? What dark path did you take here?"

Abigail heated the ground below her slightly so she wouldn't slip on the ice without Cold Snap's support. "I just want to save good people."

"Good luck finding some of those left in the world."

Abigail retreated to a kitchen seat, heating the bottom of her shoes so she could safely travel across the ice. Cold Snap's statement had more merit than Abigail cared to admit. If Tennyson City, the safest city in the nation, was plagued with corruption like Cinder claimed, then how bad was San Arbor? Abigail's fire created light, but light also created shadows and she'd be a fool and a poor hero to think darkness didn't hide in her city. When she returned, she'd have to work double time to keep her city from falling like this one.

"Everything okay?" Cold Snap asked. Her approach cooled the air.

"Didn't want to chance falling," Abigail lied. "You get back out there though; you looked really good on the ice. I doubt I could ever spin like that."

"It just takes some practice." Cold Snap pulled up a chair beside her. "I'll show you once you're all healed. As a thanks, for training me."

"Deal." Abigail didn't know why she smiled.

Cold Snap twisted her hands together, rubbing her knuckles red until she blurted out, "So that Cinder guy?"

Abigail kept her gaze straight ahead. "What about him?"

"He seemed pretty intense when I got back with you. Huffing and puffing and shouting all kinds of things at us." Cold Snap paused, either finding courage or the right word. "He seemed really protective over you."

Abigail blushed. "I'm sure he wasn't."

"I don't think so, Wildfire." Cold Snap clicked her tongue. "I came in roughed up too, and I don't think he even noticed. Or when Odo was all ripped up? This is the first time any of us have seen him, and he's the one running this operation. You don't think that's weird?"

"I'm sure it was the gunshot." Abigail tried sounding confident, to relieve Cold Snap and herself, but she tasted the lie like a lemon. "One of us dying could be difficult to cover up. If it was in the arm or something, I'm sure he wouldn't have cared. I was carved up by Bastet too, remember? Cinder didn't come down then."

Cold Snap did not believe her. One icy blue eyebrow raised in a quiet demand for more details.

"Do you know how Stretch and I got that red badge back at the lab?" Abigail didn't give her time to answer, to ask more questions about Cinder and his supposed overprotection. "He was stealing candy from the vending machine when the scientist came up. I bet it was for you."

"He slipped it onto my pillow that night." Cold Snap scratched the side of her face.

"What's that about?" Abigail asked playfully, causing Cold Snap to giggle.

"I don't know, maybe a workplace crush?" Her cheeks lit up.

"Cold! You like him, too, don't you?"

"He's nice," she admitted. "I like his company."

"But?"

"But, sometimes we don't agree on things, some big things."

The energy slipped from Abigail, and she wished they were still laughing on the ice. "Big things?"

"Promise you won't tell anyone? I want to stay on this team, and this sounds bad."

Abigail set her hand atop Cold Snap's, and the temperature difference sizzled between them. "You can tell me."

Cold Snap inhaled deeply. "Sometimes Stretch takes things too far. When it comes to our missions and training. I don't think he'd ever hurt me, but sometimes he looks too comfortable with what we do. I mean,

I want to get the sons of bitches too, but I don't want to make them suffer."

"I think it's good to know your limits." Abigail placated. "If he ever gets that way with you, if you ever think he would, find me, okay?"

Cold Snap smiled. "You're going to keep being my hero, aren't you?"

"You're a good person, Cold. I can see that."

Cold Snap slipped her hand out from under Abigail's. "Thank you."

Chapter Twenty-Three

After four more days of heavy, and forced, rest inside the subterranean hideout, the bruise on Abigail's hip had morphed from deep-plum purple, to baby-puke green, and now adopted a honey mustard hue. The medicine Hilgard provided increased her cell regeneration. The doctor didn't elaborate where he acquired the paste stored in a lime green container. She assured her team that it didn't hurt, but Cold Snap and Odo caught her wincing while moving too many times to truly believe her. Abigail still worked out to prove them wrong.

Her spiteful training also served to keep her mind unfocused on Cinder's lack of appearance in the last four days and her lack of actual decision making about him and this situation.

The evidence against the heroes at Hero Enterprises was too heavy to ignore. Between The Swordfish's *importing*, Bastet's *exporting* and Rush's dealings within the city, Abigail didn't know what other darkness Beacon or Miss Titan, the other remaining hero on staff, were bringing to the city. Abigail also didn't know the reason for it, or how these once great heroes became so corrupt. The one thing she did know was the threat it posed on Tennyson City's civilians couldn't be ignored.

She would have to pick a side. Her duty to her hero team, her promise to the civilians, or the truth she valued most. A hero saves people, and the list of those needing to be saved became incredibly long for just one hero.

Abigail returned the weight bar to the rack above her head and scooted down to sit at the end of the bench. It had been quiet over the last few days. The boys returned from their supply run without much knowledge of the upcoming plan. The only supplies Abigail had seen

Combustion

were the various junk foods stashed inside the pantry. The cheese crackers were the first to go.

Everyone was turning into a wound-up mess of boredom and anxiety. Some kind of direction would ease all of them, but each new day was as quiet as the last. Stretch liked to use his free time by stretching himself over the kitchen table like some unusable tablecloth.

"How far can you go?" Abigail asked him, walking by to retrieve a water bottle from the fridge. He'd been nice enough to let her use his *home gym* without too much fuss, but she knew he'd claim it once she looked finished.

"About nine feet on either side," Stretch answered. "I can flatten my hands to be paper thin too."

"Do your bones stretch too?"

He shrugged, or at least Abigail thought he did while draped over the table. "Haven't thought too much on the how and why of my powers. I just know what I can do."

"I bet it was weird when you first discovered them."

"Weird for me, horrifying for my brothers." Stretch chuckled. "I just kept . . . drooping everywhere. Eventually I met my limit at the time and snapped back together."

"Does anything stop the stretch?"

He unfolded himself from the table and raised an eyebrow at Abigail. "Are you asking about my weakness?"

Abigail took a quick sip of her water. "Not like that." *At least, not intentionally.*

He crossed his arms and Abigail received the message loud and clear, so she offered him a trade. "If I'm submerged underwater, I can't ignite."

It was a lie but Stretch took the deal. "The cold makes me rigid, and I can't stretch as far."

Stretch glanced over to where Cold Snap and Tech played checkers near the bunks. When she laughed, high pitched like a wind chime, he blushed.

Abigail touched his arm and whispered, "The best ones are worth the difficulty. Trust me."

As if summoned by just a fleeting thought of him, the intoxicating aroma of woodsmoke filled the room like a genie emerging from a lamp. Abigail was sure she had imagined it, his ghosts taking physical form to trick her senses, but the hideout door opened, and she couldn't stop herself from snapping her gaze to it.

Her heart fluttered and then sank as both Cinder and Warden walked into the room.

"Gather round," Warden ordered, and his soldiers quickly obeyed. The checkers skittered to the floor. "You four are getting started on the next phase of the plan."

"I'm able to fight," Abigail assured when she realized Warden hadn't counted her in his roster. "I want to go."

"I have a different assignment for you." Cinder's voice was cold, any familiarity they shared was nonexistent in his statement. "Come with me."

"You got this girl," Cold Snap offered Abigail a fist bump before she could leave their semicircle around the villainous leaders.

Abigail returned it and mouthed, "Be careful."

The stairwell heated almost instantly once she and Cinder were on the other side of the door. A hectic energy replaced the cold air usually clinging to the walls. The cavernous area was extremely vast and extremely intimate in the same head-spinning moment. Cinder slipped his hands into the pockets of his jacket and ascended the stairs. The strange energy dissipated the farther he became. Abigail chased after him.

"I really can fight with them," she said, breaking the silence. "Whatever the mission is, I'm healed enough for it."

"That's not what Hilgard believes."

"You're trusting a doctor?"

Cinder's shoulders moved ahead of her in a shrug. "I do have a different chore for you."

Abigail rolled her eyes. She reached for his arm, wanting to spin him around so they could have whatever this conversation was face-to-face, but stopped as the stairwell was imbued with wispy blue smoke escaping his pockets. He was hiding his condition from her.

From Warden.

From his team.

They climbed the stories slowly. The thicker the smoke became the slower Cinder moved. He gripped the handrail when it was there and pressed himself against the wall when it wasn't. When they reached a landing, Abigail caught a glimpse of his pale face. Sweat beaded across his forehead like he had a fever.

"We can rest?" she offered.

Cinder took the next step as a reply.

Abigail joined him on the tiny stair, their bodies pushed together between two stone walls, and looped her arm around him. "I'm helping you."

Cinder smirked; his face still free of the burns he removed the night they were together. "You won't take no for an option?"

Abigail mirrored his stubborn mood by taking the next step with him in tow. They finished the final stories in that fashion. Their breaths mingling ahead of them as the air humidified in their presence. Abigail's skin burned in the best way wherever his contacted it. The stubble of his chin scratched against her cheek. When they exited into the restaurant lobby, Cinder hesitantly removed himself from her and leaned against the sushi case. Smoke continued to lift out of his clothes.

"I want you to send HE a note," he said, before Abigail could voice her obvious concerns. "I want you to send them on a goose chase to the shipping yard. You can tell them whatever you think will get them there. Make sure it's for tomorrow night."

"Who are you targeting? Beacon or Miss Titan?"

"Titan is next on my list."

"You think the others can take out someone with super strength without me?"

"I think you're underestimating my team," he chuckled. "Would you seriously help them?"

"I have been for weeks."

"Unwillingly," he reminded. "And, getting in the way of my plans, actually."

Cinder straightened up and glanced at the golden Lucky Cat clock hanging on the wall. The feline's manicured paw tapped away with the second hand. "You better get going if you don't want to miss your bus, hero."

"You're not coming with me?"

"Think you'll miss me that much?" he teased.

"To make sure I write what you tell me to?" Abigail felt dumb saying it aloud, but knew she'd feel worse if she admitted her true answer.

"I trust you'll make the right decision. This next move is all your own."

"Right decision?" she scoffed. "You have the civilians here as hostage."

Cinder pushed off the sushi case and headed for the other door. "If you truly believe that, I may have misjudged you."

Abigail wasn't sure what she believed from him right now.

"Abigail?" he called over his shoulder after unlocking the door.

"Yeah?" Abigail stepped toward him, envisioning a hundred different requests she could fill.

"Bring me back a doughnut, would you?"

His door shut behind him and Abigail kicked an empty chair across the room. She exited Simply Sushi before she caused any property damage. She didn't think she'd regret slugging him in the mouth right now. A year had passed since they were together, and Abigail knew she may have held onto him tighter than he could have her, but that didn't remove their history.

A history that Cinder was trying to ignore.

Abigail gritted her teeth. He was doing a poor job at it.

For everything that changed in Abigail's life, the coffee shop was an odd restarting point. It remained the same her entire time in Tennyson City. The menu never offered a new special, the napkins remained rough and stamped with the coffee mug logo, the same rotation of faces still worked the counter and kitchen. The only difference were the people inside, but at every visit each person fell into a mold required by the coffee shop. A person with dark bags under their eyes emerging into semiconsciousness with their first sip of coffee. A student accompanied by a laptop and textbook taking up an entire booth. A pair of younger kids killing time at the baked goods display. Someone carefully shaking creamer out of a glass shaker into their to-go cup.

Abigail collected her usual order from the counter and plucked the newspaper from the rack. Just like every time before, her usual spot was empty, and she settled into the cracked booth. Unlike every time before, she didn't jump to the crossword puzzle to begin her message. For once, she wasn't sure what to say. The obvious answer was to tell Beacon everything. That was her job, but she didn't think that was the *right* answer. That answer was to feed Cinder's lie to Hero Enterprises so the corrupted heroes could be removed before they did more damage. But could Abigail trust a villain? Would she trust Cinder?

Nothing had stopped her before.

The evidence supported his claims, even if she didn't believe in the outcome of the vigilante system. At least one of the heroes at Hero Enterprises was involved in the criminal underworld of Tennyson City. She'd have to wait to see the rest of his evidence before fully believing his story.

Abigail sipped her coffee. It's burning temperature didn't register past her permanently scorched tongue.

Would this situation be any easier if it wasn't Cinder on the other side of it? Would she really have this dilemma if Warden gave her the task?

The answer came quick, and although Abigail didn't like it, she knew it was the truth.

She did trust him.

Abigail filled in her coded message and placed the paper back on the rack for the HE agent to collect. She returned to Simply Sushi but didn't go down to the hideout. She marched her way up to Cinder. She may have self-discovered a few answers for herself, but the last question plaguing her could only be answered by him.

And this time she wouldn't let his crooked smile distract her from getting what she wanted.

Reaching the top of the stairs, the doorknob to the loft glowed bright orange. Dark smoke seeped from under the door. Abigail kicked the door in and was prepared to extinguish a fire.

She didn't expect Cinder to be the one burning.

Chapter Twenty-Four

Cinder knelt in the center of the room. Waves of indigo flames pulsed off his body, burning the closest things around him before fading away. The floor beneath him was blackened. His hands gripped onto his face. Both his face and hands were broken apart like molten stone. The same indigo color ran like a river between the darkened pieces of flesh.

Abigail ran to him. The fire was cool, either by the last of Cinder's control or sheer luck, but the smoke billowing around him burned like a 500-degree oven. Abigail slid to his side and grabbed his forearms. He didn't release his head. He didn't look up. Abigail turned his face to her and gasped. His eyes were gone. The sockets were filled with the same blue shade. They glowed like a pair of horrifying flashlights.

Abigail tightened her grip around his arms. "Cinder! What do I do?"

He didn't answer. His body shook as another pulse expanded around him. She didn't need him to make any sounds to know the agony he was in. His face contorted. He twisted his hands inside his hair. Abigail wanted to scream for him.

She wanted to absorb this heat, to take away the fire like he was able to do.

"I'm right here for you," she said as another heat wave passed, charring the magazines on the coffee table next to them. "I'm not leaving. I'm right here."

Cinder never told her how he was able to absorb fire or heal burns. Volcanic could only speculate that it was a side effect of Cinder's initial injury. The attack that super charged his red flames to blue. Abigail was desperate. She'd try anything to take this pain away. She tightened her grip around him again and envisioned drawing the flames inside herself.

Nothing changed. Another heatwave racked his frame. The floor cracked as embers settled between the floorboards.

Abigail tried again. Cherry-red sparks burst from her fingertips in an expression of her desperation. They grew to tiny flames, and she cursed at her carelessness.

Behind the ghastly blue glow of Cinder's eyes, she caught a shimmer of emerald.

"Of course!" Abigail sucked down a gulp of air and commanded all her fire to her skin. The first thing Volcanic taught her when she was his sidekick was how to smother flames with her own. She saved so many homes with this method. Now, she would save her own.

Red fire sizzled atop every patch of exposed skin, her arms, her legs, her face, her hands, and she pressed the flames against Cinder. She smothered him with her fire. She continued to gulp down the smoke-infested air to ignite more flames. She burned brighter than she ever had before, she burned hotter than she ever managed before. She fought through the tears that pierced her shut eyes as the smoke tore apart her lungs.

"Doll." The voice shifted groggily through her mind. "Doll."

A hand that felt cold only due to her currently blazing temperature struck her cheek, and Abigail's eyes shot open. The smoke and fire were gone. The only things left were her cherry-red flames and a pair of eyes shrouded in their emerald wastelands. Her flames dropped off her like rain drops and she tackled Cinder to the floor, her arms wrapping tightly around him.

"What was that?" she asked inside the crook of his neck. His heart beat steadily below her and she found solace in feeling it, proving that he was alive.

"Me overheating." Cinder whispered.

"Does it happen a lot?"

"It has recently."

"Do I call Hilgard?"

"Not right now."

"Is there anything to help it?"

Cinder shifted under her and forced them into a seated position. "Whatever you just did seemed helpful."

Despite their embrace being disrupted, she refused to move too far from him. The floor below was charred in a wide circle, the darker center turning to ashen grey around the edges like the rings of an ancient tree. The closest pieces of furniture were destroyed. The air above them was heavy with smoke.

"Are you burned?" he asked.

Abigail checked herself over. "Surprisingly, no."

He grinned. With the backdrop of destruction and the recent memory of him combusting, it was an odd expression. "I knew you'd gotten stronger. Maybe you *are* fireproof enough for me."

Abigail shook her head.

"Not that I'm ungrateful you're here," Cinder placed a scarred hand atop her knee. The molten form had hardened into the familiar crisscrossing of burns that was just as much Cinder as was his crooked smile and duster jacket, "But, why are you?"

Abigail felt the blush surface across her face but refused to look away. "I wanted to know why you keep pushing me away."

"Pushing you away?"

Abigail sighed. The admittance was turning painful. "Why won't you kiss me? If . . . things have changed and you don't feel that way about me anymore, I won't—"

"Stop." Cinder interrupted her.

"Cinder, I—"

"Please." Cinder's face was either red from his near-death experience or something emotional. "You're reckless. I didn't want you recklessly coming back to me. I wanted to make sure it was real."

"Real for you?" Her throat burned.

"Real for you," he answered, squeezing her knee cap. "It was always real for me."

"Then prove it."

Cinder didn't hesitate. He gripped the meager collar of her T-shirt and pulled her into him. He kissed her hungrily. Abigail kissed him back all the same. Oxygen fueled her fire, but he fueled her.

Every kiss from before evaporated as this reckless, desperate, starving kiss took over their memories. The heat between them was a flash fire. It scorched Abigail before she ever realized it.

Cinder pulled away too soon. Abigail was about to complain until she heard footsteps above them.

"Who's that?" she asked when a skylight rattled open.

"A guest." Cinder pulled Abigail to her feet, kissing her quickly. His lips sparked against hers before he took a step to separate them. "My ally."

A large man leapt from the open skylight to the floor with more grace than Abigail expected. The damaged floor should have given away under his massive form, but the loft held firm. Unlike Abigail did when he turned to face her. Her legs threatened to collapse at the sight of the hero.

"You alright?" Volcanic asked Cinder, glancing around the damaged living room. "This looks like a bad one."

Volcanic gestured to the scorch marks on the floor, clearly knowing about his illness. He collected a charred piece of newspaper off the ground and returned it to the desk where it had fallen from.

"Nothing she couldn't handle."

Abigail would have blushed at Cinder's compliment, but she couldn't stop staring at Volcanic. He wasn't in his costume; he hadn't worn it in years since retiring from Saves the Day Hero Company, but did wear a black domino mask that poorly hid his identity from someone who had worked alongside him.

"Who's the girl?" Volcanic upturned his wrist at his side, ready to ignite a fireball if he needed to. Abigail recognized the stance and was appalled he'd threaten her with it.

Cinder chuckled. "You don't recognize your old protégée?"

Volcanic's eyes widened. His throat moved like he was swallowing a large bite of clam chowder. "Abigail?"

"She's going as Wildfire right now. Kind of a full circle thing, eh?"

"You're involved with *this*?" he asked.

"*You're* involved with this?" Abigail fired back.

"Volcanic was the first hero I employed." Cinder crossed the loft to stand beside him.

At one time they stood like this often, as hero and sidekick. Helios and Wildfire. After the accident, Abigail never thought they'd be on the same side again. Especially as they did now. Cinder, rouge antihero, and Kenneth, retired super hero. It should have been a laughable image, perhaps it would've been if Abigail wasn't realizing what their partnership actually meant.

"You knew all this time?" Blue sulfuric smoke marked her statement. "You knew he was alive and didn't say anything? We went to the funeral together! I was devastated and you watched me, knowing he was still alive!"

"I didn't know until half a year ago," Volcanic defended without success.

"Why didn't you tell me then?"

"I didn't know how." The hands at his side dropped, the fight in him leaving. "If I told you I knew he was alive, I would have to tell you why."

Abigail turned to her next target. "We're you ever going to tell me that you were alive? Or was I just in the right place to find out?"

"You know now."

Cinder's answer infuriated her. Blue fire slipped between her bared teeth. She wasn't sure who her next statement was aimed at. "I trusted you."

"You still do." For as soft as he said it, Cinder's voice snarled against her. "You wrote my code as I asked."

"You have the city as your hostage, of course I did."

Cinder shook his head. The action so carefree despite almost burning alive moments ago. "You know I wouldn't hurt someone innocent."

"He's right," Volcanic chimed in. "Abigail, I know this sounds crazy, but it's all true. The heroes here, in other cities, they're abusing their power and making things worse for the people inside their cities. I was almost like them. Saves The Day was going to make me into something like that."

"If you knew, then why didn't you stop it?"

Cinder said to Volcanic, "She thinks we can get rid of the corrupt ones with the legal system."

"If enough heroes stood up to them, then yes. We could," Abigail said.

Volcanic sighed. "One hero, one civilian and one villain wouldn't be enough."

"Abigail, I meant what I said," Cinder spoke up, "You're not a prisoner here. If you want to leave, you can. If you want to try and stop me, you can. But I'm moving forward with my plan, and if you're going to get in the way of it, then I will ask you to leave."

Combustion

Abigail crossed her arms. "I'm staying."

Cinder smirked. "Good. Volcanic, how are things in San Arbor?"

"San Arbor?" Abigail echoed, pushing inside their bubble. The air heated 20 degrees around the three flamed-powered individuals.

"That's where I'm going next," Cinder explained.

"San Arbor isn't corrupted."

"You really think that?"

"Yes." Abigail answered. King Arthur could be an asshole, but that didn't place him in the same ranks as the heroes in Tennyson City.

"Okay," Cinder gave in quicker than Abigail expected. "I'm willing to discuss that further after were done here. You would be the expert on The Round Table Knights."

"I thought the mission was already finished?" Volcanic asked.

"The attack on Miss Titan is for tomorrow," Abigail answered.

Cinder scratched the side of his face. "It's actually happening now. I was testing you Abigail, to see if you would write my code. Sorry about that."

"So Cold Snap is—"

"Absolutely fine. You've trained her well," Cinder assured. "They should be getting back soon."

"Then you'll sick her on Beacon? Cold shouldn't be a killer."

"Beacon's not on my list. He's clean. He didn't even know what the others were doing."

"I find that hard to believe," Abigail scoffed.

"You'd be surprised what some teammates are kept in the dark about."

"Are you keeping me in the dark about something?"

"Are we teammates?" Cinder challenged back.

"I'll come back when we're ready to discuss San Arbor." Volcanic decided, taking a step away from his two ex-sidekicks.

The sparks that passed between Abigail and Cinder passionately moments ago now sparked wildly at their fingertips, ready to be unleashed but falling to the tormented floor like depleted fireworks instead.

"So will I," Abigail agreed. "You're not marching to *my* city without me."

"When Tech gets back bring him up here," Cinder said. "We'll talk then."

Chapter Twenty-Five

The hideout was empty when Abigail entered, slamming the door behind her. The crash that probably dented a hinge did little to dent her anger. She breathed out a sulfuric cloud of blue smoke and flames. She unleashed a few fireballs into the air that burst into a shower of sparks. She kicked the side of her bunk. She collapsed onto the crappy mattress with an agitated scream muffled by the sheets.

The betrayal of Volcanic knowing Cinder was alive and not telling her seeped out of her skin like a terrible toxin and absorbed into the bedsheet. Having to keep her own and the other heroes' identities a secret should have made her more understandable to the situation. Keeping secrets was a huge requirement in a profession whose dress code demanded a mask, but she'd gladly throw away her secret identity if it meant easing the pain of one of her friends. She thought Volcanic thought the same.

Volcanic hadn't been unsure of how to tell her. He was only being selfish.

Abigail gritted her teeth and forced the anger to flee her system. She needed to keep a level head. Not just for her cover, but to be prepared for the talk about San Arbor and whatever Tech had to do with it. Dox-Con had just paired up with the Knights so perhaps that was the corruption Cinder assumed was in her city. The technology company would be easily hackable to Tech and perhaps he would reveal the dark plans of the company. Abigail flipped onto her back. Taking down a technology company would be far easier than any Knight.

Not that she believed any of her team could be on Cinder's hit list.

She'd once seen Excalibur shed a tear for a squirrel hit on the road during patrol. Lancelot was his own caricature of a good-boy superhero. Merlin volunteered at every high school's science fair and hosted her own chemistry theme club.

The Round Table Knights were nothing like Bastet.

She kicked at the bunk above her, showering herself in dust. If she didn't do something productive, Abigail feared she'd do something . . . reckless.

To help waste time until the other's arrived, Abigail cleaned the hideout. Despite its small size, she had depleted the supply of paper towels and multi-purpose cleaner, and resorted to using an unused bed-sheet to unsuccessfully mop the floors. She was almost done with the terrible job when Odo flew into the room, chanting excitedly. The others followed him, but with their combined voices Abigail couldn't make out their victory shriek.

Abigail ditched her sheet in the kitchen sink and strode right to Tech, but was intercepted by Cold Snap and Stretch, catching both of her arms in theirs. Cold Snap's bubbly energy tried to entangle with Abigail, and although she was glad to see her friend in one piece, she didn't let her mood distract her.

"It worked like a charm!" Cold Snap announced.

"It couldn't have gone better," Stretch agreed.

The rips in their clothing and grimy mixture of dirt and blood across their skin didn't match their attitude. Stretch was missing a shoe.

"You missed a great fight," Odo added, coming back to the ground. "I'm glad you're back on your feet."

Warden appeared behind them. If he was happy with their success, he didn't show it. He glared at Abigail. "Titan had no idea we were there."

Abigail didn't like what his gloat implied.

"Cinder wanted me to take Tech upstairs when you all got back," Abigail said, eager to leave for more than one reason.

Combustion

Warden stepped to the side to allow her passage. Abigail would have rather walked barefoot through a valley of scorpions than turn her back to him.

"Is everything okay?" Cold Snap asked before Abigail could move, keeping their arms locked together.

"For sure." Abigail thought she was telling the truth, but her voice dipped like she was in the middle of an interview. "We'll be right back."

"Good," Cold Snap squeezed Abigail's arm before releasing her, "because I think we deserve a big victory dinner."

"Where could we go?" Odo fluttered down beside them.

"We can order in."

Abigail collected Tech and his ever-present laptop before the others could decide between pizza or curry and hurried up the stairs. Tech didn't ask questions as he followed Abigail, and she was thankful for it. She wasn't sure how to answer them, not to mention if she'd be able to with the mixture of emotions roiling inside her gut. She didn't think she'd ignite during this, but she still wasn't sure what to expect. They reached the top of the stairs and Abigail knocked twice before entering the loft.

All evidence of Cinder's overheating episode was erased. The smoke was aired out, most likely from the opened skylights. The burned papers on the floor were gone, the charred furniture rotated to hide their disfiguration. The scorch marks on the floor blended in with the falling shadows. Cinder stood from his seat at the couch looking every bit like the crime-boss he claimed to be. He adjusted his coat, the high collar hiding his expression.

"Tech," he greeted. "Warden said the plan worked?"

"Yeah." Tech shifted his laptop in front of him as a shield. "I mean, yes, sir."

"Do you have the video I asked you to hold on to?" Cinder gestured them to follow him to the desk. He shoved away books, pens, and other documents to create a semi-clean space.

"Of course." Tech set his laptop down and started to work. With each keystroke his freckles flashed orange. The computer screen resembled something out of a spy movie. She peered over Tech's shoulder as he typed strange symbols onto a black screen. "Would you not hover?"

Abigail stepped back, startled. "My bad."

Cinder snickered at her.

"Where's your *ally*?" she asked about Volcanic.

"Something came up. He'll be back later."

Neither of them made eye contact.

"Here it is." Tech stepped away from his laptop. The video on the screen waited for someone to hit play.

"Part of Tech's ability is accessing the digital network," Cinder explained. "If something's ever been online, or stored digitally on a device, he's able to access it."

"What's this going to show?" Abigail asked, fear leaking into her question.

"Cell phone video of a partial building collapse in San Arbor a few months ago," Tech answered.

"Dox-Con Tower?"

Cinder nodded at her deduction, then signaled Tech to hit play.

The footage instantly brought Abigail back to the scene. The tower's debris scattered around the fallen prong protruding from the lawn. Bodies moved frantically in and out of the frame. Dust erupted like smoke bombs from the videographer's position inside the tower. They moved forward so that the screen captured the chaos on the lawn. Abigail found herself as the dust cover settled. The remains of her golden cape flapped in the wind. She stood next to King Arthur. His hand wrapped around her. Abigail felt the grip, as if the video was occurring in real time.

At the time, she hadn't noticed it. Even if she had, there would have been nothing she could've done to stop it. Amidst the grainy footage, the smoke, the shake of the camera, Abigail saw the undeniable shift in King Arthur's eye color. The flash of purple was gone in an instant, but the color stained Abigail's vision. It had never been her decision to let the kid go. His death had always been on King Arthur's hands. He commanded her to let Gerald die.

"This can't be possible," she whispered as the video stopped, gripping the edge of the desk. "I would have known . . . This has to be doctored."

Tech gasped. "I would never tamper with this."

"The video is real," Cinder told her. "King Arthur brainwashed Avalon."

Hearing her name reminded Abigail of who she was supposed to be right now. She pinched the inside of her wrist to stable herself. Tech couldn't know her connection. She asked, "How did you get this?"

"Tech pulled all the footage the night this happened."

"Why didn't someone do something?" Abigail asked the universe. "Everyone in San Arbor knows what happens when King's eye color changes, the person taking this should have said something." King Arthur never should have done this.

"I'm sure he would have tried," Cinder said, "But someone got to him first."

Abigail paled. "What do you mean?"

Cinder nodded to Tech who continued the video. Moments later, the phone fell to the ground and was crushed by a blue boot.

"Lancelot."

"I'm not sure if he was actively aware of what he was doing," Cinder confirmed.

"What happened to the person taking the video?"

"Unsure."

Abigail backed away from the desk so she could lean against the couch, her legs wobbling. She squeezed her arms together, still processing what this meant. Cinder walked Tech to the exit and dismissed him before joining Abigail. The couch scraped against the floor as their weight leaned against it.

"What else has he done?" she asked in a horrified whisper.

"Volcanic is bringing the rest of the evidence. I know watching that wasn't easy for you."

"You knew since it happened?"

Cinder nodded.

"How long have you been watching the Knights?"

"Since the beginning," he answered. "I've been watching a couple of major cities."

"Why didn't you start in San Arbor?"

"Tennyson City was worse off."

"But you planned to come to San Arbor?"

"If I needed to, yeah."

"Would I have been on your list?" Each word crashed around her. Her world felt very far away and so very close at the same time.

Cinder turned to her, lifted her chin, and forced her to look at him. Their eyes seared each other's. "You would never be on that list. I didn't need that video to know you're innocent. One of the good heroes."

Abigail shook her head free of his hand. "No one is innocent."

Cinder sighed. "In the grand scheme of things, you're pretty damn close to it."

Abigail didn't respond. The air around her chilled and she ran her hands over her arms.

"Abigail," Cinder said, looking straight ahead. "I would have told you. Told you everything when I had the chance, when this was over."

"I'm finding that hard to believe. Every time I see you, you've kept something else from me. How am I supposed to know your truth from your lies?"

"Is it too cheesy to say I've done it all to protect you?"

"You wouldn't be protecting me if you came to San Arbor and tried to kill my friends."

"I never wanted to drag you into this, but I'm glad you found your way here." Cinder reached into his pocket and handed its contents to Abigail. "I know I can create light, but only when I'm with you does the darkness go away."

"That's pretty cheesy." Abigail rolled her eyes but accepted his gift. Her breath caught. The melted pendant of her engagement ring shook in the palm of her hand. Through tears she said, "I thought I lost this."

"I took it while you were recovering," he admitted. "I didn't think I got such a cheap ring. The gold didn't even stand up to a little heat."

"That fire was way more than a little heat."

Cinder fished back inside his pocket for the chain and slipped the ring through it, lowering it back into her waiting palm. "You've worn it all this time?"

Abigail punched his shoulder without any force. "I missed you. It's all that I had left."

"You have the full me now," Cinder promised, opening his arms to her. "I mean it, no more secrets and no more lies."

Abigail tightened her hand around the ring, feeling the familiar bite it caused against her skin. "I won't be able to kill King."

"Would it be easier if he were a villain?" Cinder raised an eyebrow, his twisted smirk reclaiming his face. The soft moment between them fading to something more comfortable.

"Nothing would make it easier."

"Hear me out first." Cinder's response was interrupted by Volcanic leaping down from the skylight. "This may change your mind."

Volcanic dusted off his tan jacket after he straightened. He still wore the black mask that looked too small for his face. His entire civilian outfit, matching tan pants and collared shirt, constricted him more than his physical form. Abigail wondered if he ever missed the job. When she was his sidekick it was all he cared about.

Volcanic handed a large mailing envelope to Cinder, who greedily tore into it. Whatever the documents were inside pleased Cinder. He nodded to himself, slapped the papers against the desk, then handed them to Abigail.

She examined the various photocopied documents and photos, but Cinder explained the contents with a disgusted vigor.

"Aside from you, King Arthur has been using his power of sway to gain access and favor with several of San Arbor's business and political leaders."

The statement didn't shock Abigail. From how freely he'd been using his abilities, it was a natural progression. Abigail flipped through the documents, photos showing a purple-eyed King Arthur meeting privately with sharply dressed congressmen, and asked, "What is he gaining from it?"

"Power and allies." Volcanic supplied.

"A run for mayor," Cinder said.

Abigail barked a laugh. "King hates the mayor."

"He hates Benton," Volcanic corrected. "Imagine what he'd do in that position."

"Without anyone able to stop him," Cinder said.

King Arthur's voice crept out of Abigail's memory like a summoned demon. *". . . once we have full control of the city."*

Abigail paled. "Creating a city run by heroes wouldn't be that bad, would it?"

Cinder's face darkened. "Ask any of the people that know about the truth of Tennyson City."

"He's teamed up with Camellia Diaz and Dox-Con without abusing his power," Volcanic added. "There are people who will support him without him brainwashing them."

"What does Dox-Con have to do with this?" Abigail asked.

"If Dox-Con's energy grid becomes San Arbor's only source of power, communication, and personal freedoms, what could happen if a tyrant king controlled it all?"

Abigail stared at Cinder. His words crashed against her in icy waves. "You don't know that for certain. That he would do that."

"I get it," Cinder said. "You don't think he would because he's a *hero*. What if he wasn't? Would you hesitate to stop some unnamed person?"

"I don't think he would because he's my friend." Abigail spat the lie.

Cinder saw through her as he did every time before. He crossed his arms and waited.

"A what-if scenario doesn't give you the right to kill someone."

"When San Arbor is in ruins, you'll wish someone had."

Abigail shoved him, and Volcanic placed himself between his two ex-sidekicks.

"Things are getting *heated*." Volcanic raised Cinder's arm up by the cuff of his jacket, revealing blue smoke seeping out. "Let's take a break."

Cinder yanked his hand free. "No. We're making a plan tonight. With or without you, Dragon Slayer."

Abigail mirrored his fighting stance and pinned him with her most furious glare. "San Arbor is my city, it's my rules. We'll take down King Arthur. We won't kill him. Or any of the other Knights. Excalibur can probably help us, or at least not get in the way. He's been the best one of all of us. I can't see him involved with King Arthur."

"What about your boyfriend?" Cinder's twisted smirk wasn't as charming as it was a moment before.

Abigail refused to acknowledge the wrongful title. "Lancelot is wrapped around King too tightly, so is Merlin. Even if they don't know what he's doing, they'll support him." Abigail continued flipping through the pages of evidence. "I'm taking these to organize them. They'll need to easily explain what King Arthur is planning. Volcanic, will you get better evidence of what Dox-Con is doing with their energy grid? Something to show it's going to take over completely?"

"Already on it."

"Tech can probably pull more wrongful uses of King using his power." Abigail was disgusted by her own words, but the video of King Arthur abusing his power on her disgusted her more. "The video proof will look better than the photos."

"He'll find you whatever you need," Cinder agreed.

Abigail pulled out a sheet of paper from the stack. "Bank statements?"

Volcanic nodded. "King Arthur has been sending large amounts of money to a shell account."

"Do we know the real holder?" The amounts listed on the statement became comically large. If given that amount of money, Abigail wasn't sure she'd be able to spend all of it.

"A company marked with this logo." Volcanic gently took the page from her and flipped it over. A lime green six-pointed star stared up at them.

Abigail gasped.

"You recognize it?" Cinder asked.

"It was on the sonic boom device. On the ointment Hilgard gave me."

"A weapons manufacturer?" Volcanic asked.

"A super manufacturer," said Cinder. "The ointment was made from reworking the cells of someone in India who could heal themselves." He shrugged when Abigail stared at him. "We tried it on me first, but it didn't work. I didn't realize the doctor gave it to you."

Volcanic brought the conversation back on track. "If King Arthur is funding this group . . ."

"He's having something made," Abigail finished. "Something with his ability."

The air thickened around them. Abigail slid the documents back inside the folder.

"Are you ready to go back home?" Cinder's voice made her jump.

"No," Abigail answered. "But, I made a promise to San Arbor when I accepted my mask. I won't let her down."

"You're a good hero." Cinder smiled. "I'll get the team ready."

"No," Abigail shook her head. "I won't let them get hurt. I can handle this on my own."

"Our own." Cinder corrected. His voice was as soft as the smoke coming from the fingers that brushed hers. "You're not going in there alone."

Chapter Twenty-Six

Sneaking into Hero Enterprises was easy. Abigail was inside Beacon's office within fifteen minutes under the guise of attending a tour. She slipped away from the tour group before they made it off the first floor. She found the office by following the building's directory posted outside every elevator. Beacon's office reminded her of a corporate employee's more than a hero leader's. Instead of weapons lining the walls, Beacon's office contained a few bookshelves with old and dusty textbooks. A snow globe sat on his desk with a tiny Eiffel Tower imprisoned inside. Two framed photos rested on either side of it. One showed all the HE heroes at some masked event, and the other showed a maskless Beacon surrounded by what looked to be his family.

The Hero Relief Center was a guarded castle in comparison.

Abigail sat at the desk and rifled through the drawers until she found a sheet of paper and a pen. She had to be quick—someone other than Beacon could walk in at any minute—but made sure to keep her handwriting neat and legible. The strange symbols of the cypher were easy enough to mess up when she wasn't in a hurry. Once satisfied with the note, Abigail placed it in the center of the desk. The message was cryptic, her plan was complicated, but she needed to speak to Beacon before she left town.

According to the tour guide, the heroes were in a meeting with Tennyson City's public sanitation committee and couldn't meet them for photos. The absence of the heroes and the chance of selfies and autographs made the tour group mutter in annoyance, but set Abigail's plan into motion. Finding Beacon's office empty was the first step.

Waiting on the fire escape was the final part.

Combustion

Abigail left the window behind Beacon's desk cracked so she could hear his return. From her position about three-quarters up the side of the building, Tennyson City faded in and out of focus as the heat obscured her vision. Below her, citizens the size of specks continued with their daily lives. She knew she'd look the same to them if anyone looked up. Bits of sand carried up by the wind scraped against her bare skin, but Abigail didn't mind it. Finally, she could see the ocean. The blue surface shimmered under the sun, and foamy waves crashed onto the rocky edges of the land.

There were worse places to wait.

Sometime later, the chair scraped against the floor as someone sat down. Abigail froze. The window whined as it shimmied the rest of the way open. Beacon poked his head out and looked down at her. He hadn't changed since the last time she saw him. That meeting at the Round Table felt like a year ago rather than two months. Too much had happened, too much had changed. It seemed everything around her had transformed while he remained constant.

Beacon frowned. It was clear he didn't recognize Abigail as she did him. Her pulse quickened. She hadn't accounted for this. She racked her brain for some clever thing to say. Something that would hint at her identity without actually saying it. She needed to ensure his deniability.

Slowly, Beacon's face morphed into the man she met in San Arbor. The friendly expression he wore in all of his photos. The one that matched his yellow costume.

"Can I come up?" Abigail asked.

Beacon backed away from the window, and Abigail pulled herself inside the office. He locked the office door and pulled an extra seat from the corner to the desk. Abigail didn't move from the window, choosing to lean against the frame rather than take a seat. She risked a lot being here. He risked a lot letting her in.

"This seems pretty elaborate." Beacon tapped the note on his desk. "I hope it means you have better news than I received earlier."

Abigail swallowed, knowing he meant the news about Miss Titan. "There won't be any more attacks. The gang is moving out. You're safe."

Beacon slammed his hand on the desk. If the piece of furniture wasn't between them, Abigail figured the blow would have been directed at her. The sudden noise sucked the sound from the air. "You kill all my heroes, all my friends, and run off to the next city? I trusted you, Avalon. You failed me. You failed Tennyson City. You failed your fellow heroes."

Abigail didn't flinch. "Your heroes weren't who they claimed to be. They were doing terrible things to the city."

"I know my team."

"You didn't, and that's not your fault. They kept themselves secret." Abigail spoke quickly so he couldn't interrupt or leave. "Swordfish was importing drugs, and Rush was running them through the city. Bastet was trafficking the people of Tennyson City, and Miss Titan was using portions of all the profits to fund a weapons manufacturing facility across the border."

Beacon stared at her. Abigail knew he didn't believe her. She slowly reached into her pocket and retrieved a flash drive. She set it on the desk.

"That has all the evidence."

Beacon picked up the drive and examined it. "You joined them? The villains?"

"They aren't villains. I never agreed with their vigilante justice, but I do agree that corrupt heroes need to be stopped."

"Why stop now?" Beacon set the drive back on the desk. "Slay the final hydra head."

"You're not corrupt," Abigail answered simply. "Good heroes still exist."

"Is that what you are?"

Abigail didn't accept the label. "I just want to save people."

"Is that what you'll do next?"

She nodded. "We're going to stop the next bad guy."

"And what do I do with this?" Beacon pointed at the drive.

"Up to you. They're your friends. It's your call how you want them remembered, but I wanted you to know the truth." Abigail straightened. "My intention was never to fail you or Tennyson City. You and I didn't know the whole truth when this mission started."

Beacon rounded the desk to sit down. He clasped his hands together in his lap. A large vein bulged from under one of his yellow gloves. The gravitas of the room deepened. The weight of Abigail's accusations settled on his shoulders.

"Titan had been taking a lot of vacation recently, never told me where she was going. Never brought back any new snow globes for her collection. I thought that was weird." Beacon kept his gaze on his hands. They twisted together. "Rush, before he died, kept acting strange; paranoid and jumpy. The toxins found in his autopsy- do you think he was using the drugs he was selling?"

Abigail nodded. "The chemical makeup is the same. There's a file on the drive. It affected people with abilities differently than those without."

"And that girl you found in the research center?" Beacon dragged his hands across his face. "God, Bastet put her there."

Abigail squeezed his shoulder. "We got her out of there, and now you can keep everyone here safe."

His next statement surprised her. "Thank you. Thank you for keeping my city . . . No. It's not my city. Thank you for keeping Tennyson City safe."

Abigail smiled. "It's what I do. But, Beacon, please believe me. I didn't want to hurt any of them. I believed that they deserved a proper trial. But apparently, someone in the justice system is bought, and the charges would have been dropped. If you can, if you choose to act on the evidence, please start there."

Beacon shrugged her hand off his shoulder. He plucked the flash drive from the desktop, placed it inside a drawer, and then handed the coded note to Abigail. "Would you mind burning this?"

Abigail pinched the note and seared the edges until the paper and the message vanished in smoke.

"You took a big risk coming here, giving me this," Beacon patted the drawer where the drive now sat, "But you should probably leave before someone sees you."

"One last thing, you need better security on your second floor. Key codes on the stairwells or something."

Beacon's voice was hollow; he sounded detached from this conversation. "I'll mark that down."

Abigail was halfway out the window when the intercom buzzed, and a panicked voice carried through the air. "Attention. Attention. Intruder alert. I repeat, a large man dressed in a suit has entered the building. He's demanding Beacon's head. He's attacking—"

The intercom fizzled out. Silence filled the room.

"Warden," Abigail said his name like a curse and stepped back inside the office, heading for the door. "A dangerous guy from the gang."

"You can't go down there," Beacon said. "Your cover."

Abigail paused, her hand already on the door handle. "I'm not letting you go down there alone."

Beacon didn't protest and ran out of the office.

Abigail followed him through a series of secret hallways taking them to the ground level quicker than she could have on her own. Finding Warden wasn't difficult. He left a trail of broken furniture, damaged drywall, and bloodied employees as he traveled deeper into the building. Abigail tried assessing their injuries as she passed them. The worse of it was torn skin across tender cheeks and swelling eyes. Abigail's skin sizzled.

"Medic is on the way," Beacon explained, lowering his hand from his ear and the earpiece inside.

Fire licked up her arms. "Can you cause a distraction? I'll get him out of here."

"Keep your eyes covered."

Abigail stepped behind Beacon, and they entered a gallery space. Photos of the heroes looked onto the massacre that the room had become. The mid-century decor was in ruins. Chunks of glass littered the floor from broken frames and windows. Dark soil marred the walls like blood as large tropical plants had been slung from their pots. Warden stood at the center, his fat fingers coated in the flesh and blood stuck under his rings.

Warden lunged at Beacon. The mass that allowed him to deliver carnage with simple punches hindered his speed. Beacon used it to his advantage. His skin glowed until it shone like a spotlight pouring out of his costume. He peeled away a section of fabric from his chest and blinded Warden with the full force of light.

The light eliminated every shadow in the room. The glass shards created an infinite number of rainbows. Beacon unleashed the illuminance of a tiny sun. Even with her eyes on her feet and standing behind the main source, Abigail felt the intensity.

Warden yelled out and covered his eyes.

"You're up!" Beacon shouted, covering himself.

Abigail leaped around him with her fists blazing. She walloped into Warden's chest knocking his disoriented self toward the windows. Her flames chewed away pieces of his clothing, filling the space between them with smoke. Warden dropped his hands to smother the fire starting on his vest.

With his face exposed, Abigail nailed a solid blow to his nose and a final kick into his gut sending Warden out a window. His large rump cushioned his fall. He didn't seem to notice the fire burning away his tie, the wailing of sirens, Beacon's approach, or the glass digging into his arms and legs. Warden glared at Abigail with sunburned eyes.

His stare was heavy. It was meaningful.

Beacon yanked her arm before Abigail could follow Warden outside. "Go now," he ordered. "Before anyone else comes."

"But . . ." Abigail turned back to Warden, but he was gone. All that remained were the rainbows filtering around the glass.

"I'll take care of this." Beacon shoved Abigail gently forward. "Save the next city, I'll clean up Tennyson."

Chapter Twenty-Seven

The hideout stirred up a strange mixture of sad farewells and relieved departure as Abigail packed her bag. It didn't take long. The short list of belongings she brought fit inside her backpack, and other than her heightened stress levels, she hadn't picked up any souvenirs. She hadn't picked up any *fun* souvenirs. The scar on her hip would be a constant reminder of her mission. So would the bonds she forged with the hired killers. So would her betrayal to King Arthur.

She shook her head. King Arthur was betraying her and their city.

She held onto the small hope that after his arrest he could rehabilitate. That whatever evil had wedged its way into his heart could be exorcised. That a two-month sabbatical could reset his mind and King Arthur would return as the leader of the Knights that Abigail knew him to be.

Thought him to be. She suffocated that hope in her hands, holding on to it too tightly.

Abigail moved to the exit. The others were gone and wouldn't know about her leaving until they returned. This was better than having to say goodbye. If the hideout was difficult to leave, she could only imagine how the others would react. Tech and Stretch wouldn't care too much, but Abigail knew Cold Snap would usher out some water works. Abigail always thought she wanted a little sister, but she never expected to find one like this. Odo, despite his indifference, had developed a kinship with her. One that wouldn't evaporate over time. If their lives weren't wronged by the hero world, Abigail believed their futures would be different. Ones far away from crime.

She climbed the stairs to meet Cinder at the restaurant level. With each step forward, Abigail shed the layers that morphed her to Marie

Barret until she reached the top landing as Abigail Turner, as Avalon: The Dragon Slayer. The fading dye job on her hair would have to go the moment she was back. She would protect her city as herself. Not as this false identity.

She owed it to the citizens of San Arbor and herself to take down King Arthur and disrupt the heroic status quo of San Arbor as herself. She couldn't hide behind Wildfire. She couldn't blame some villain.

She made this decision by herself.

She opened the door and found Cinder leaning against the sushi case with a backpack at his feet. In another time, his fur lined coat meant they were headed for a weekend away at a cabin in the mountainside. Today, their trip warranted a more important destination.

"Ready?"

"I guess so," Abigail answered. "It'll be nice to be back in my own place."

"Don't remind me," Cinder grumbled. "I asked Volcanic to watch over my place here, but you know how forgetful he can be."

Abigail bumped her shoulder against his. "I'm sure your loft will survive."

"We better make this a quick trip." He winked. "Just in case."

The dimly lit, fishy smelling restaurant front should not have been a backdrop to any romantic moment, but knowing Cinder was coming back, with her, to their home, made Abigail a little giddy. She leaned up and stole a kiss from his chapped lips, pulling away just as the front door chimed opened.

"We're closed." Cinder said, keeping his darkening gaze on Abigail.

"You didn't think I'd find out?" Warden barked, as something wet slammed onto the ground.

Abigail turned around and gasped. The meek frame of the Hero Enterprises' agent lay piled onto the floor. His bloodied chest faintly raised with shallow breaths. Both eyes were blackened. Three fingers were missing on his left hand. Abigail kneeled beside him. Unsure of how to make him better, but desperate to try. The agent whimpered in her arms.

"That's the damned Dragon Slayer from San Arbor," Warden continued.

Cinder blew out a displeased breath. "You know I have heroes employed."

"Not snitches. She's been sending messages to Hero Enterprises. Meeting with Beacon."

"She's been feeding them false information," Cinder defended.

"Not the whole time, and you know it." Warden's temper spiked until Abigail was sure he'd be able to breathe fire like her. She shifted herself between him and the wounded agent. "I knew something was up from the beginning. I recognized her moves from the news."

Cinder, either unafraid or unaware of Warden's murderous abilities, approach the large man. Dangerous air rolled off his shoulders with blue smoke. He was a predator: dangerous, wild, unhinged, and intelligent. This was Cinder, the Flame Villain. "Do you really think I'd let a snitch into our operation? Do you think I'm that stupid?"

"I think you're soft." Warden spat. "Or else you wouldn't stop once things are *even*."

"Is that what this is about?"

"I won't let some hero ruin this for me."

"Or someone soft?" Cinder flicked his hand to unleash a mighty stream of blue fire into the sushi counter exploding the glass and wood. "Don't test me, Warden."

Cinder's eyes burned hotter than the flames behind him. More fire encircled his hands. He loomed over Warden despite their height difference and, unhappily, Warden stepped down. Cinder kicked the heel of Abigail's boot signaling it was their time to leave. She slowly brought the agent to his wobbly feet.

"He's going to the hospital," she declared with the same strength of Cinder.

"Fine," he snarled for the sake of the standoff with Warden. "Clean this mess up."

They were out of Simply Sushi before Warden could confirm his task or attack their backs.

Not much was said as Abigail and Cinder delivered the agent to the hospital, leaving him in a bloody, yet thankful, heap just outside the security doors. Abigail would be happy when she could actually deliver people inside of the hospital. She'd be happier when she wasn't taking people to the hospital at all. Cinder had paid for their train tickets in advance, even spending the extra money so they could bypass the crowded public check point, opting to do all the registering online.

Abigail inserted her false identity at the kiosk for hopefully the final time.

Cinder claimed a booth in the very back car and stacked their bags on the empty seat next to them, building a privacy wall of backpacks and jackets. Abigail settled in for the long ride back home. At least this time she wasn't alone. At least this time she knew what was waiting for her on the other side of the train platform. The train's intercom voiced their destination and safety guidelines in a fuzzy female voice before pulling away from the station. Tennyson City glistened goodbye.

Combustion

Once the noise of the commuters and railcar wheels filled the space, Abigail turned to Cinder. He opened one eye as their knees bumped together.

"We should probably use this time to sleep." He adjusted his furry hood between his head and the seat back.

"I want to use this time to talk about Warden."

"That brute? Why?"

Abigail's mouth hung open at his dismissal, but she recovered. "He didn't seem too happy with you."

"That's nothing new." Cinder maneuvered in the seat so his body faced Abigail, their conversation better contained. "I hired Warden for his skills, not his personal charm."

"Skills? He's never in the missions, just sort of a babysitter. Do you need someone as unhinged as him looking after your operation while you're gone?"

"The operation is wherever I am. This about Cold?"

Abigail chewed the inside of her cheek. "I do worry about her."

Cinder grabbed her hand and squeezed her fingers. "What happened to the HE agent won't happen to anyone on *our* team. Warden's only power is his unnatural size. If it came to a fight, Cold Snap has the advantage."

It was a small comfort, but a larger one would be knowing Cold Snap wouldn't be anywhere near a threat like that. Abigail pressed further, knowing she had Cinder trapped in their conversation while their hands were linked. "What was the thing he said? About you being soft?"

Cinder rolled his eyes. "Difference of opinion is all."

"A difference of opinion is liking honey mustard more than barbeque sauce. Who are you getting even with?"

Cinder didn't reply. He tried to turn away, but Abigail yanked his hand to keep him facing her.

"You said you wouldn't keep anything else from me."

"I'm not getting even with someone; I'm making things even. With our society. Leveling the playing field with those who have powers."

Abigail nodded. "Making sure situations don't label people as villains, I understand. You've told me this already."

"Warden doesn't want to stop at being even. He want's those with power to be on top. A villain society."

"How is that any different than what Tennyson City was?"

"It's not. Except for who's on top."

"He wants to be the top dog." Cinder awarded Abigail's correct answer with a nod, and she continued, "Why is he following you?"

"You don't think I'm a good leader?" he feinted a pout.

"You know what I mean. If Warden wants to be the one in charge, why is he taking orders from someone who doesn't want him in that position?"

Cinder shrugged. "My guess is he thought I could get him close enough."

"Close enough until he eliminated the person in his way."

"Good thing I have a hero who can watch my back for me." Cinder's playful smirk was everything but comforting in the face of a possible attempt on his life.

"Did you know all of this before you teamed up with him?" Abigail asked.

Cinder nodded.

"Then why did you?"

"It's hard to find an up-right citizen that'll go along with your evil plans," he teased before stealing his kiss back from Abigail. "I promise we can talk more, when we get home, but I do want to sleep, okay?"

Combustion

"One more question."

Cinder raised an eyebrow but didn't protest.

"Do you have an actual plan for King?"

"I do."

"What is it?"

"I'll tell you later."

"Cinder—"

"I'm not keeping it from you," he cut in, "I just don't want to say it out in the open."

Abigail frowned but accepted his reasoning. "It better be the first thing you say when we get home."

Cinder smiled and it blew away her frustration. Abigail smiled too, her stomach twisting as she realized what she said. *When we get home. Together.*

"I have 'one more question' for you," he mimicked her earlier tone. "What did Warden mean about you meeting with Beacon?"

Her stomach dropped, but knew Cinder deserved her honesty. "I had to see him before I left. To let him know the attacks were over. To tell him the truth."

Cinder's features darkened to storm clouds. "That was dangerous."

"I didn't give him any of your names."

"Dangerous for you, Abigail. What's stopping Beacon from calling King and giving him a warning?"

"They're not working together," she answered. "You were right, he didn't know what his team was doing. He has no reason to tip off King."

Cinder sighed, rubbing his thumb across Abigail's knuckle. It was still bright red from an earlier injury. She'd lost count of the number of times she'd bloodied up her hands. "I wish you would have told me before," he whispered. "I could have backed you up."

"I needed you to trust me." *I needed to trust myself.*

"I do," he promised.

"I trust you, too." Abigail sealed her vow with a kiss.

Chapter Twenty-Eight

Avalon stared back at Abigail from the mirror inside her office at the Hero Relief Center. The red hair dye was stripped from her shortened curls that now brushed her shoulders. She tightened the golden bracers around her wrists and made sure her cape was straight. She did a spin to see the costume in its full glory. To see herself in full glory. This was how she was supposed to look. This was who Abigail was. A hero. Despite everything that happened, despite everything that was going to happen, she was excited.

For a moment, she allowed the feeling to override the anxiety in her blood stream.

She attached her sword, its weight anchoring her to the ground, and headed for the Round Table. She shouldn't look forward to the normality that would come with this day, but she allowed the feeling to envelop her as she rode the elevator anyway. After her and Cinder's plan, everything would be different; either for better or for worse. She could have one last day.

"Avy!" Lancelot greeted as soon as she stepped off the elevator. "I knew you were back but wanted to let you settle in before I came to see you. How are you? I like your hair."

"I'm ready for it to grow back," she answered, twisting a tiny curl that could no longer be restrained by her mask's hair bow feature.

Lancelot surprised her with a hug, hoisting her a few inches off the ground and squeezing her tightly. "I'm glad you're home."

His statement was a relieved whisper. A prayer atop marble steps. A confession to a faceless listener.

"It's good to see you too," Abigail wheezed. She wasn't the only one who changed physically. Lancelot's arms looked like they were stuffed with potatoes, and his costume stretched across his chest. There was no psychic residue from his hold; he kept her suspended with just his strength. "How have things been here?"

"Incredible," he beamed, setting her back on the ground. "I've been running both of our patrol routes. I didn't realize how many flammable things there are, but I've modified my shield to clear paths for people to escape the fires and first responders to get in. That's been really helpful. There was a string of car thieves stealing catalytic converters, but we got that taken care of pretty easily . . ."

Abigail listened to Lancelot ramble on about his successes from the previous months with pride. Pride in him for becoming such a decent hero, and pride in her city for raising one. Lancelot never lost the zealous drive to do good that he showed when the Knights first hired him. He climbed the ranks from sidekick to hero without any trouble, and Abigail knew great things could be in his future if he kept on this path. Maybe he wasn't too far under King Arthur's corruption.

". . . King has some pretty big plans for us," Lancelot's current story snapped Abigail back to attention. "His plan is starting to take shape, and just in time too! I can't really say anything yet, but I'm sure he'll tell you himself later. I couldn't have handpicked a better leader for us," Lancelot stopped to laugh, "I guess that's why he's in charge."

Abigail's heart sank. She had been right; Lancelot *was* too enamored with King Arthur. Her sidekick had so much potential, and King Arthur had used it for his own misguided plans. How long had Lancelot been under their leader's charm? She wondered if King Arthur had ever needed to use his power on him. If Lancelot even knew he used it on her.

Lancelot's thumb brushed under Abigail's eye. She blinked rapidly, realizing that she had started to cry. Started to mourn the Lancelot she knew.

"You don't have to cry, Abbs." Lancelot ran his thumb under Abigail's other eye. "I missed you too. I'm not going anywhere."

She didn't correct his assumption about her tears. Abigail stepped back and composed herself. Lancelot wouldn't get hurt in Cinder's plan, except a blow to his pride that would have to heal on its own. She hoped in that time he could morph back to the hero-worshipping kid she met years ago in his blue puffy pants and feathered cap that kept blowing away in the wind.

"We should get to the meeting." Abigail led their way inside the room.

Abigail had no reason to believe the Knights or the Round Table would change in her absence, but she was relieved to find them all the same. Merlin tapped a plastic straw against the side of her coffee mug before setting the stir stick back on the tray. Her red hair, looking far more natural than Abigail's box dye job, was braided over her shoulder while the long tip of her witch's hat hung over the other. She gave Abigail a slight nod in greeting as she took her seat next to Excalibur, who tapped his knuckles against Abigail's.

"And the Dragon Slayer returns." His automated voice rang out through the mouth guard of his helmet.

"Did you expect anything different?" Abigail joked.

"Glad you're back," Merlin admitted after taking a sip of her no doubt chemically enhanced coffee. "Now 'Xcal will stop whining about his coffee being bad."

"I'm sure he'll find something new to complain about," King Arthur teased beside Merlin. "Welcome back, Avalon."

Abigail's stomach churned as she said, "Thanks, King."

"I assumed you'd want to take a few days to get settled before coming back to work," King Arthur said. "No one would judge you."

"I've been away from San Arbor for too long," she replied. "I don't think I could wait a few days if I even tried."

"Have you met with President Samuels yet?" King Arthur asked. "To discuss the conclusion of your mission?"

"Yeah, Avy," Lancelot encouraged, "Tell us how everything turned out. Did you stop the bad guys?"

"We're meeting tomorrow," Abigail answered King Arthur. "After he gets back from his trip. I guess he wasn't expecting me back this soon, either."

"I don't think any of us were." King Arthur's smile didn't reach his eyes, and Abigail wondered who the act was for. "Would you mind paying me a visit first? After your patrol today. There's a new advertising campaign I'd like to bring you up to speed on."

"Won't Samuels go over that with me?" Abigail's skin crawled thinking of being alone with King Arthur for any amount of time. "Or marketing itself?"

King Arthur waved away her concern. "It'll be easier if I do it. Cut out the middleman."

"Sure." Abigail returned his fake smile. "I'll come by after shift."

Cinder's plan required getting King Arthur alone. She hoped this wouldn't be too soon. They may not have another opportunity like this.

"Where are we going today, King?" Lancelot's chipper voice broke the tension unintentionally building between Abigail and King Arthur.

King Arthur hit a few buttons on the remote control and turned on the monitors. Without President Samuels, King Arthur took over his role in leading the meetings. He delivered the Knight's patrol assignments while shifting through road maps and police reports for them to watch out for. After the presentation, Abigail was happy to leave the Hero Relief Center with Excalibur and start their shift together.

Combustion

Although there was beauty in Tennyson City with its colorful flowerpots, arid landscapes, and the salty taste permeating the air, no city would compare to San Arbor. Living up to its nature inspired name, the meticulously planted trees every few feet were in full bloom. The green foliage was a striking contrast to the metal and brick buildings that climbed into the skyline. The fresh smell of trees mixing with the community gardens in the parks overpowered the scent of car exhaust and other usual stink that lived in a city of this size.

Abigail couldn't have picked a prettier city to work in. Or a friendlier population to protect. Her prerecorded videos had fooled the residents into believing she really was on desk duty. The entire city had been captivated by her fall and recovery. Her desk was covered in get well cards and tiny packages of chocolates that Lancelot and Excalibur took turns eating, and beautiful flower arrangements that Shannon enjoyed on the front desk.

Since the start of patrol, Abigail had returned countless waves and smiles to people who were surprised to see Avalon back on the streets. She was trending online before lunch.

"I guess we weren't the only ones who missed you," Excalibur chuckled as a fan jogged back across the street after taking a selfie with them.

"I'm sure they'd do the same if it were you who . . . broke their leg," Abigail assured.

"I don't want to chance it. My popularity numbers are the lowest of the five of us."

"Even below Merlin?" Abigail gasped dramatically.

"She gets the fanboy vote, but still."

"You were always my favorite."

"I think you have to say that."

"I would never lie to you," Abigail promised. "Even before I was your sidekick, you were my favorite."

"Well thank you, Avalon." Excalibur straightened his shoulders. "You're my favorite too."

"You always seemed to know what was right," Abigail added as she pushed the crosswalk button. "You never doubted your position or your morals. Even when other people challenged you."

"We're heroes," Excalibur peered down at her, "We don't have the luxury to second guess."

Abigail kicked a pebble into the middle of the road. A car quickly ran it over. "If you had to do something that maybe people didn't think was right in order to do good, would you be able to?"

"Is this about Tennyson City? You know that anything you had to do there doesn't make you bad. You were undercover, and I'm sure there were situations you had to be in to keep your cover."

"It's not about Tennyson City." Abigail kept her eyes on the pebble.

"You can talk to me, Avalon."

For the tiniest moment, Abigail considered telling him everything. She wanted to tell him what happened in Tennyson City and what she planned to do here. She wanted him to tell her it was okay, that he believed her, that he was good, too. But she didn't. Excalibur held onto his secret identity the most to protect his family; she would never purposely put him in any more danger. "I just don't want to disappoint you. You gave me the second chance I needed to become who I am."

"I knew the kind of person you could be if given the right tools to succeed."

Abigail looked up from the road. "Person? Don't you mean hero?"

Excalibur placed a hand on her shoulder. "It's a good person that makes a good hero, not the other way around. You're a damned good hero, A. Without my guidance, I know you still would've done great things."

Abigail's eyes welled with tears, and they spilled out behind her mask. She hugged Excalibur. His armor digging into her. "Thank you, boss."

Chapter Twenty-Nine

Abigail was careful not to cut her tongue on the edge of the envelope. She pressed down the flap and added two pieces of tape for extra security. The details of her undercover mission, the actual truth of Hero Enterprises, the *villainous* organization, and the evidence against those heroes and the evidence against King Arthur were enclosed. Everything that would justify what was about to happen was stored inside the white envelope with the HRC address header. Abigail had to believe it would be enough. There was no room to hope anymore.

The Hero Relief Center was empty this late at night. The civilian staff had gone home hours ago. The silence was equal parts comforting and concerning. If her attack on King Arthur went wrong, then no one in the building would get hurt. If her attack on King Arthur went wrong, then no one would know what happened to her, either.

The door to Excalibur's office was open like it usually was even after-hours, allowing Abigail entrance without any fuss. Before his main office space was a tiny, bathroom-sized room that was his assistant's office. Abigail ran her finger across the desk she used to claim. The current assistant decorated the space with cohesive rose gold and pastel purple office supplies. This tiny room was where her second chance of becoming a hero began.

Now, it was where she was potentially ending it.

Abigail moved into Excalibur's office. The number of weapons on the walls had somehow grown in the years. She didn't think there was enough wall space to begin with, but there were several long swords, ornate bows, and dual-headed axes that she didn't recognize. Thankfully, Excalibur's desk wasn't cluttered, and the white envelope was

Combustion

stark in contrast against the dark surface. She scripted his name across the envelope with a black marker.

Abigail left his office, hopefully not for the last time, and returned to hers. As she shut the door behind her, the lamp on her desk flipped on. She sucked in a breath and readied a fireball at the intruder.

"It's just me, babe," Cinder said from the desk chair.

Abigail extinguished her flames. Her heart rate settled back into a normal rhythm. "Did anyone see you?"

He shook his head. "This place is too easy to break into."

Abigail crossed the space and perched herself on the desk next to him. "I gave you my entry codes."

"Are you ready?"

"It's a little too late if I'm not."

Cinder scorched her with his twisted smile before pulling a duffle bag from the floor on to the desk. He removed two pairs of dark tinted glasses about the size of dollar store swimming goggles and a small canister with a pull top.

Abigail examined a pair of goggles. "What're these for?"

"My master plan." Cinder snapped the other pair over his head, and the straps tangled inside his messy hair. He pointed to the canister. "That's a flash bang and it'll create enough noise to deafen you for a few minutes."

"So I won't be affected by King's powers."

"Bingo. The goggles are just to help you see after. They're just a precaution, I hope you don't have to use either."

"You're worried about me." Abigail said smugly.

"Of course, I am." Cinder didn't hide the worry in his rumbling voice. "I'll be just outside if you need help. If I think you need help, I'm coming in."

Neither of them liked the idea of Abigail going in on her own, but it was the better option. If King Arthur saw Cinder at her side, he'd issue a command without hesitation. They'd be brainwashed before they passed through the door. They both refused to become a weapon against each other while in King Arthur's control.

Abigail put both the goggles and the canister inside her jacket pockets. She glanced at the clock. There were a few minutes before she was supposed to meet King Arthur. A few minutes to fit a lifetime of conversations inside.

"I love you," she said knowing it nowhere encompassed everything she wanted him to know.

Cinder blinked, as if the statement confused him. "I love you too, Abigail. I always have."

"Some nights I laid awake wondering where we'd be if things had been different from the very beginning. If anything would have changed if I hadn't been Inferna and you hadn't been Wildfire."

Cinder grabbed her hand and rubbed his thumb over the top of her knuckles. "If you hadn't been a hero, and I hadn't been a villain."

His corrected statement hung heavily between them.

"After tonight," he continued. "After this job is completed, other people won't have to wonder that about themselves. Once we can all be equal."

Abigail closed her eyes and imagined that world. She imagined a world that didn't bully Cold Snap away from her normal teenaged life because her skin was different. She imagined a world that accepted Odo despite his bug-like appendages. She imagined a world where Excalibur could do hero work without the fear of his family being hurt because of it. She imagined a world that didn't force Cinder into being a villain after a single breakdown. She imagined a world that didn't demand you rise above *normality* because you possessed a superpower.

Combustion

She imagined a world that was protected by all people. She imagined a world that didn't need protecting. It was a good world.

Abigail opened her eyes and saw her world. Cinder held her gaze before leaning forward to kiss her. It shouldn't have been a kiss goodbye, but as he pulled away, Abigail's eyes shed two tears.

"After we complete your mission," she said, "We're completing mine."

"What's yours?"

Abigail flipped his hand over and dark blue smoke raised into the air. "Getting you better."

Cinder slipped his hand out of hers, hiding it and the smoke inside the fold of his coat. "Let's finish this."

Abigail reluctantly slid off her desk and headed for the exit. She knew Cinder would be right behind her, but she still watched him over her shoulder until she could no longer see him. His ghost had haunted her for the last year, and now seeing him lounge in the shadows of her workplace made her fear he may still be a ghost. An entity shifting in and out of her reality.

Outside of King Arthur's door, Abigail reached for her sword out of habit but remembered it was missing from her hip. Left in her office with the rest of her Avalon costume. This was just a meeting after all, there was no need to come armed. A foolish thought when both she and King Arthur were deadly without the help of conventional weapons. Abigail inhaled deeply, filling her veins with fire, and entered the office. King Arthur occupied one of the love seats, tossing the decorative sphere between his hands. Lancelot sat across from him, laughing at part of a conversation she walked in on.

Lancelot joined Abigail on the floor with a big grin. "Hey Abby."

"Lance," she greeted a little louder than necessary, hoping Cinder was outside to hear her. "I wasn't expecting you."

His grin faltered slightly.

"I wanted him here." King Arthur set the sphere on the coffee table and joined them. "My new branding affects both of you."

"You're going to love this," Lancelot added, lengthening the vowel in *love*.

Abigail found it difficult to believe him. "We're not ditching the Camelot theme, are we?" she asked with a laugh, wanting to keep the air between them light as the devices inside her pockets grew heavy.

"No way," said Lancelot.

"I propose we change your moniker," King Arthur began. "The Dragon Slayer seems too aggressive for someone like you."

"Someone like me?" Abigail questioned.

"You've really grown into your own, Abigail," King Arthur continued. "The recklessness about you has evaporated. I don't want people to keep seeing you as a sidekick."

Abigail hadn't been a sidekick for years. San Arbor *did* recognize her as a full hero. "Shouldn't Lance be getting the make over? He's been in the hero business less than I."

"Lancelot has also grown into his own." King Arthur smiled at Lancelot. "Like the legendary knight for which he's named. San Arbor recognizes the names of the characters in the legends more so than the locations. I want you to consider changing your hero name from Avalon to Guinevere, the Knight Queen."

Abigail gasped, and dove behind the first defensive shield she thought of. "Shouldn't Merlin take that title? You two are the closest ones on the team. It'd make more since for the two of you to be king and queen."

King Arthur shook his head. "Arthur and Merlin are more recognizable than Arthur and Guinevere."

"In the polls," Lancelot added, "People were more likely to connect Guinevere and Lancelot. It'd make total since for us."

"For us?"

"The rebranding would keep the Knights in pairs."

"There's an uneven number of us, what about Excalibur?" Abigail asked.

"Did no one tell you?" King Arthur asked with fake surprise. "We're getting a new teammate. She comes recommended from Hero Enterprises. Miss Titan sent in her application weeks ago. The younger sister of Rush who wants to take up her brother's mantle to honor him. Keep his legacy alive."

"'Legacy' would be a cool hero name." Lancelot snapped his fingers. "If we could spin it to the Camelot theme, I mean."

King Arthur patted Lancelot on the shoulder, reassuring him that he was on track for a good idea.

Abigail stared at them. She watched the corruption leak from King Arthur into Lancelot. The corruption didn't stop there. Even if this sister came to the HRC without knowing the truth behind Rush and Hero Enterprises, she wouldn't be immune to King Arthur's plans. He needed to be stopped. She wouldn't let him taint another hero.

"What do you think?" Lancelot asked her. "Ready to be my queen?"

"I think that Lancelot was the knight who betrayed the real Britannia king," Abigail stared down King Arthur as she said it.

"I think that king didn't have the power I have to keep his court in line."

Abigail reached inside her pocket and pulled out the canister. She slipped her thumb through the pull tab. Before she was able to activate it, her body froze.

"Stop her." King Arthur's eyes didn't change as he issued the command to Lancelot.

Abigail's arms were pinned against her body by the cold touch of Lancelot's powers. He didn't look at all guilty about his actions.

"I didn't want to believe you, King." Lancelot said, shaking his head. "But you were right. Abigail did turn against us."

Abigail gasped, struggling against the psychic chains around her.

"I hoped I had been wrong too." King Arthur had been practicing his sympathetic looks, because the one he passed between Abigail and Lancelot was almost believable. "Perhaps she didn't turn on her own, perhaps our Abigail is still in there."

"Lance, don't listen to him!" Abigail shouted, losing a bit of breath as each word allowed the pressure to build around her chest. "This isn't what it looks like. King is the villain. Ask him about Dox-Con, about his run for mayor."

Lancelot's eyebrows knitted together. "King being mayor is the best thing for the city. He knows what's best for all of us. I thought you knew that?"

Abigail's attempted protest was squeezed out of her by the building psychic pressure.

"I bet another villain got inside her head," King Arthur speculated, walking toward the phone on his desk. "Maybe she wasn't the best person to send under cover. With Abigail being so easily manipulated and all. I'll call security. We'll need a collar to detain her."

"I'm really sorry, Abbs."

Abigail didn't buy Lancelot's apology. If he was, then he'd try to stop King Arthur as he dialed the phone, or at least pause to hear her side of the story. With the remaining breath inside her lungs, Abigail tried to spit out a blast of blue fire but only bits of molten spit dribbled down her chin.

Behind her, the office door smacked the wall as it burst opened. Lancelot's eyes widened but he didn't have time to react as Cinder

Combustion

rocketed in and sucker punched him in the gut. The psychic hold around Abigail severed. She landed hard on her knees and sucked down oxygen to refill her tank. Cinder flew past her, slamming into a wall, and Lancelot regained his psychic hold over her.

"Lance, please," Abigail rationed the little oxygen she had left, "You don't understand what's going on."

"I understand that this Flame Villain tricked you," Lancelot's voice shook. "He's done it over and over again."

Cinder barked a laugh as he returned to his feet. "I'm going to enjoy this."

King Arthur's eyes shimmered purple, but his command was drowned by the *whoosh* that came from Cinder and the torrent of blue flames he shot at Lancelot.

Lancelot raised a hand, and his psychic energy caught the blue flames. Cinder stepped closer, increasing his fire, and Lancelot's mental hold on Abigail loosened. Blue flames piled in front of Lancelot as his shield kept the flames from burning him. Cinder was a step away. Abigail dropped back onto the floor as Lancelot directed all his power to stop Cinder.

It wasn't enough.

Cinder rushed through the flames and tackled Lancelot, pinning him to the ground and walloping a series of punches to his face to keep him too distracted to summon his powers again. With the commotion of flames gone, King Arthur's eyes turned purple again. Abigail squeezed her eyes shut and pulled the tab on the flash bang. Blinding light submerged the room.

The proximity to the bang created a terrible ringing in Abigail's ears that brought her momentarily to her knees. She gritted her teeth and pulled on the goggles. The opaque whiteness softened, and she saw the shapes of the other occupants of the room. Cinder still had Lancelot on the ground and King Arthur was using the edge of the desk for support to find the exit. Abigail pounced at him, hands burning brilliant red.

Through the goggles, the activation of his powers became two ghostly orbs of purple. The ringing in her ears could fade away at any moment. She refused to be submerged inside that purple ocean again. She refused to become his puppet. Abigail clutched his throat and seared away his vocal cords.

As the ringing subsided, Abigail heard King Arthur's final scream dwindle into a whispered wail and he dropped to his knees.

"I won't let you destroy San Arbor." Abigail bashed her knee against King Arthur's jaw, knocking him out. She lowered him carefully onto the ground and tied his wrists together with the zip tie stored in her pocket.

It became harder to see with the goggles, so Abigail pulled them around her neck. Seeing everything with her real vision solidified what she had done. Her leader lay unconscious on the floor with his neck charred and hands tied behind his back. The threat to her city was detained. After tomorrow, when Excalibur found her note, the threat to people like her, to people like all of them, could be stopped.

The facts of a better world didn't ease the guilt of her actions. King Arthur had been her friend. She didn't know how they became the villains in each other's lives.

"I've been wanting to do that for a while."

Abigail turned to find Cinder standing over an equally unconscious and bound Lancelot. He picked pink bubble gum out of his ears. Steam lifted off his back either from his illness or the rocket launch from before.

"Is he . . ." Abigail couldn't say it, panic slipped into her voice.

"He's not dead." Cinder confirmed and tossed his self-applied earmuffs to the ground.

Relief surged through her. "Will you help me move them?"

"To where?"

Abigail pointed at the two couches. Cinder chuckled.

"Do you think they'd do the same for us?" he asked. "Make sure we were nice and comfy after taking us down?"

"We're not them." Abigail looped her arms through King Arthur's and waited for Cinder to help. "We're the good guys, remember?"

Cinder sighed, but helped Abigail move both King Arthur and Lancelot to the couches so they wouldn't spend the night on the cold floor. Cinder used the remaining zip ties to rope their feet together and tether them to the coffee table.

"He needs line of sight for his powers," Abigail explained as she strapped her goggles to Lancelot's face.

"If you didn't like the gift, you could have just said something," Cinder teased. "What now?"

"We wait for the aftermath," Abigail decided.

"Lucky for you," Cinder grinned, "I'm an expert at laying low."

"Lucky for you, I have a safe house not too far from here."

Chapter Thirty

The seventh-floor unit of the Phoenix Apartment Complex finally had a reason to smell like woodsmoke. The open floor plan welcomed its missing occupant as if no time had passed. Cinder threw open every door, opened every cupboard, left the bathroom light on, convinced the cheap coffee pot to come to life, and laughed at the empty fridge. Some things never changed, and with Cinder claiming the back patio like before, Abigail could forget that everything had.

This was where it began. The intertwining of their lives started on this small balcony with the San Arbor skyline leaning in to hear their secrets. The gutter was still dented from when Abigail used it as a foothold to access the roof. The concrete wall around the patio still sported scorch marks from a misplaced fireball. Cinder still picked the gold and blue coffee mug with a crack in the handle.

Abigail leaned against the patio ledge next to Cinder. He wrapped his arm around her waist and hauled her closer to him. They stared at San Arbor and her cotton candy-colored sunrise. The beautiful and jagged cityscape stared back, still hungry for their secrets. Abigail only offered it their future.

A tiny promise made up of tiny pleasures like old coffee, soft pajamas, and casual touches that still enticed goosebumps. A future that could include growing snow carrots outside a mountain cottage and selling them overpriced to tourists at a roadside stand. Abigail leaned deeper into Cinder. Their body heat sealing the promise of her dreams.

Of a future together. Like they had before.

A future they could obtain after the ramifications of tonight came forward.

Abigail pulled her phone from her pocket. There were no notifications. She knew not to expect any until morning, until Excalibur found her note. Until someone found King Arthur and Lancelot. Knowing that didn't stop her from opening the news application and searching for anything related to King Arthur and their attack against him. The application mirrored the coming dawn around them: stagnant and quiet.

"You'll drive yourself crazy doing that, doll." Cinder's jaw moved against Abigail's head as he spoke, looking down at her phone. "All we can do is wait."

Abigail slid her phone back inside her pocket. "I'm a terrible waiter."

"Don't I know it," he chuckled.

Blue smoke hadn't stopped rolling out of the collar of his shirt since they left the HRC. In the dark, Abigail could almost pretend it wasn't happening, but this close to him there was no denying it. Not when it shifted in front of her, blocking her vision, tangling inside her hair, or buzzing across her ears. She laced their hands together.

"Are you okay?"

Cinder smiled. "No."

Abigail's hands tightened.

"I will be though, promise."

"Was it from the fight?"

"The rocketing, I think." Cinder's low voice drifted around them like the smoke. Some words coming into focus easier than the others. "I try not to ignite that much of me anymore."

Abigail slipped a hand free and pressed it against his forehead and recoiled back. "You're burning up."

"We do that."

Abigail frowned at his attempted joke. "I meant as in a fever."

Cinder reclaimed her hand. "I know."

"You should lay down."

"With you?"

Abigail knocked her shoulder against his, causing them both to laugh. The joyous sounds like lightning bugs in the darkness. Like hope in the face of illness.

"I love you, Cinder," Abigail said before the fireflies could vanish.

"I love you, Abigail. Forever."

Suddenly, forever felt too short.

Abigail kissed him. It felt like a car crash. Her heart jerked. It sounded like a car crash. Crunching metal ricocheted around them. It was a crash. Too real and too close.

She pulled away and looked over the patio ledge. A car's engine smoked from where it rammed into a stoplight pole. Sparks rained down from the power box, striking the dark street in flashes of color. From her distance, Abigail didn't see the driver, but she did see someone standing in the middle of the street, dusting his hands together.

"Warden," Abigail gasped.

"Shit." Cinder mirrored her panic.

"What's he doing here?" Abigail looked between Cinder and him. "Did he cause that crash?"

"Probably." Cinder pulled away from her, reaching through the patio door to claim his jacket.

"What's he doing here?" Abandoning her coffee mug on the ledge, she caught the red domino mask Cinder threw at her.

"Not sure, but whatever the reason, it's not a good one."

The dark street shimmered alive with brilliant colors as rainbow sparks clashed against the pavement. It was too bright to come just from the power box. Abigail leaned over the patio to better see the street. Three people merged out of the shimmering vortex of color and stood with Warden. One of them handed him a megaphone. Cinder muttered a second curse.

"Do you know these guys?" Abigail asked.

"Unfortunately. They were Warden's top picks for my operation, but I didn't hire them. The Mora Brothers are loose cannons and money-hungry mercenaries. They'd ruin my plans."

"I guess they lined up with Warden's."

"I know you're there, Cinder," Warden's megaphone-amplified voice carried over the building. "Abigail too."

Abigail's eyes widened. Not only did Warden know her address, but he knew her name. He knew Avalon's secret identity.

"Tech." Both she and Cinder whispered to each other.

"Make this easy for me," Warden continued. "Come down here and surrender. Your ideas are too weak to do any good. You've aligned yourself with the heroes, and now you're my enemy."

The Mora Brothers conducted an intimidating show of their abilities: one created an arc of colorful sparks that jolted to the nearest electronic and shorted it out, one fired metal balls from the tips of his fingers into the side of the car sounding like a machine gun, and the third bashed his fist into the asphalt, forming a crater around him. The Mora Brothers were starving wolves, and their all-you-can-eat buffet was San Arbor.

"Making things equal won't make anything better," Warden shouted. "We were born better for a reason and we're going to be on top because of it."

"He's a mad man." Flames encircled Abigail's wrist. Staring down at the crazed criminal she saw a flash of King Arthur. They were different sides of the same coin. Both needed to be stopped, but Abigail was certain this man could never change like she hoped King Arthur could. "We need to free King and Lance."

"What?" Cinder snarled.

"These villains are being set loose in San Arbor and two of the strongest heroes are tied up on a couch!"

Cinder grinned; in the face of pure chaos, it was pure beauty. "San Arbor has the best hero right here."

"Now's not the time." Abigail still smiled at his compliment.

With his thumb on the megaphone's trigger, Warden's orders to the Mora Brothers floated to the patio. "You two, do your worse in the city, flush out all the heroes. Kill them all."

Two of the brothers disappeared in a vortex of color.

Cinder leapt onto the patio ledge. "I'll buy you some time. Do you have your gear here?"

Abigail shook her head. "My suit's at HQ, but I have some flame-resistant prototypes."

"I'll see you down there." Cinder stepped off the ledge. Brilliant blue fire encased his boots and allowed him to walk to the street like he was on an invisible staircase.

The prototypes hidden inside a shoebox on the top shelf of Abigail's closet had been made as a favor from the HRC costuming department. The T-shirt and jeans looked normal but were made with material similar to her Avalon cape to prevent them from burning away if Abigail needed to activate her full powers while off the clock. Once President Samuels found out about the project, he canceled it, claiming it would be better for Abigail to control her abilities when not on patrol. Abigail didn't know why she hadn't returned the clothing pieces at the time, but she was grateful for it now.

Once dressed, she followed Cinder's exit and jumped off the edge. On the street, Cinder summoned a fire wall to separate himself from Warden and the Mora Brother who shot metal from his fingertips. The

Combustion

flames caused the villains to pause and allowed Abigail a safe opportunity to land beside Cinder.

"Do you think there's more Warden supporters?" she asked.

"If there are, I haven't seen them." Cinder added more fire into the wall so it could sustain itself. "Can you take Mora? I'll keep Warden distracted?"

"I'll help you as soon as I'm done."

"Take your time," Cinder smirked, but it didn't hide the discomfort in his eyes. More smoke lifted off him than the wall of flames.

"Leave some of the big guy for me." Abigail knocked her knuckles together, igniting them with blazing cherry-red fire. Her real request hung unspoken between them: don't push yourself.

Abigail commanded her flames over her forearms and used them as a shield to bypass Cinder's wall and then tackled the Mora brother before he could unleash a metal barrage. They tumbled to the ground. Warden shouted at them but was cut off by Cinder's assault. The Mora Brother bit down on Abigail's arm as she pinned him to the ground. The bite was more intense than she expected and warm blood slid down her wrist. She yanked herself free and saw a flash of metal inside the Mora Brother's mouth before his teeth phased back to bone. She leapt up and kicked him hard in the ribs.

Her toes ached and a sharp pain shot through her foot. Hobbling backward, Abigail created her flame armor around herself.

"If you can believe it," the Mora Brother returned to his feet, spitting Abigail's blood from his mouth, "I've got the strongest punch between my brothers. Want me to demonstrate?"

"The problem with punches is that you have to reach me first."

Abigail exhaled the sulfur building inside her throat and smothered the brother in blue fire. Whatever metal the Mora Brother was able to produce was surprisingly flame resistant, and a series of tiny bullets shot through the fire and banged into Abigail. The armor rendered the shots to paintballs. She gritted her teeth and leapt at him again. She hammered a combo of fire covered punches against his burnt face and neck.

She did a better job at singeing away his hair and shirt collar than slowing him down.

The Mora Brother slapped the side of Abigail's head with a hand that felt more like a cast iron skillet. She crumpled to the ground. The star splattered sky drifted so close to Abigail that she reached up to try and catch one. Instead of a hallucinated star, she caught a metal ball shot by the Mora Brother. The pain snapped her back into reality.

With her body covered in flames, Abigail slammed into the Mora Brother. She increased her temperature until the asphalt turned sticky under them. The Mora Brother melted into a puddle of bone and metal. Pieces of flesh bubbled and popped. The image was grotesque, but the victory was required.

Further down the street, Cinder still battled Warden. Chain gauntlets wrapped around Warden's arms with tubing connecting them to a power supply on his back. The lime green device amplified Warden's attacks tenfold and absorbed all the fire Cinder shot at him.

Worse than all of that, Cinder was slowing down. He took more hits than he could dish out. Blood smeared across his face and down his shirt. He dropped to a knee.

Abigail tried to run to him, but a hand wrapped around her ankle. She looked behind her, fearing the undead heroes from her nightmare but found the Mora Brother instead. The metal in his exoskeleton was reconnecting and fresh skin grew out from the charred remains of his face.

Abigail would have preferred the zombies.

Combustion

"We're not finished yet." The Mora Brother's jaw trembled with each word.

Abigail kicked him hard in the mouth, but the Mora Brother continued his reconstruction and stood up. It didn't matter how many times she would burn him down; Abigail wouldn't stop until the regeneration met its limit. She spat her Dragon's Breath on her knuckles turning the fire blue, and readied her next attack.

A scream behind her stopped Abigail. She turned to see Cinder lying face down on the street. Warden, sadistic and sick, loomed over him. Blood dripped off Warden's hands like the sparks of Abigail's flames did hers.

A handful of metal bullets assaulted Abigail's back. The pain caused her vision to spot, and blood filled her mouth as she bit her tongue.

"Wildfire!"

The call came from above. Cold Snap dropped toward Abigail and blasted the Mora Brother with ice until he was encased completely. The glacier steamed in the heated night. Cold Snap landed beside it and Odo fluttered down on his dragonfly wings. Abigail had never been so happy to see a pair of killers.

"What are you doing here?" Abigail asked, then shook her head. "We need to help Cinder."

Abigail turned just in time to see Warden leaping through a doorway made of rainbow light. On the other side of the portal, she glimpsed one of the other Mora Brothers and a downtown fountain. Cinder struggled to his feet. Dark blue energy pulsed out of him, and his skin flickered with the same glowing energy. The glowing orbs of his eyes searched the empty street for something.

For her.

"What's happening?" Cold Snap asked, covering her mouth with her hand.

I'm overheating. Cinder's admission echoed in Abigail's head. She needed to cool him down, and fast.

Abigail grabbed Odo and Cold Snap's hands making them both look at her. "I need you two to help my city. Warden and two more of his goons are downtown. The heroes won't get there in time so it's up to you. Please."

"What about him?" Odo asked.

"I'll take care of Cinder."

"We'll take care of San Arbor," Cold Snap promised.

Cold Snap squeezed Abigail's hand before linking her arm through Odo's who lifted them into the air.

"I'll find you when I'm done!" Abigail shouted up at them.

Cinder stood statuesque on the dark asphalt. Blue energy pulses reflected haunting shadows against him. The fire inside him cracked through his skin, marring him in a road map of lines. His hands gripped the sides of his head, trying to hold himself together. Energy waves lapped against Abigail. The cerulean waves should have belonged on a tropical beach where they both sat together in the sand. Instead, they burned her.

San Arbor faded away as Abigail approached him. The cosmic level heat singed the hairs on her arms, but she didn't care. Nothing would keep her from him. Cinder slowly devolved into a supernova. Abigail reached out to catch the falling star. In the dreams where she was unable to do so, she finally caught the brilliant light. Cinder's face was as soft as petals on a stargazer lily. She slid her hands between his and held his face.

"Cinder."

Combustion

His glowing eye sockets flickered until the emerald wastelands returned. The cracks in his skin lifted and he managed a smile, leaning into Abigail's touch.

"Hey doll."

Abigail heated her hands, like before in the loft, and pushed her flames into him but nothing happened. The pulsing increased. Energy waves slammed into her chest. Each impact hotter than before. The air between them grew thin. Abigail's eyes watered.

"It's not working," she said, panic rising.

"This feels different." Cinder shivered, his entire body shaking, as the energy escaped his body in double time. "Dr. Hilgard said this may happen."

"What would happen?" Abigail rushed through her question while Cinder had chewed over each of his words.

He didn't remove his gaze from hers, his eyes switching between ethereal blue and solid green. "I'd overheat to a point where I couldn't cool off."

"What does that mean?" Abigail knew the answer, but she clutched onto the hope of her caught fallen star.

"This is killing me, Abigail."

Tears erupted from her eyes. They burned away the moment they landed on her face.

Cinder cupped her cheek, mirroring her touch. They gripped each other as solar flares tried to pull them apart. Red and blue sparks drifted into the air above them. It probably looked beautiful to an outsider; to someone who couldn't feel Abigail shattering.

"Unless something stops me," Cinder said with an otherworldly calmness to his thunderstorm voice, "This energy will explode. It'll kill a lot more people than just me. I don't want that to happen."

Her tears made Abigail's voice raw and hoarse. "Tell me what to do."

"Kill me before this disease does."

Abigail couldn't breathe. Her entire world crumbled beneath her feet. The only thing holding her up was his scarred hands. His shifting eyes searched hers. She wondered if he saw the snapshots of their lives together and their lives to come filling her subconscious. She had lost him once before, and now he was asking her to lose him again. Forever.

"Abigail, please," he whispered. "We're running out of time."

Either she kill him and save San Arbor, or this energy rips through him destroying both. Either way, Abigail was losing her home.

"I'm tired of saying goodbye," she choked out.

He squeezed her cheek. Flakes of darkened skin on his hand broke away in a wave of energy. "This is the last time."

"How should I do it?"

"The least painful way would be nice." Cinder still managed to smile, and it forced more tears from Abigail.

Abigail kissed him for the final time. His rough lips sparked against hers as she pulled him close. The scent of woodsmoke consumed her. His scarred hands ran up her arms. Abigail kissed Cinder goodbye for the final time.

As she pulled away, tears and soot dirtying her face, she summoned her flames, her very soul, into her hands and pressed them against the side of Cinder's head. He placed his hands over hers and nodded, his crooked smirk claiming his face. Red sparks shimmered like a summertime sparkler against him but had no effect. The blue energy carried the fire away in quickening pulses. Abigail inhaled and tried harder.

The cherry-red sparks morphed to purple before becoming blue. The most brilliant blue flames danced around her fingers and poured into the cracks of Cinder's skin, smothering the fire inside him. Cinder leaned into her hands, sighing as the fire singed away his pain.

Silent tears raced down Abigail's face as her fire snuffed out his life force.

"I love you, doll."

Cinder spoke his final words with smoke oozing from his mouth and eyes before the fire inside extinguished completely. He fell forward into Abigail's arms. She shook violently as sobs wracked her body. She fell to her knees and clutched Cinder's burned and lifeless body to herself. He dissolved to ash in her arms. Blowing away with a gust of wind.

Her city was saved, but at a cost she could never recover from.

Chapter Thirty-One

Abigail forced herself to stand. Her body smothered with ash in a heartbreaking suit of armor. Blue fire burned around her wrist, licking up her skin as familiar as her original cherry-red flames. The high temperature bit into her palms and kept her conscious enough to move forward. The coveted blue flames she quested after her whole hero career were finally hers. She'd give them back, give everything back, to rewrite the last few minutes of her life.

Good job, hero.

Even in death, she heard his voice so clearly in her mind.

The fire bit into her skin again, bringing her away from unobtainable wants and foolish hopes.

"A hero saves people," Abigail reminded herself. "And right now, this city needs saving."

Fueled by a calm rage burning up her sadness, Abigail headed for the downtown. Only one person was to blame for Cinder's death. Abigail was ready to return the favor to Warden and whoever else he brought to San Arbor.

Finding Warden was easy. He and his goons left a trail of breadcrumbs in the form of upturn vehicles, trashcan fires, broken ATMs, and frightened civilians. Abigail extinguished the fires she encountered and tried to ease the cowering civilians' fears, but without her sword and costume, she looked like one of the deranged villains causing the damage. The trail led to downtown, as she expected, and she found the fountain depicted inside the portal. The angel's outstretched arms were broken off and drowning in water. Ice covered half the fountain's pedestal.

"Wildfire!"

Combustion

What little remained of her hope drained away knowing she would be the only one responding to his name. The real Wildfire was dead.

Abigail turned in the direction of the voice. Cold Snap and Odo hovered in the air. Below them, one of the Mora Brothers laid on the ground, impaled with icicles. Cold Snap created another spear in her hands.

"Where's Warden?" Abigail called out to them.

"Right here." Warden dropped down from the fountain, hidden behind the angel's marble wings. The strange contraption around his arms glowed green before connecting into the battery pack. "San Arbor is the perfect place to begin my reign."

Abigail's blue fire encased her arms and snapped wildly around her. "You're not the first villain to threaten my city."

"I will be the last." Warden's arrogance scraped down Abigail's spine. He eyed the downtown buildings with a predatory hunger. He stepped out of the fountain, crushing one of the discarded arms under his boot, and approached Abigail. "Where's your partner?"

The disgusting glint in his eye was proof he knew exactly the type of state he left Cinder in.

"This ends now." Sulfuric smoke escaped Abigail's mouth and she unleashed a shimmering breath of fire at him.

The water turned to steam and covered the plaza in thick fog. Abigail tracked Warden by the flickering lights emitted by the battery pack. She attacked him recklessly and relentlessly, slamming her burning fists into his chest, head, arms, into every inch of him. Warden tried to grab her. Abigail increased her fire, and Warden whirled away before the flames could burn him too severely.

Abigail chased him, rounding the fountain as he tried to flee. An enhanced fist waited for her behind the angel's gown and punched her in the nose. Her vision spotted and blood dripped down her chin. As she blinked away the pain, a second enhanced punch connected with her gut and knocked Abigail down. Warden cackled in the fog. On her hands and knees, Abigail scrambled backwards to get out of range of a third attack. She desperately and unsuccessfully tried to inhale, her broken nose blocking her airway. Part of the fountain shattered, adding more dust to the fog, and Warden howled painfully in the debris.

A pocket of air cleared around Abigail as Odo lowered Cold Snap to the ground. Her icy hands pressed against Abigail's face without consent and cracked her nose back into place. Abigail inhaled deeply and her fire returned to her veins.

"Thanks." Abigail stood with the support of Cold Snap.

Cold Snap spoke quickly. "There's one more Mora Brother on the loose and we've seen some looters breaking into stores. I've never seen Warden this . . . crazy."

"Leave Warden to me," Abigail ordered. "Find and take down the other brother."

"You don't look good." Cold Snap said.

Abigail didn't feel good. "I wouldn't be a good hero if a few super strength punches kept me down."

"Hero?" Cold Snap's eyes widened.

Abigail didn't give her time to process the reveal. "Stay with Odo, keep each other safe."

"We can keep you—!"

Abigail shoved Cold Snap away before she finished her statement. A massive hand tangled inside Abigail's hair and hauled her out of the dust cloud. Abigail slammed onto the plaza ground. She summoned a shield of fire before Warden stomped down on her rib cage. She rolled to the side and sprang up. Warden had said he recognized her fighting style so he would know how to counter it. Abigail needed to improvise. She needed to be reckless.

Commanding blue fire to her hands, Abigail propelled herself into the air and slammed into Warden, wrapping her hands around his tree trunk of a neck. Ignoring the fire, Warden peeled her hands off him, squeezing her wrist so tightly she thought the bones would snap. Abigail heel kicked him and scrambled out of his grasp. He shook out his scorched hands. The machines on his back flashed. The veins on his throat crawled onto the sides of his face. He charged Abigail like a missile.

Abigail charged back.

She shot her brilliant blue flames out of her palms and tried to burn him away before Warden made impact. The machines absorbed as much of the fire as they could, but they shrilled and wined, and Abigail knew they had reached their limit. Warden ducked to the side to avoid a head on collision with Abigail.

Refusing to let him escape, she forced her flames into a dome around them. Dangerous looking solar flares burst through the blue dome and shattered like lightning above them.

Abigail wiped the blood off her face with the back of her hand. "I'm placing you under arrest for your crimes against San Arbor."

"Think a little cage will hold me?" Warden spat. "Besides, once I tell the world Avalon helped kill the heroes in Tennyson City, you'll be sitting in a cell yourself. Unless, you plan on bending the law for you, too."

"If my people find me guilty, I'll arrest myself."

"There's no way in hell you're going to stop me!" Warden rushed her, both hands pulled back and ready to strike.

Abigail summoned flames to her feet and used the extra force to flip over Warden, yanking out the tubes on his power supply. The machine sparked violently, and chemicals poured from the pipes, soaking Warden. The flames leapt at the fuel like wild dogs.

The explosion was instantaneous.

A ballet of dark blue and bright orange light forced Abigail out of the dome and shattered the construct. She slid several feet on her back until the remains of the fountain's base stopped her. Blinding sunlight curved around the angel's remaining wing above her. If it wasn't for the pain, it would have been a beautiful morning.

A crowd of people had formed around the plaza by the time Abigail stood, pulling herself up with the remains of the statue. She shielded her eyes from the sun and tried to smile at them. She needed to reassure them that things would be okay. Her smile was stained with blood. Her thin mask slipped around her neck. She was too tired to notice.

"Please stay back." Abigail's voice sounded like her insides felt, raw and pummeled. This was nowhere near the voice of a hero.

A police officer didn't listen and cautiously approached Abigail. "Avalon? Is that actually you?"

She nodded. "A villain is still here. It's not safe. Please, stay back."

The plaza shifted around her. The sky spun like a tilt-o-whirl. Abigail braced for a fall, but the officer caught her.

"It looks to me like you got him."

Abigail tried to turn around and see where Warden ended up, but the officer stopped her.

"I'm not sure you want to see that."

He was probably right. From the horrid expressions of the people around her, Abigail was sure Warden did not survive the blast. Abigail leaned into the police officer as her legs began shutting down. "Sorry," she muttered, closing her eyes.

"It's okay." The officer adjusted his arm to better support her. "For all you do for us, it's nice to help."

The air around them dipped in temperature and Abigail heard the soft humming of Odo's wings. She opened her eyes and readied herself for her next fight. She readied herself to defend Cold Snap and Odo from the crowd.

But a fight didn't come. Only applause.

"That's the lady who saved my life!" someone shouted.

"And he helped save my store!"

Abigail smiled. The last thing she saw was Cold Snap waving at the crowd, shouting, "Hi'ya everybody!"

Chapter Thirty-Two

Abigail hobbled up the ramp to the backdoor of the San Arbor police station, gripping the handrail to help ease pressure off her injured leg. Her Avalon costume hid most of the bandages wrapping around her torso and limbs, but her mask didn't hide the bruises blossoming under each eye from her broken nose. Looking down at her hands, her knuckles slowly scabbing over, and the backs of her hands cut and scraped, she wished she wore gloves.

As the backdoor opened, she straightened, gritting her teeth to appear strong and stable. When it was the same officer who had caught her the morning of the battle, she relaxed. Officer Matteo Hardin helped her the rest of the way into the empty hallway. The warm area comforted Abigail and she was probably the only one grateful for the broken AC system.

"I really appreciate you doing this for me," Abigail said as he moved the brick away from the door that kept it open. "I won't be long."

"We'll have to record the meeting," Matteo explained, "But it won't be leaked anywhere. Just for legal reasons."

"I understand." Abigail followed him through the precinct. "Do they need a lawyer?"

"Depends." Matteo talked over his shoulder, leading her deeper into the station. "Is this an interrogation?"

Abigail swallowed. It wasn't for him, but she imagined he would have questions for her. She hoped she had sufficient answers. Something to make him understand. Their plan hadn't included anything after the take down. Either because the outcome could've been too messy to successfully plan around, or because Cinder knew he wouldn't be a part of it.

"I'll be there too."

Officer Matteo's voice pulled Abigail from her encroaching thoughts. The overhead lights burned too brightly, the warm and stagnant air pressed around her too tightly, the memories of Cinder's death choked her. She shook her head, attempting to reset her mind. She was here with a purpose. She needed to complete it before submerging herself into his memories. She needed to submerge the foolish hope that he had escaped this death too.

"With us being collared, you'll be the strongest person there. I'm glad to have you on my side of the glass." Abigail wasn't sure if it was fear or uncertainty she heard in Matteo's tone, but she tried to address both.

Matteo unlocked a steel door, and they entered a holding room. Three of the walls were constructed with iron bars. "You don't mind wearing one?"

"Not at all," she lied. The idea of losing her flames twisted her stomach in terrible knots. To have her fire removed, even temporarily, worried her. She'd be defenseless. She may not get it back. She may lose her final piece of Cinder. Her hands heated and blue sparks tickled the inside of her palms. "If this is the only way to talk to him, I want to do it."

Matteo handed her a power collar. It looked identical to the one Warden made her wear in Tennyson City. It sapped away her powers in the same way. Goosebumps ran up her arms. She snapped her fingers and produced only sound. Matteo continued their path through the holding cells. Several contained people caught looting the city, and two of the Mora Brothers were collared, stored behind glass and steel.

Abigail paused at the second to last cell. He didn't need to activate his powers to command her; Abigail became ensnared by his cold and hateful glare. King Arthur didn't look at all like the king of legend locked inside a prison cell. His boyish brown curls matted against his forehead, matching stubble crawled across his cheeks, the orange jumpsuit hung off him like it tried to get away. The dark purple rings under his tired eyes matched the dark purple burn encasing his throat. She doubted he needed the collar with his vocal cords still damaged. Abigail didn't know if they would ever heal.

She hurried past his cell.

Officer Matteo rapped his knuckles against the last cell. The sound matched Abigail's heartbeat currently residing in her throat.

"You have a visitor."

Lancelot glanced at the door from his seat at the attached metal desk. He had rolled his orange sleeves over his elbows. It was the only piece of personality in the cold room that matched King Arthur's. Lancelot's cold eyes matched their leader's, too. When they connected with Abigail's, his gazed morphed into a matching glare.

"Why are you here?"

Abigail was surprised he spoke at all. She was not surprised he fixed his gaze in front of him, refusing to look at her.

"I needed to see you."

"I don't want to see you." His statement slapped her.

She would take it. "You can just listen, please."

"Listen to you lie your way out of this? Avy, you're a villain. You're as bad as them all. I can't believe you folded under him so easily. We were heroes together."

If she wasn't collared, Abigail knew fire would have raced up her arms. She exhaled like she might still combust anyway. "I was still helping people, taking out the bad guys."

"I wasn't a bad guy!" Lancelot snapped his attention from the wall to Abigail, his eyes rimmed in red. "Not to our people. My friends. Never to you."

"I don't think you are." The softness of Abigail's voice clashed against his outburst. "But I think you were being used. By King Arthur. I think he was using all of us to take over San Arbor in his own way."

Lancelot shook his head. "Do not pin this on King. He knows what this city needs. I believed that when I joined the Knights, and I do now. I bet you did too."

"King used his powers on me so that I couldn't save Gerald. He made it a show against Benton. I was his pawn."

"Is that why you turned on us? Because King hurt your feelings?"

Abigail pressed her hands against the glass wall between them. "Lancelot, please, think about this. I know you; I know you're a hero. You want to do good, and King probably made you think doing things his way was the only way to do good. You're better than that."

Lancelot was still. Abigail hoped he was returning to her. Returning to the Lancelot she knew as her sidekick.

"Why are you telling me this?" he asked coldly. "It won't make me forgive you."

Abigail dropped her hands. His words hurt her deeper than she expected them to. She backed away from him. "I just wanted you to understand why."

Abigail followed Matteo away from her old teammates. Neither of them felt chatty after the exchange with Lancelot. Both were silent as Matteo unlocked the collar from her neck. While his back was turned, Abigail snapped her fingers and breathed in the warmth of the blue flame dancing atop her fingers. On the other side of the cell block, the door marked *Evidence* tempted Abigail closer.

"Did you all get a copy of the documents?" she asked Matteo.

"Two," he answered. "One the HRC sent over and a second set that Mayor Benton dropped off. I guess he didn't think you'd give us one."

Abigail sighed. "I can't say I'm surprised."

"We also tracked down the shell account you flagged."

"You found the weapon?" She turned to him. "Do you know what it does?"

Matteo looked around, double checking the expansive hallways on either side of him, and beckoned her forward into the evidence room. Matteo swiped his badge against the caged door and nodded at the officer sitting at the desk.

"Careful, Hardin," the officer at the desk warned. "Chain of custody and all."

"Nothing's going to leave a box," Matteo assured. "Just need to confirm this is what Avalon saw."

"Right." The officer eyed Abigail but allowed them through.

Matteo approached the nearest shelf. Wrapped in a plastic bag was a lime green personal recorder with a six-pointed star emblazoned on the side. "Don't touch."

Abigail raised on her tiptoes to better see the device. "What does it do?"

"Don't know, none of us want the King to test it. But the tag it came with read 'digitalize.' What do you think it means?"

"Nothing good." King Arthur's powers were limited to line of sight and his target hearing his original voice. If this thing could reproduce his commands on a digital scale, then no one would be safe from King Arthur's control. "You should destroy it."

"Don't," commented the officer from the front of the room.

"I can't," Matteo said, then lower for just Abigail to hear, "Maybe after their trial."

Abigail smiled.

Chapter Thirty-Three

The news anchors didn't look any different in real life compared to the digital counter parts Abigail was used to seeing. Without the flashy studio lights their makeup lines were harsher. Channel 9's Greg Grindle didn't seem to enjoy the summer heat and kept checking his suit jacket for sweat stains. His co-anchor, Isadora Banks, held her composure far easier than him and made small talk with other new station personnel between guests.

The plaza fountain still lay in ruined piles. The gathering press and civilians made themselves comfortable in the small areas deemed safe by the city. In the days since the attack, the reveal of King Arthur, the arrest of Camellia Diaz, the death of Cinder, no one had picked up the rubble. Supposedly, the broken fountain was a symbol that although San Arbor was attacked, she was not defeated. Abigail was sure it had something to do with a shortage of manpower or leaving it for the backdrop for the press conference.

The media loved making a scene.

Cold Snap and Odo sat to the left of the stage. They were being honored as San Arbor's saviors. In the crowd of people someone was handing out handmade T-shirts with their faces on them. Mayor Owen Benton and President Quin Samuels were currently at the Channel 9 mobile news desk sandwiched between the two anchors.

According to the schedule, Avalon was supposed to make a speech after this segment. She didn't have a clue what she'd say. Hiding inside the shadow of a building corner, she hoped they'd forget about her.

"President Samuels," Isadora Banks prompted. "What will happen to the Hero Relief Center now?"

"I wish I had a better answer Isadora, but right now we're not sure." President Samuels wore matching cherry-red cufflinks, tie and handkerchief. "Obviously, we want to continue serving San Arbor and relieve the duties of her first responders, but I know some major changes will need to be made. I don't think anyone expects us to start back up like normal after what happened."

"After your golden hero tried taking over the power grid," Mayor Benton butted in.

President Samuels frowned. "Yes. King Arthur appears to have been involved with some questionable actions that are still being investigated."

"Now that King Arthur and Lancelot are out of the Knights, will a new leader take their place?" Greg Grindle asked.

"When we are ready to make that announcement, you will all have a first-row seat." President Samuels smiled.

Isadora Banks absorbed his charming energy and shifted the conversation as her producer held up his hand signaling them to wrap up. "If the HRC is looking to recruit any new heroes, I bet I know where two new applicants could be found."

"Yes," Samuels agreed. "It would be foolish to let those two go too far."

From the side of the booth, Cold Snap gave the stage two thumbs up.

Greg Grindle turned to the camera and said, "Coming up next, we'll have a word with San Arbor's Avalon. She not only defeated the dastardly villain who attacked this very plaza three days ago in an attempt to take over the city, but also has created a winning record of taking down corrupt heroes here and in Tennyson City. Stay tuned, Channel 9's exclusive coverage will be right back."

Abigail pushed herself off the building's cool wall. Apparently, they hadn't forgotten her. Her Avalon costume and the makeup applied by HRC media hid most of her injuries from the fight before, but the crowd still parted as she approached the stage. President Samuels waited at the walk up for her, and waited for Benton to pass before asking, "Any word from Excalibur?"

Abigail shook her head. He and Merlin were at the correctional center with King Arthur and Lancelot. "I doubt we'll hear anything for a while."

Samuels ran his hand through his hair breaking it apart in a frenzy. "I never in a million years thought this would happen when we first started the HRC. Arthur only wanted to help people."

Abigail touched Samuels' arm. "I think, in a way, he was still trying to. Tennyson City's heroes couldn't eliminate crime, so they controlled it. The power became too good to pass up. King's plan would have eliminated the crime, but also San Arbor's freedom."

Samuels sighed. "I guess even being a superhero you can still make mistakes."

"We're still humans, sir."

"Save some face for us?" Samuels asked with a grin. "I'm not sure how we'll recover from this."

Abigail nodded, unable to confirm a promise she doubted she could keep, and joined the anchors on their mobile stage.

"Avalon," Isadora Banks greeted, reapplying her lipstick while the cameras were off. "Thanks for coming on, are you feeling okay?"

"Not in the slightest."

Both anchors stared at her, fear brimming in their eyes.

Abigail chuckled and lied, "I'm kidding. Yeah, I feel fine."

Greg Grindle chuckled back, it sounding as awkward as hers and finished his prep work. The cameras flashed on, and Abigail still hadn't decided on what to say, or how she was supposed to help the HRC.

"Welcome back," Greg Grindle said into the camera lens. "As promised, here is Avalon herself, the Dragon Slayer. Welcome to the show."

"Thank you for having me."

"We'll leave the stage to you, hero." Isadora Banks scooted her chair a few inches away from Abigail.

Abigail glanced between the cameras and the crowd. She should recall the fight with a smile, entertain the audience and keep them distracted from the horror laying around her. The fountain wasn't the only thing yet to be cleaned up, and Abigail saw the dark smear that had once been Warden's obliterated body. She wasn't a good hero.

"The events in Tennyson City and my assault against King Arthur were not legal," she began. "I will face any legal action and punishment that San Arbor sees fit for me. Heroes are not above any law, and those with powers who don't choose this profession aren't below any law either."

"Avalon, I hardly think anyone blames you—"

Abigail cut the reporter off. "My involvement in Tennyson City came about because I believed in a man who said there needed to be equality between those with powers and those without. That those who abuse their position needed to be stopped. I've murdered, I've stolen, and I've lied to all of you."

The excited demeanor of the crowd dropped, and hushed whispers filled the air. President Samuels gaped at her. This was clearly not how he thought she'd help the company. She still wasn't sure how to do that, if the company could even be saved. If being a superhero was even the answer.

Abigail stood up, her heart thumping in her chest, and ripped off her mask. "My name is Abigail Turner, and I am no hero."

Both Greg Grindle and Isadora Banks gasped. The cameras zoomed onto Abigail's face. President Samuels leapt onto the stage. Abigail ignored all of them and addressed the crowd.

"We can all be heroes, we can all be good people, and that doesn't require special powers or a mask," Abigail rambled quickly on, her words coming faster than her mind could filter them. "This is the future I see for the HRC. A future that isn't celebrity endorsed. A future that doesn't pit San Arbor's protectors against each other. All of us together can make San Arbor the best city. All of us can be heroes."

The plaza was quiet. The reporters stumbled for a proper reaction. President Samuels shook his head, his mouth mirroring a fish's searching for air. Abigail's face heated; perhaps she'd gone too far.

"Yeah!" Cold Snap shouted. "I want a future like that."

The harsh mummers morphed into agreements and applause.

Abigail beamed at all of them. Not her citizens that needed protecting, but her equals. The officer who had caught her whistled loudly. Even Mayor Benton added in a few claps.

Greg Grindle composed himself and set the show up for a commercial break. Abigail, with a strange bounce in her step, joined President Samuels.

"That wasn't what I expected," he admitted.

Abigail patted his shoulder. "I'm sure you can clean it up, sir. Also, I'm resigning effective immediately."

"What?"

Her decision shocked both of them, but Abigail held on to her conviction. "I think I can do a lot more as just me."

"Vigilantism is a crime. Avalon you can't be—"

"Abigail. My name is Abigail," she corrected with a grin. "Thank you for every chance you've given me, but I think I have to do this next part on my own."

"At least sleep on it," President Samuels grasped for straws. "I can't file any paperwork until Monday. At least sleep on it."

"You're the president and you can't push paper until Monday?" she chuckled.

"We do have rules," his expression softened. "Rules that are in place to keep us from going out of line."

"I'll sleep on it." Abigail said. "But I probably won't change my mind. There needs to be change."

"And this change starts with you revealing your secret identity and turning in your mask?"

"Pretty reckless, right?"

"It's pretty you," he corrected.

Good job, hero.

Epilogue

Abigail ushered the group forward. Several of the people she knew from the weekly meeting sessions, several more she recognized from sporadic visits to the center, and several more were live-in residents at the Cinder Center for Powered Individuals. Excited chatter raised above the crowd, especially from the younger attendees. They rapidly fired questions they wanted to ask the coming guest. A girl clutched a magazine to her chest. The cover matched the poster she had in her dorm room. Abigail would make sure she had one of the front row seats.

Opened for almost a year, The Cinder Center for Powered Individuals became a safe haven for people first developing their powers. The center provided training and education, a support system, career networking, and college prep. The city of San Arbor funded part of the center while the retirement package of Avalon, Dragon Slayer, covered the remainder.

"Find a seat everyone," Abigail instructed as the group spilled into the gymnasium. The training dummies, practice targets, and volleyball net were pushed against the back wall allowing room for a small stage and folding chairs. It was nothing compared to the lavish displays held by the Hero Relief Center, but Abigail liked that.

This was not a hero company recruiting center; this was a place where people didn't need to feel alone. A place where people didn't need to be afraid of their powers, or of how the world may see them. Here, they were just people. There was no pressure to be anything else.

But when she was able to use her past connections to the hero world to help those who considered a hero career or wanted to meet the current top star of San Arbor, Abigail was happy to pull some strings.

"Hi, Sydney." Abigail stopped at the little girl and her magazine seated two rows back. "How about we move you to the front?"

"Really?" Sydney leaped from her chair.

"Of course, come with me." Abigail moved Sydney's folding chair to the front row next to two other boys. "Sit tight, he'll be here soon."

Sydney hugged her magazine tightly to her chest, crumbling some of the pages together. The damage didn't register though, probably because seeing the real hero up close trumped the doctored image on the cover.

"Hey Abigail, they're ready for you." The blue-skinned center volunteer jogged over to her. The air dropped several degrees, and the two boys made a show of shivering and rubbing their hands over their arms. The woman playfully stuck her tongue out at them.

Abigail liked watching Cold Snap, who had returned to her original identity after Warden's attack on San Arbor, interact with the kids of the center. Julee took a part-time job at the local roller rink and got half price on all rink time. She somehow convinced Abigail to join their roller derby league.

"I better go welcome our special guest." Abigail knocked her knuckles against Julee's, creating a dusting of frost over each of their hands.

Abigail had a lot of final say in the design of the Cinder Center for Powered Individuals, but the interior design team truly made her vision a reality. As she exited the gymnasium, following the interwoven blue and red floor tiles to the front entrance, she passed her favorite room in the building. All four walls of the sitting room were covered in photos of everyday people doing extraordinary things with or without powers. Everyone could be a good hero, and Abigail wanted everyone who came to the center to find a role model. She ran her fingers across one of the photos. The wooden frame had faded where the oils of her fingers disrupted the tarnish. The selfie of a soot-covered Avalon and Thomas always made her smile.

She wore that smile all the way to the front where her special guests waited. Excalibur hadn't changed and she doubted he ever would. His metal frame was a staple piece at the center as he made routine visits to see the kids and talk with people who considered following a hero path. Standing at his side was a face Abigail was still getting used to seeing in a mask. The costume suited Odo. Hero work suited Odo.

"Hey guys."

"Abigail!" Excalibur plucked her off the ground in a hug. "It's good to see you."

"Likewise," she smiled at him, then asked Odo, "Are you ready?"

She was glad his mask didn't cover his extra eyes. His dragonfly wings extended behind him with pride.

"A little nervous," he chuckled.

"Don't be. You're the hottest sidekick in San Arbor right now, a couple of kids and teenagers shouldn't frighten you."

"I'm not sure what to say to them."

"Don't worry." Abigail swatted his arm. "They've got plenty of questions."

Odo sighed, but a smile crept along his mouth. "I guess I should get in there."

"If you don't, one girl may cause a riot." Abigail pushed him gently forward.

She fell into step next to Excalibur. Being able to be herself without the mask was freeing. She didn't think it would feel this real to just be Abigail. She didn't need to hide behind her mask to do good anymore. Odo entered the gymnasium with a big smile and waved at the assembled group. From the back, Julee whistled loudly.

"Lancelot says 'hi' by the way," Excalibur whispered as Odo started his speech. "He's sorry he couldn't make it."

"With you and Odo here, someone needed to be at the office."

"I told him on his next patrol day he should come by."

"The kids would like that." Abigail watched Odo. He demonstrated how his wings could reflect light. "It would be nice to see him, too."

Excalibur clapped his gloved hand over her shoulder. "You've done really good here, kid. Don't tell anyone, but you're still my favorite sidekick."

"I don't think you can say that, boss."

"I can say whatever I want," he huffed. "Being the leader of the Knights comes with that power."

"They'll never have a finer leader."

"And San Arbor will never have a finer hero."

She looked up at him, his helmet hiding his expression. "You know I'm not coming back to the HRC."

"I mean as you. As Abigail Turner," Excalibur nodded around them. "You should be proud. Of yourself and this place."

She was proud of all good work she'd done as a civilian, no mask required. Abigail smiled.

Acknowledgments

My unwavering gratitude to Kurt and Erica at Speaking Volumes and Nancy at AAA Books Unlimited for helping my dream become a reality. Thank you.

I am so grateful to my writing group, The Queen City Fiction Writers, for your constant guidance and advice. I'm so happy you guys can finally finish the series.

I would like to give a huge thank you to all the local Cincinnati bookstores who have carried Ashes Over Avalon on their shelves and invited me to author fairs. If you're in the Queen City, check out my favorites: The Cincy Book Rack, The Bookery, Scarlet Rose Books, Rockin' Rooster Comics and Games, The Hidden Chapter Bookstore, and Joseph-Beth Lexington.

Thank you to my mom, Maja, who never missed one of those fairs or signings. I was so nervous to tell you I was trying to write a book all those years ago. Thank you for your constant support and cheerleading. Thank you to my husband who pushed me to chase this dream. You told me you wouldn't read the books until they were published. You better start reading.

And thank you to everyone who has read the Ashes Over Avalon books and for going on this journey with me. We did it! We became heroes.

About the Author

Jordan S. Keller is a Cincinnati based writer whose love for stories started at a young age when she preferred to write in a spiral-bound notebook rather than play outside at recess.

The thirst for stories grew in college where she majored in print and radio journalism, sharing the lives of the incredible people who live in Eastern Kentucky through the city radio station and multiple area newspapers. She possesses a bachelor's degree from Morehead State University for Convergent Media.

She sharpens her writing skills while recounting the heroics of her Dungeons and Dragons characters over dinner and co-running The Central Cincinnati Fiction Writers Group.

Jordan S. Keller lives with her husband, their bearded dragon, a goblin disguised as a cat, a puppy with airplane ears, and fourteen koi fish inherited when they bought the house.

Upcoming New Release!

JORDAN S. KELLER'S

FAILING GRAVITY

**Roman Koa knows
to survive in the Slums he has to be ruthless...**

When presented with an opportunity to take from the wealthy sky city, Icaria, he accepts the job despite it being offered by his ex-best friend Oliver—the only person to ever leave the Slums and live in Icaria. If Roman completes the job, he can have whatever he wants and he wants Icaria for himself.

**For more information
visit:** www.SpeakingVolumes.us

Now Available!
JORDAN S. KELLER'S

ASHES OVER AVALON TRILOGY
Book One – Book Two – Book Three

**For more information
visit: www.SpeakingVolumes.us**

Now Available!
MARK E. SCOTT'S

A DAY IN THE LIFE SERIES
Book One – Book Two – Book Three

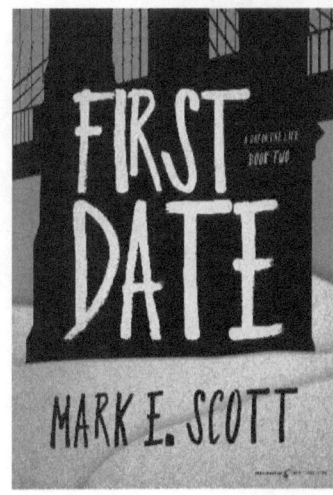

**For more information
visit:** www.SpeakingVolumes.us

Now Available!
TONI GLICKMAN'S

BITCHES OF FIFTH AVENUE SERIES
Book One – Book Two – Book Three

For more information
visit: www.SpeakingVolumes.us

www.ingramcontent.com/pod-product-compliance
Lightning Source LLC
LaVergne TN
LVHW091628070526
838199LV00044B/988